CW01643374

I read this book in one sittin
since I fell in love with the gir
page turner, I just kept wanting to know. I loved the mystery, I loved the characters, I loved the setting, I loved the writing, I loved the sugar cane.
Benjamin Zephaniah – poet, playwright, author, included in *The Times* list of Britain's top 50 post-war writers.

I loved the element of mystery and suspense, which kept me guessing and turning the page. I didn't see the ending coming, and I love it when that happens!
Kimberly Llewellyn – The Indie Book Review

Set in Mauritius, Sugar Cane evokes all the rich sights and scents of a tropical landscape - a sensuous feast.
Penny Morgan – Author

It is hard to believe this is a debut novel as the author writes in such a compelling way and clearly has a natural gift for storytelling. I have read some amazing books this year, one of my favourites being The Help, I would put Sugar Cane right up there in the same league and would highly recommend you discover it for yourself.
Charlie Plunkett – Author

For more Sugar Cane reviews please visit:
www.sandybredpublishing.blogspot.com

Sugar Cane

By E.E.Fry

Best Wishes
Emma
xxx

Copyright

SandyBred Publishers
59 Bryants Hill, Bristol

Printed in England by Dolman Scott Limited
First published by SandyBred publishing in June 2012.
This edition published by SandyBred Publishing in June 2014.

ISBN 987-0-95729838-0-9

For Mum and Grand-mère

A glossary of Mauritian Creole (Kreol) is provided at the end of the book.

Prologue

Tifi

I'd taken the afternoon off work to give my mother a break from the hospital. She hadn't left my father's side in the two days since he'd been admitted for respite care. I drew back the curtain, took her coat off the back of the chair and placed it on her shoulders. She was too shattered to argue with me as I ushered her out of the door. I slipped a twenty pound note into her hand and told her that a taxi was waiting for her outside the main entrance. I kissed her on the forehead and watched as she slowly walked away, still gripping the carrier bag full of fruit that she'd bought in the hope that he'd regain his appetite.

In the run up to his finale, my father had babbled incessantly about angels and three foot tall rabbits. I do believe that in some respects, he actually spoke more during his last weeks on earth than he had in the thirty odd years that I'd known him. The morphine, of course, had a lot to do with it. That day, like any other, I'd been expecting the usual banter, a few rude jokes about the nurses, an enquiry into the football scores. I returned to his side and noticed instead that his favourite cotton pyjamas bagged around a protruding collarbone. His beautiful ebony skin, having already lost its healthy sheen months before, had further diluted to the colour of dirty dishwater. Drips with different coloured taps fed the bruised yellow veins that protruded from his shrivelled hands. His face sank into the mass of pillows that framed his head, proud features slowly caving into the skull that had once supported them. That day, for the first time since the doctor had provided her prognosis, my father's eyes laid bare the fear that the drugs had so carefully concealed.

He held my hand tight for the four hours that I was there and didn't say a single word. He stared at a section of ceiling above my head. I tried to meet his gaze but gave up after the first hour. At ten to nine on the dot, a disembodied voice heralded the last ten minutes of visiting time. In that same moment, my father pulled his hand violently across him, yanking me onto his chest. He brought his free hand over and held me still with the little strength that remained in his body. He strained to plant the dry touch of lips on the back of my neck. Lying with the side of my head pressed against his heart I noticed that his skin smelled sweet, like syrup. He whispered urgently into my ear.

'Tell me that I am forgiven! Please tell me that I am forgiven!'

I tried to move my head without hurting him but he held me firmly in place. Managing to mumble through the cotton of his nightshirt, I asked, 'Forgiven for what Dad?'

He remained silent for a good while before he grasped me painfully by the shoulders and pushed me away.

'I need you to tell me that I'm forgiven,' he growled, 'I need you to tell me now!'

His conduct betrayed him and I reacted as any terrified child would when gripped by a stranger.

'It's alright, Dad. I forgive you. Everything's alright. You're forgiven, OK?'

His features softened instantly, slumped back into his bed, exhausted. In that brief moment I saw a flicker of the man he used to be. My big strong dad, my protector, my comfort, my kin. A beaming smile lit up his face. The glint returned to his eyes.

'My black angels are silver swords in disguise, Elizabeth. They live in the sugar cane. I can hear them calling my name.'

I felt the cold blade pierce my heart as he spoke. I reached out for his hand in a futile attempt to stop him from leaving, but he placed it on his chest, caught his breath and fell soundly asleep.

My father, George Labelle, died at 8.59 p.m. 20th January 2005. It was cancer and he was only 52 years old.

Part One

Revelations

Chapter One

Tifi

The memories of my first taste of sugar cane are as vivid as if it were yesterday. I was six years old. In fact, it was my sixth birthday, the 14th April 1978. My father bought me the strange looking stick from a market stall on a visit to London. It was a reasonably chilly day and the black man with the dreadlocks who served us looked thoroughly uncomfortable in his thick duffel coat and finger-less black mittens. He bobbed from one foot to the other, rubbing and blowing on his bare fingertips as my father took his time searching out the correct change from his purse. I can remember the sound that the cane made as I squelched it between my teeth. A lollipop stick made the same noise when you broke it in two and created the same jaw tingling paralysis. Then that unforgettable initial sensation as the sweet concentrated liquid poured over my tongue and down the back of my throat. It was the kind of sweetness that children dream of in fairy tales. An experience that left me full of wonder and yet quietly anxious that another brief taste would send me to sleep for a hundred years.

I took great pleasure in grinning my approval at my father, if only to watch his eyes dance and to listen to the earth trembling laugh that would follow. He picked me up in his expansive arms and spun me around in the air. I was his princess and he was my bear, my friend. Back then, there didn't seem to be anything in the world more important than making him happy. We depended on each other for our very existence. The sugar cane became a part of this affinity, just as chicken curry, salt fish, chilli peppers and the strange patois phrases he taught me were to become as I grew nearer to adulthood.

He cut an impressive and overwhelming figure, drenched in dark cocoa skin and garnished with massive hands. My mother, Shelly, referred to them as 'his mixed grills', ten butcher's finest and two prime cut steaks. While I looked forward to the security that they provided, others imagined them crushing human bones to dust. He was a man of few words never speaking unless it was entirely necessary to do so. His rich bass voice would only rarely resonate through the floorboards of my childhood bedroom and lull me to sleep. He earned his keep as a chef in a small restaurant in town and when he wasn't working he spent most of his time growing vegetables and watching cookery programmes. He embodied everything real and safe and true, this remarkably enlightened spirit who lived in the house with my mother and me.

Shelly, my mother, always played the part of my connection with the world outside the windows and spun her web around us as though we in turn had given meaning to her existence. She brought me up in a small working class town in Hampshire, although she's actually a born and bred Londoner. She's the one responsible for introducing my palate to pickled herring and 'liquor', a green glutinous liquid, in which she still likes to saturate my chips. She has wide voluminous hips that once matched her wide engaging smile and slate grey eyes that used to sparkle when it rained. Her favourite piece of motherly advice is that 'you should never judge a book by its cover'. Although she usually adds, with a touch of her own indeterminable logic, that 'if it walks like a dog and barks like a dog, then it probably is a dog'. She was my accent, my thoughts and my feminine wiles; the other half of me, the half that no one could see on the outside.

My mother had always had a penchant for falling in love with men who would make her life difficult. At the tender age of fourteen, she fell in love with a Russian sailor who promised her an exciting life away from the Bourgeoisie suburbia in which he said she was suffocating. He serenaded her with vodka and placed a stolen fur coat around her shoulders. Why a Russian sailor was living in a bed and breakfast in Walthamstow, she can't explain, but he'd been romantic enough to induce her to run away with him. They got as far as a bed-sit in Portsmouth. He made sure he'd had his wicked way with her before he disappeared like a 'fart in the wind', as she so eloquently puts it.

Too fearful to return home, she hitched a ride to Eastleigh and begged the help of her Aunt Brenda, who was thankfully sympathetic to her niece's plight. Ten years later, Aunt Brenda passed on and left my mother the house and all of its contents. Shortly afterwards she decided to rent out the back room for a bit of company and to help with the household bills. And that was how Shelly met George Labelle.

My father never spoke about where he came from, nor about the life he led before he arrived in England in 1971. On the one occasion that I persisted in my interrogation, he had grown bleary eyed and walked out of the house. I was only about five years old at the time and this is my earliest memory; watching him from the front window, the net curtain framing my head like a wedding veil.

'What's wrong with daddy?' I asked my mother.

'Nothing, dear,' she replied over her crossword, 'There are just some things that your father doesn't like to talk about.'

'But why not?'

'Because.'

'Because, why?'

'Just because!'

I had to learn to content myself with knowing nothing more about my father than what I saw and heard with my own eyes and ears. So you can imagine how I felt when, at nine years of age, I discovered the passport nestling between the pages of a pornographic magazine. Hiding in his garage, I didn't even query the fact that the passport said that his first name was different. I didn't even study the photograph. All I needed to know was bundled into a nine letter word. I hid a scrapbook under my bed from that day forth and for five years, surreptitiously collected, cut up and glued into it any holiday brochures or magazine articles that I could lay my hands on that mentioned the elusive island of Mauritius.

I discovered that it lies in the Indian Ocean, some 800 kilometres east of Madagascar, 1200 km south of the Seychelles and 5854 km west of Australia and is only 58km by 47km in size. The island itself is so small that you can travel around it by car in the best part of a day and is littered with extinct craters, volcanic lakes and tropical forests. In a geographical magazine I found a picture of a chain of magnificent mountains that scarred the skyline, framing whole towns and cities. I learnt that spring actually falls between the months of September and December and that temperatures rise from a chilly 22 degrees Celsius of August to a liquefying 42 degrees by the beginning of January.

I cut out a picture of a bedraggled roadside vendor hacking off a whole branch of lychees to pass them illicitly through the car window of a waiting buyer. I sank into the images of the clear blue and turquoise lagoons that I found on the centre pages of a diving magazine. I stared enviously at the self-satisfied grins of rich businessmen in trophy photos, celebrating the landing of barracuda, wahoo, sharks and the infamous Mauritian blue marlin. The long sandy stretches of coral white beaches framing their expensive and exclusive hotels. But above all, it was the Mauritian faces that truly captured my imagination. Faces that looked just like mine; small noses and crimson lips, thick wiry black hair and curly eyelashes, dark eyes with dark patches and freckles, chocolate brown skin and puppy pink palms. They smiled up from the pages with bright white teeth, inviting me in, asking me to join their party.

Outside of this world, I liked to pretend that I was a pretty normal kid. I enjoyed the usual friendships with neighbouring ruffians and school bullies and by the time I was ten years old, I had someone who I could call my best friend. Samantha Phillips. We were in the same class at primary school and we were put in the same tutor group at the local comprehensive. We even held hands on our first day at big school as our mothers waved us forward from the school gates, our hearts and smiles filled with trepidation and excitement. However, it was the disquiet murmur of our peers as we walked into the assembly hall that I remember most about that first day at secondary school. That, and of course, the way that Samantha had dropped my hand like a hot potato by the time we'd reached the second row. I hadn't thought much of it then. Hindsight, I've come to appreciate, is a 'many splendored thing'.

I did reasonably well at school, keeping my head down and studying hard until the onset of puberty brought about the usual hormonal trials and tribulations. My particular affliction was huge breasts. Unfortunately, they don't appear to be that big now, but I can assure you that at the tender age of fourteen, they were simply devastating and their mutation coincided with my first encounter with puppy love. I spent most of my time daydreaming about Paul Connors, (muscular, slim hips, blond hair that flopped on his forehead, sultry blue eyes), the toughest boy in our year. The cruelty of my predicament was that he fancied my best friend, Samantha, (porcelain pale skin, amber locks and an easy walk), and therefore I understood that he'd never look at me, Beth, (gangly, awkward, Paky looking girl, who's always getting in the way of an easy snog).

One fine day he asked Samantha out on a date to the rec. She was pouting at the mirror, over her deserted desk, her pink pleated ra-ra skirt barely covering her cleverly chosen black underwear as she leant forward to retouch the red lipstick that she'd taken from her mother's dressing table when she informed me.

'He says he wants you to come along too,' she'd said with a shrug. 'I can't understand why, probably got some Indian friend that he wants us to double date with.'

Unimpressed by the lack of forewarning and quietly distressed by the fact that I was still wearing my school uniform, including my mother's hand knitted grey sweater, I watched and waited as Samantha finished getting all dolled up. Eventually, but before I'd had a chance to finish the lemonade and salmon spread sandwiches that her mother had been kind enough to offer me, she strode out of the bedroom, across the landing, down the stairs and straight out the front door. I, as always, skipped along a few feet behind, breathlessly and unquestioningly following her across the desolate park towards the abandoned youth club.

Within minutes of our arrival, Samantha shouted, 'You know it's not her fault she's coloured! Her mother's white, so that only makes her half Paki.'

Paul pushed Samantha out of the way.

'Well, if you ain't gonna give out, let's 'av a look under 'er shirt then.' Moving towards me, he sneered, 'Let's see if she's got pink or brown nips on those big tits of 'ers.'

Beside me, I heard his sidekicks, Graham and John, jeer their approval as he took hold of my sweater and yanked it, sending grey buttons flying.

My best friend, Samantha, her black eye makeup smeared like a cartoon burglar, sidestepped away into the darkness.

Ultimately, I did fight back; the judo lessons that my father insisted on dragging me along to finally coming into some practical use. I managed to knee Paul in the balls and make a run for it. I ran and ran and ran. I ran home clutching my ripped blouse and flaying cardigan shut in the aftermath of his successful dirty nail scratching enquiry. I ran up the stairs and into the bathroom, yanked off the offending garments and jumped under the shower. Without a second thought, I reached for the nailbrush along with the green bar of Palmolive soap and scrubbed at my skin until it screamed; desperate to destroy the sickeningly superficial layer that imprisoned me and reveal to the world my truly acceptable whiteness.

I passed my father as I crossed the landing to my bedroom. I was wrapped from top to toe in a large beach towel so that he couldn't witness my shame, but he still averted his eyes, as if he knew what had happened, as if he knew I was made wrong in some way. I ran for my room, flung myself on the bed and wept. I lay there feeling sorry for myself long enough for my sadness to be replaced by a boiling rage, my lungs inhaling and exhaling, growling like a wolf trapped in a snare. Searching for something to blame and destroy, I knelt on the floor and extracted the scrapbook from its hidden lair. I opened it and I tore every page from the spine, shredding each one into a million tiny pieces that could never be stuck together and vowed that I would never think of Mauritius ever again.

That was the evening I put away childish dreams of ever understanding why my skin was a different colour. I became aware of the ridiculous predicament in which I was living; of being and feeling English and yet looking like something else, of belonging and yet not being allowed to belong, of wanting to be proud yet knowing that my efforts would never be appreciated. The realisation that white people would always believe that they were doing me a favour and that black and Asian people would never recognise me as one of their own. My hair wasn't curly enough to be considered Afro and my skin too dark to be considered Indian. Old ladies in saris looked at me distastefully in my western clothes. Old Afro Caribbean women made a point of ignoring me as I passed them in the street. I could be from anywhere and nowhere at the same time. Lost.

I never spoke to Samantha again and I could tell from the red in her cheeks each time she passed me in a corridor that she was happy about my decision. Thankfully, I went on to college in a different town. I studied French, History and Politics and then travelled another ninety miles west to Bristol to partake in higher education. I discovered liberal friends and intelligent men and realised that I could create my own family from within their ranks.

Out of term time, I let my hair down on the party scene in Ibiza and Cyprus. I met my present best friend, Kitty, a seasoned loafer, in a bar in Aiya Nappa. We made a point of making many male friends who we didn't need to stay in touch with. I finished reading all the French and history that

I could stomach and Kitty and I went travelling to India, Hong Kong, Vietnam, Thailand and Mexico. Loved up, we became blood sisters on a beach in Goa. We ate foreign food and danced a lot. Once I'd successfully sated my wanderlust, I returned to England and landed an effortless job as a civil servant while my best friend kept on floating.

I met, fell in love with and married Patrick, an architect with a passion for foreign cuisine. It was his fine Roman nose that first attracted me to him. That and the way he'd kept his cool when I crashed my beloved D reg. Golf into the back of his brand new Audi A4. My mother adopted him into her brood immediately, while my father remained as always, eternally passive. Patrick and I invested in a large mortgage so that we could have dinner parties with friends. We enjoyed three holidays a year, had two cars and an espresso maker. Sunday evenings we dined at my parental home. Monday and Wednesday nights we went to the gym. Kitty came back to the UK to do a few photography exhibitions and sort out her finances, so every other Thursday evening we'd meet in a pub and inevitably get pissed. Friday night therefore, commanded 'hair of the dog' at our local and Saturday, a night in with a film. This familiar rhythm continued unabated until the day we all found ourselves sat in the front aisle of a Crematorium.

As I watched my father's coffin disappear behind the red velvet curtain the day of his funeral, something snapped. I broke. I wasn't expecting it and suddenly everything was too late. The aisles around me contained representatives of my mother's family and my father's faithful work colleagues. A swathe of pasty faces, speckled with red noses and weepy eyes that looked back at me with pity as I surveyed the turnout. All I could comprehend was that there wasn't a single brown face in the room. Well, except mine of course. I was alone and conspicuous. Not even Kitty's glistening emerald eyes could befriend me.

Patrick squeezed my hand and screwing his face up in consternation had asked, 'Are you alright, Beth?'

And I'd snapped despicably back at him, 'Well, my father's dead, what do you think?'

I'd hurt him but I didn't feel guilty. The only thought encased in my head was how I despised him along with every other colourless face in the room. And so it began.

I knew it was a ridiculous and selfish reaction. The faces that I unexpectedly found intimidating were the same faces that witnessed the marital vows that I'd declared only two years before. These faces represented all the people who had unwaveringly visited my father in his final days at the hospital. These faces belonged to friends and relations who were sharing my pain. My mother, my husband and my best friend. In an instant, they were all alien to me. The whiteness of my world was suddenly overwhelming. Throughout his illness, I hadn't conceived that he could possibly leave me. Now here I was, still without knowledge, solitary and betrayed. He'd invited me to taste the sugar cane but had held the roots of the plant well out of my reach.

Chapter Two

Papa

Regret.

It is a word that has haunted me for as long as I can remember. During the darkest days, when ghosts played in the shadows around me, I made myself regret everything and everyone.

Régré.

I cut myself off from the ever rising sun and disappeared into a place where no one was able to find me. I stayed there until the panic set in, then yanked on the cord that attached me to the world, as it had to be. Each time this happened I remembered that which I had forgotten. I remembered that my rope was attached to my daughter.

Elizabeth.

Now I am dead. There is no cord and I find myself alone in nothingness, just blank and me. I do not like it here. It is neither light nor dark, hot nor cold, black nor white nor Technicolor. I am neither floating nor standing nor lying. I cannot see any limbs. Come to think of it, I am not quite sure whether I can see. I cannot feel anything and there is nothing to touch.

Bez sa!

The only thing that I am sure of is that I understand what is happening. I know that she holds the key to my redemption. I am reminded of the moment that she wrapped her minute fingers around my little finger the day that she was born. It was the first time that I was touched by religion – a blinding faith that only she knew why she had come to stay and that I was now merely a servant to her cause.

My story?

Do I have to?

Of course.

From the beginning?

Mo mama fell pregnant with Frank the minute papa placed a ring on her finger. The proposal itself was not a romantic event. If I remember correctly, papa described it as a rather brief and stammered discussion over a weak cup of vanilla tea. *Mo mama,* a good Catholic, strongly believed that God, *le Bondyé,* preferred those who lived a difficult life. It was for this reason, she told us, that she accepted his offer on the day he left for the desert in 1942. *Mo papa,* in contrast, did not care for religion, but he said he knew a good woman when he saw one. He swore that it was love at first sight, cupid having scored a direct hit the day he fell into *madam's* lap on the 46 bus home from Port Louis.

Papa came out of the war in the desert without so much as a scratch, although it took him a rather long time to find his way home. The happy couple married on a rainy day in April 1949 surrounded by hundreds of family members that they did not know. They said that it was a joyous occasion, further tempered by the consumption of litres of white rum. Within nine months, mama was proudly displaying a fine protuberance while papa worked dayshifts, nightshifts and any other overtime that was available at a factory in Phoenix. Frank was born at 7.45 one humid morning in *Zanvyé, sori*, January 1950.

Frank was a lively baby. He was into everything from the moment that his muscles provided him the strength to move and would have proved a handful even to the most experienced and youthful of parents. Unfortunately for my parents, who were neither of these things, Frank tested their nerves and reflexes at every turn. He demanded their undivided attention and they gave it willingly. He knew how to play them right from the start. Born on 11th October 1953, in sharp contrast to *mo frer*, I was a lazy baby. I was also smaller and more fragile, because, I was told, I would not take to the breast. I often slept so soundly that several times in the first six months of my life I made *mo mama* scream with terror under the belief that I had passed away in my sleep. Dr Balgobin insisted that this was quite a common ailment among some Creole children and assured my parents that I would grow out of it by the time I reached adulthood.

I grew out of it by the time I was six years old. However, by this time, Frank now nearly ten years old had already won the heart of my father. Unlike Frank, I discovered that I was not capable of making decisions for myself and that I was too fragile to be allowed out on my own. Over time I had to come to terms with the fact that I was not a normal child and that was just the way it was. I would never be like Frank. I would always be the second son. When Marie came along in December 1959, I was quietly demoted to child number three, behind *'tifi surpriz'*, their surprise little girl. Then in January 1961, Juliet, *'zanfan zoli'*, the beautiful child arrived and I was firmly repositioned as child number four.

We lived in Quatre Bornes, a small town to the south of the great city of Port Louis. Nestled in the Plaines Wilhems, it sits alongside an area called Rose Hill at the foot of Corps de Guarde Mountain, at the bottom of which stood our tiny corrugated iron home.

Lakaz.

Lakaz Labelle was small yet adequate. Our front door sat in the middle of the front wall and entered onto a white living space large enough to contain a black plastic sofa, a laminated floral dining table with four mismatching chairs, a sideboard with one door hanging from its hinges and a homemade coffee table supporting a wooden radio. To the right of this room was a dark blue kitchen with an un-tiled floor, an old laminated table, a low firewood stove and an empty gas cylinder. My parents and my sisters had their own bedrooms. Two coconut husk mattresses without bed frames were propped up in a corner for Frank and me to drag into the living room in the evening. At the back of the house, there was a hole in the ground shielded from view by a sheet of bamboo. A nearby cold water tap supplied *dilo* to the houses twice a day and next to that laid the old tin bath.

Our house was neighboured by four others of equal size, each with a front door that faced onto a makeshift square and each constructed from planks of wood and covered in corrugated metal sheets that rattled when it rained. A tall palm separated the boundaries of one house from the other, under which we tied our *chien méchants* with heavy duty rope. Those children, *banzanfan*, not yet old enough to go to school or clean, played in the dirt in the middle of the square, while one or more of the mothers polished their tiled doorsteps with coconut husks. When the floors finally gleamed, the women would go outside and sit in the seats that their husbands and fathers would inhabit when they returned home from work. They'd take advantage of the respite from their chores to gossip about the goings on in the square alongside their own, where their lives were mirrored as if in a parallel universe.

Moris.

The tropical climate fed a vibrant flora and fauna that drenched the land in a rich green. Palm trees provided us with dignity and majesty. Plump imperial princes squatted in the shade of their slimmer female cousins, who in turn reached up to the heavens and danced in the easterly breeze as the orange dust of the volcanic earth plumed in annoyance at the trucks that awoke it from its chosen resting place.

The St Jean Road split the town of Quatre Bornes in two. A bustling market and busy bus station worked to keep the trading centre alive and vibrant. Men propped their bicycles on the side of the road and sold guavas covered in *disel pima* from baskets resting on the worn leather seats. *Goyav de Chine*. Women with burnt fingers stood hunched over immense fat filled woks, serving the masses with *gato-piman, gato-brinzel, gato-pomdéter* – spicy fried treats filled with enough chilli to make grown men weep. Tables lay ablaze with multicoloured mountains of *pom damours, zak, papaya, pima, zallot, sousou, ziromon, gros pois* and succulent *mang lakord.*

Manz manzé.

The cry of *'poisson salé'* rose above the perfume of spices, as the salt fish vendor desperately waved the flies off his produce, hands and clothes wreaking, eternally perfecting the art of the quick sale. The mouth-watering aroma of vegetable *kari* mingled in the thick air as the *dal-pouri* salesman fought off the dusty workers clambering for a taste of his delicacies. Buses as ever flooded the area with the progressive stench of industrialisation, while taxi drivers opened the doors of their small rusting chariots to allow the twenty five perspiring passengers crammed inside to escape into the midday sun.

Kann.

And then there was the sugar cane - so sewn into the fabric of Mauritius that it is impossible to contemplate my home without them. A tall swathe of immortal soldiers that covered the land, they told people where and how to live and reminded them daily that their lives depended on the success of the crop. How different would all of our lives have been if it were not for the sugar cane? A double edged sword that could bless you with one blade and damn you with the other.

Chapter Three

Tifi

My mother and I received an unexpected invitation to the solicitor's office two weeks after the funeral. Wrapped up warm against the freezing February elements, she'd looked shockingly like a bag lady as she shoved me through the glass doors marked, *'Johnson & Partners'*. Glancing back at her, I had to remind myself that she'd once been a very beautiful woman. Her steely grey eyes and brunette curls had at one time complimented a creamy complexion and wide ruby smile. The cancer had succeeded in leaving her in much the same state as dad had been when he left her. Wrinkles, white hairs, dry lips and pallid skin, which once upon a time, she'd have gone to so much trouble to camouflage, now flourished in all their glory.

Ushered through to a Mr Bolton's office, we sat down in two leather chairs opposite an expensive mahogany table. Mother fidgeted with her hair, her handbag and her fingernails. Mr Bolton strode into the room clutching a green paper file under the arm of a style-less brown jacket and an anxious glance from my mother reminded me that she now expected me to take the lead.

'You said in your letter, Mr Bolton, that my father had written a last will and testament.'

'Yes, that's correct,' he replied.

'Well, to tell you the truth, it's come as a bit of a surprise.'

'These things usually do.'

'But you see, as far as we're aware, my father didn't own anything of any value and my mother is adamant that she had absolutely no idea that he'd written a will.'

Mr Bolton rocked on his heels, 'I see.'

'So, what I'm trying to get at is whether it's at all possible that you might have contacted the wrong family.'

He stepped back aghast, 'I can assure you that we at Johnson and Partners are not accustomed to making mistakes about something as serious as the reading of a last will and testament.'

'So you're absolutely sure?'

'Yes, now shall we begin?'

My mother didn't acknowledge the question, so I shrugged and told him to continue. Opening the green folder, he cleared his throat, brought out two envelopes and placed them on the table in front of him.

'To my wife, Shelly Labelle, I leave two letters marked A and B,' he read aloud, 'It is my final wish that you read letter A to help you to decide when and how you intend to use letter B. I leave it to you to make the right decision.'

Turning to me, he continued, 'To my daughter, Elizabeth Stephens, I leave this key.'

Mr Bolton withdrew another envelope from the folder and placed it on the table alongside the others.

'The use of which will become apparent over time and in trust that you will do the right thing with whatever you discover.'

I reached over and slid the envelope towards me. Tearing it along one side, I tipped the tiny metal key out into my palm. It wasn't extraordinary, just a common two tooth key that you could pick up almost anywhere. I looked to my mother for some indication that she knew what this was all about but instead met a stony wall of silence that she maintained while I finished off the legalities, thanked Mr Bolton for his time and escorted her out to the car. She didn't speak throughout the whole journey home. I waited as she pushed open the front door and watched as she disappeared behind it with a heaving of coats. I felt for the fragile key in my pocket. My father, never full of surprises had certainly pulled this one out of the bag.

I'd made a point of visiting her every couple of days or so after that. Patrick would make some excuse about needing to work late and I'd take the opportunity to check up on her. She shut down every time I tried to mention the meeting. So, instead, we'd end up watching TV cuddled together on the sofa, usually accompanied by a take away of some comfort eating description. I managed to endure two weeks of this strange taciturn dance before she finally asked me to help her go through his belongings.

It was four o'clock on a drizzling Sunday afternoon. She shuffled away into the kitchen as I entered, still in her blue cotton dressing gown, her hair a dishevelled greying mess on her shoulders. I walked through to the living room and discovered an encampment of dirty cups and plates on the coffee table, accumulated in the three days since I'd last visited her. Two empty tubes of cheese and chive Pringles and an empty tub of Haagan Daaz Cookie Dough ice cream lay at the foot of the sofa. Picking up what I could, I followed her out to the kitchen.

She was making a pot of tea. Three cups stood in a line and I watched her pour a little milk into each. Placing the debris on the draining board, I walked over to her and rested my head on her shoulder. She patted it soothingly and poured tea into only two of the mugs.

'Force of habit, pet. I'm sorry,' she explained.

'Your dad liked a good cup of tea didn't he? Couldn't live without it he said...Best thing we English knew how to make...Ten times better than our cooking...Still he never drank it with less than three sugars in it...I thought it ruined it, but he'd just laugh at me and say that I didn't know what I was talking about.'

I pulled two chairs out from under the kitchen table.

'Come and sit down, Mum. Let's have this cuppa and then get you and this house sorted out, OK?'

She duly obliged, tugging her dressing gown down to cover her knees.

'How's Patrick?'

'He's fine.'

'Good,' she said, placing her hand on top of mine, 'remember to tell him that he's allowed to visit me as well.'

'I promise I'll ask him to come with me the next time I visit,' I lied.

The truth was that Patrick and I weren't even talking. Ever since the funeral, 'Beth n' Pat' had undergone a radical metamorphosis. We lived in the same house and slept in the same bed at night but that was about all we had in common. Somewhere along the line he'd turned into a patronising git and, although a part of me couldn't blame him for thinking such a thing, I was apparently no longer right in the head. Anything and everything he said grated on me like sharp nails down a black board. We rarely ate a meal in each other's company. I'd lie in bed at night and cry for no apparent reason and he was too frustrated to care. In the heat of an argument he laid blame on my hormones and then on my inability to cope with my grief. I missed my father, that was true, but there was something else missing that I couldn't quite put my finger on. I tried to explain that it felt as though I'd left the iron on but didn't know where to look to check whether I'd turned it off. Suffice to say, he didn't understand.

I was deep inside the walk in wardrobe of my parent's bedroom when I finally found it.

'Hey, Mum, what's this?'

I pushed a large wooden box full to the brim with paperback books to one side and discovered a small metallic panel.

'I don't know, dear,' she replied, her backside protruding from a chest on the opposite side of the room.

I dragged a chair over and jumped on top. The panel was actually a door to a built in safe, just like the ones you get in hotel apartments, the ones that you're supposed to hide your passports and traveller's cheques in, so that the maid knows where to find them.

'It's a safe. Did you know it was here?'

At length, she arose from her scrimmaging.

'Oh, yes,' she said flippantly, 'it was your father's idea. I haven't a clue what he hides in the damn thing. It was always off limits to me.'

'It's locked,' I told her, tugging at the handle. 'Shall I try that key he gave me?'

I awaited her approval but no response came so I trotted off downstairs to get the key from my coat pocket. When I returned, her face had visibly paled, a look of resignation quietly seeping through its pores. It was obvious that she didn't want me to open it, but something inside me assured me that I had to be cruel to be kind, that whatever it was she was scared of would be far better out in the open, that in this strange role reversal, I'd have to be the grown up. I clambered back onto the chair and reaching into the dark depths of the cupboard, placed the key in the lock and turned it clockwise. I heard the satisfying clunk as the mechanism fell into place, then discovered that the wooden box alongside it stopped me from accessing my treasures.

'You'll have to give me a hand bringing this down,' I said shifting my stance to take the weight of it off the shelf.

'Careful with your back, dear. Maybe we should call Patrick and get him to take it down for us?'

The box slid off the shelf as my back clicked in protest.

'It's OK. We can do this without him.'

She raised her hands to take it from me and just as I loosened my grip, she stepped backwards, allowing the box and all of its contents to fall to the floor. She looked up at me with exactly the same expression that she'd used at the solicitor's office. Resolute, I returned my attention to the matter in hand and opened the safe door with reassuring ease. I reached into its black belly and pulled out a rusty blue tin that had once held a selection of 'Fine English Butter Biscuits'. I stepped off the chair, sat down on the bed and lowered the tin carefully to my lap.

'Are you sure, dear?' My mother asked, sitting down beside me, unwillingly drawn into my father's plot.

I nodded without lifting my eyes from the box. I have to confess that I'd half expected it to explode as I lifted the lid and was very relieved when it simply fell back on its hinges. I emptied the contents of the container onto the sheets:

- A bundle of tea stained envelopes that appeared rather worse for wear, a tired piece of raffia string holding them together.

- A small black leather purse fastened by a soft leather cord that snapped as I pulled it open to peer inside, unleashing an array of brightly coloured glass marbles all over the sheets.

- A rosary bead necklace attached with sticky tape, now brown and peeling, to a prayer card with the 23 Psalm written upon it.

'Although I walk through the valley of the shadow of death, I shall fear no evil,' my mother mumbled through paper lips.

- A bundle of sepia stained photographs that displayed the stark and staring faces of members of a family dressed up to the nines in suits and stylish hats.

'Do you know who these people are?'

The answer was obvious, I know, but it was important that I involve her. She took the photos from me and after a few moments, she tapped the corner of one of them.

'I think that boy maybe your father,' she said, holding the picture so that I could see four children; two little girls and two older boys with not a smile between them. The boys were crammed into ill fitting brown suits and the girls into sepia stained mini meringues.

'See, look at his eyes,' she continued, 'He's got the same eyes as my George, the same eyes as my darling George.'

A tear welled in the corner of a dark eye. She was right. The face that rebelliously glared back at me was most surely that of my father, albeit when he was a boy. She handed back the picture and asked me to translate the French inscription scrawled on the back.

'It says, 'Frank, Marie, Juliet and me 1968. Marie and Juliet's first Holy Communion. Mama had just smacked me when this picture was taken.''

Spellbound, I realised that this was the first piece of my father's past that I had ever been allowed to touch.

'Is there anything else in the box?' She asked.

'Just this melted lipstick and this blue Saint Christopher pendant,' I replied, holding the box so that she could see. Uninterested, she took the photo from me and shuffled it back amongst the rest.

'These letters,' I asked, 'do you want to read them with me?'

‘I don’t think that I should,’ she snapped.

That strange mask descended again as she began to knead at her stomach.

‘Mum?’

She stared at the pictures that now lay in her lap.

‘Mum? What is it for goodness sake?’

She pushed herself up off the bed, scattering the photographs amongst the books on the floor.

‘I think we’re going to need another cup of tea,’ she muttered as she staggered out of the door.

Chapter Four

Papa

Is Shelly OK? I did not have time to say goodbye.

Of course it matters!

Yes.

I do not know. I suppose you have to understand my home.

Surely, you know this?

Bann dimounn Morisyen.

It was the Dutch who first bought slaves to the desert island. They ripped African, Malagasy and Indian men, women and children from their homes and rammed them into vessels destined to make port in the rich city of Port Louis. Ships would be replenished, cargoes swapped, money exchanged, lives and minds lost. They brought rats and dogs and killed off the Dodo for good measure. Then the French came and in a spirit of *fraternité* refused to free their slaves, even after the abolition of slavery was decreed in Paris in 1794. Instead, they set about creating a hybrid that they would later endearingly refer to as Creoles.

Then the British played their part, claiming the island as spoil of the Napoleonic wars in 1814. Unsure of how best to exploit the sugar cane industry on the island, they waited a further twenty-one years to free the slaves in their care. As thoughtful as ever of the lives of those they exploited, they swiftly refilled the fields with legalised servitude from India and China, rapidly making the Creoles redundant in the only land that they knew.

Kot Anglé pasé, larzan pousé.

For many years, the British, who were reliant on cheap workers to corner the international sugar markets, poured thousands more Indians into the country, saturating its resources. Consequently, the Indians – or Hindu's, Tamil and Muslim's – took over the island and therefore our lives. The arrival of Chinese merchants further reduced us to fourth place in the division of Mauritian wealth; a wealth that most of us Creoles believed had been born through the blood of our ancestors.

Arc-en-ceil.

In 1968, Mauritius acceded independence from the Crown and every Hindu, Muslim, Creole, Franco-Mauritian, Chinese, Sino-Mauritian, Tamil, Telugu, Marathi, Indian or Catholic, had something to say about it. And they said it in English, French, Kreol, Hindi, Urdu, Hakka, Mandarin, Cantonese, Gujurati and Bhojpuri. Approximately one million people, divided by ethnicity, religion and caste, were now faced with living alongside each other as Mauritians in an area of no more than 788 square miles. At a time when we should have been growing together, we chose to tear ourselves apart. Violence and hatred claimed the lives of at least twenty human beings, left hundreds injured and many others simply disappeared.

That year, my father got into politics and warned the workers of the 'Hindu peril'. My brother saved himself by winning a scholarship to study in England among *bann blan*. My sisters were taught how to fear the Muslims, *bann lascar*. My mother decided to renounce her *madras* ancestors and forbade us to accept food from our Indian school friends. The world around me was imploding with paranoia and I decided to fall in love.

Chapter Five

Tifi

'Mum, what is it, for Christ's sake!'

When she hadn't return to the bedroom, I'd left the box on the bed and gone downstairs to find her sitting in the kitchen.

'Mum, what is it; you're starting to scare me.'

She dropped the teaspoon that she'd been using to stir her cold cup of tea and slowly plunged her hand into her dressing gown pocket. She dragged out the two envelopes and placed them on the table in front of me. She turned her head away, opting instead to watch the pots and pans balance on the edge of the kitchen sink. I sat down opposite her and opened the envelope marked 'A', carefully unfolding the paper within. It was hand written, on cheap lined paper; my father's unmistakable script in dribbling blue ink.

My darling Shelly,

Alas, it is not up to us to decide how and when we depart this world and it is hard to describe how sorry I am to leave you in this way. You have always been my rock and I do not know how I will be without you near. I want to thank you for being my lover and my best friend. I want to write across the sky in stars and tell everyone what a wonderful woman you are, what a wonderful wife you have been and what a wonderful mother you are to my daughter. You have been more than I could ever have hoped for and I cannot thank you enough for finding us and saving us. Against the wishes of everyone around you, you stood by us. You, a white woman in a white world, showed my daughter and me the true meaning of love. And no, I am not being silly. You helped us to feel at home in your land. You helped us to understand it and find our place within it. You brought my daughter up well, taught her how to be a woman and accepted her into your heart as your own. You have shown us all what is possible and taught us all how much better we can be. I wish that I did not have to leave you in this way. I wish that I could stay forever but I am finding it harder as each day passes. I can hear you say, 'chin up darling,' as you English always do and I am trying my best. But if I must keep my chin up, then you must not be sad. You must make one of your cups of tea and remember as you drink it that I am always with you. I know that we shall see each other again in time so please do not worry about me. There are plenty of souls on the other side awaiting my arrival, I will not be lonely. In the meantime, look after yourself, eat well and try not to watch too much television. Please try not to miss me.

Letter B, as I am sure you have already guessed is a letter for Beth. It is my final wish that you be the one to give it to her. I would not presume when or how you should do this. I know that this final request will be very hard for you both, although I know that you have always known that this day would come. I am also sure in my heart that you will do the right thing by her and keep an eye on her. She will need you now more than ever. Throughout it all, please, please remember that I love you and that this is all for the best.

Yours forever,

George x

I folded the letter neatly and pushed it back into its envelope.

'I'm not your real mother,' she mumbled.

'Don't be daft,' I chuckled, 'of course you're my real mother. Your name's on my birth certificate for goodness sake.'

'It's a fake.'

My vision blurred, 'I said, don't be daft.'

'Your father had a friend who was a cleaner at the Registry Office.'

Her face swirled in a frenzied kaleidoscope of greying hair and teacups.

'Beth?'

Her enquiring voice slowed ridiculously like a 70 on a 45.

'I tried to stop you.'

She struggled up from her seat.

'I tried to stop you, you silly little girl'.

She returned seconds later with a glass of water and one of her 'special' pills.

'Here, take this. It'll make you feel better.'

I was in no mood to argue and popped the little blue pill into my mouth. I turned the other envelope over in my hands. My logic ran wild, screaming through no man's land - *it can't be true, it can't be true, it can't be true* - until it was hit with the cold white flag of surrender. I heard her say something.

'I'm going to lose you too.'

I took the second letter out of its envelope.

My Beth,

If you are reading this letter then you will already know some of what I am about to tell you. Do not be angry with Shelly. She has been a good and loyal wife and a loving parent to you from the minute she saw you. If she did not tell you the truth before, it was through no fault of her own. She was simply being loyal to my wishes. I was the one who denied you. I suppose you will be thinking it unfair of me, to leave you to cope with this revelation alone, but please believe me when I tell you that I had no other choice. It is hard being a parent. You must try and get everything right and I assure you that I spent a long time worrying and trying to figure out the best way to let you know.

Your real mother, or more correctly, your biological mother and I lived at a time when we were not supposed to love each other. Her name was Sahana and she died bringing you into the world. In not succumbing to the wishes of others, we lost more than we bargained for and when we discovered that you were inside her, we had to run away, if only to keep you safe. We came to England to start a new life. We were young and full of hope and fear and we did what we had to do to give you a proper start in life. Then God decided to take my Sahana from me and left me all alone to look after you. Now there was no way that I could return and if it had not been for Shelly, I do not know what would have happened to us.

There are things that happen in this world that should not happen. Things that have remained the same way for centuries that people are too scared to question. Your birth was a miracle that proved everyone wrong but at the same time, I did not comprehend the full price that would have to be paid for going against them. We decided that it was better that you grew up how you wanted to be and it broke my heart to know that one day you would have to find out who had given you your honey caramel skin and straight black hair.

If you have not already found it, the lock that your key fits is hidden in the walk-in wardrobe in my bedroom. The box it opens is full of the memories that I was able to bring with me from Mauritius. It feels right that you should have them to look after now. There has not been a day that has passed where the wrench of the call home has not pulled at my heart and sometimes I think you felt it too. I could see it in your eyes, whenever you tasted a delicacy from our homeland. Subconsciously, you knew you belonged somewhere else, even when you tried to resist it. This is why you must be the one to take me home. I want you to spread my ashes on my homeland. There is a place in the sugar cane where I would like you to leave me. If you read the letters in the box, you should still be able to find it.

Please do not be angry and please remember that I did this for your own good. You are the reason why all of this happened and you are the reason why I carried on. I would have been nothing if you had not entered my life. I love you Beth. Never, ever forget that and no matter what you chose to do I will always be looking out for you.

Your loving father, forever and a day

Dad x

'I fell in love with your father and his little girl the first time I saw him struggle up the front step with you in your pushchair.'

Her voice filtered through the fog.

'I was living alone at the time, Aunt Brenda, God rest her soul, having left me this big house to move into when she passed away. I can't have children you see. An accident the year before I met your father put paid to that. I met the wrong type of man, the kind that doesn't know how to treat a lady right. I didn't tell anyone about it, not even my mam. I was so ashamed and upset with myself for allowing it to happen after everything else. A year on, and I was still rattlin' around this big old house on my own and a mate of mine says, 'Why not rent out one of your rooms for a bit of company and a few extra pennies?''

'So, I put a sign in the window and your father, God bless him, was the first to knock on the door. I remember his face as though it was yesterday, all flustered and frustrated. He'd been turned away from every door that he'd been to. They didn't like black men in those days, let alone one with a baby. But I couldn't just turn him away. Besides, you were peering up at me out of your pushchair, smiling like the sun would never stop shining.' She reached over and caressed my cheek with her rough hand, 'You had the face of an angel. You were my second chance, Beth. God had smiled on me that day and I didn't care what colour you were or where you'd come from. You were going to be mine, my own little daughter.'

'We married 'cos it made things easier. I could adopt you, and your father was allowed to stay in the country. We were good friends and we grew to love each other. Neither of us wanted passion. We'd both had that,' she laughed nervously, 'and look where that had got us? Nah, what was important was that you were brought up proper and given a good home. I know some things about your real mother, but not much and I'm supposin' that most of what you need to know is written in that letter or packed in that box.' She pulled a crinkled tissue from her pocket, 'He never really talked to me about it properly. I asked, of course I asked, but he never really answered. You know what he was like. He'd clam up like an oyster; zip that mouth of his tighter than batman's pants.' She dabbed at her nose, 'He loved her though,' I heard her choke on the words, 'no denying that. He loved her more than he could ever have loved me-'

My reaction was unforgivable.

'-Why tell me now, for fuck's sake!' I bellowed.

The anger surged through me, exploding from the pit of my stomach where it had been subconsciously stored for all those years.

'For fuck's sake, I'm 33 years old or at least I thought I was until five minutes ago!'

My tirade was met by a stunned silence, an unstoppable force slamming into an immovable object.

'I am 33, aren't I?'

She stared at me with that same blank expression.

'I can't believe this. No, I don't want to believe this,' I went on. 'It's got to be a fucking joke, hasn't it? Mum? Please, please tell me this is just one big horrible fucking joke!'

'Don't you think I didn't worry about the consequences of not telling you,' she retorted, slamming her fist down on the table, 'I warned him. God I warned him, but he made me promise not to tell you. For all these years it was our secret. But then he wrote those bloody letters. Don't you see?' She cried, 'He wanted you to know. After all this time, he wanted you to know. He just left it up to me to have to tell you on my bleedin' own. The letters, the box, the key, don't you see?' She threw her hands up into the air, 'the bastard left it up to me to tell you all on my own.'

Chapter Six

Papa

Yes, I am scared. I am accustomed to the silence now, but I am scared that if I stop thinking I will cease to be. This is it – the great mystery of the ages – hell is the unforgiven. It is not what I was expecting.

Kozé bayo!

Alright!

They score certain laws into your heart from the minute you are intelligent enough to tell friend from foe. Every child learns the dance the moment he or she can walk. There is an order to things, a pattern that should never be flaunted because, otherwise, things might change. And change, we are told, is a dangerous thing. Sahana and I happened to learn our lesson at exactly the same time.

We were in the market in Quatre Bornes with our mothers. A tiny brown hand clasped in a rough potato peeling one, I was six years old when I spotted her across the glistening red mountain of *pom damours*. Sparkling brown eyes met twinkling brown eyes and we exchanged smiles. With my free hand, I pulled a face at her. She reciprocated – a cross-eyed grimace mirrored in another grubby face.

Both of our mothers were waiting to be served by the broken lady in the navy blue sari. Mo mama had her plastic colander of fruit ready for weighing. Sahana's mother, Mrs Sundaram, was taking her time picking out which succulent ones she was going to buy. It became clear after a long while, that we had to wait for Mrs Sundaram to finish picking her fruits before we would be served. Mama did not know that the old woman in the navy blue sari knew that Mrs Sundaram was married to Detective Inspector R. Sundaram. So, she grew more and more upset the longer she was made to wait.

Alala!

Like a thunderclap, she threw her plastic colander down on the ground, scattering the once unblemished tomatoes to the winds. Narrowing her eyes, she looked down at me and yanked my hand away from my face.

'Don't play with that damn *malbar*!'

Then she dragged me away. I tried to pull back but I did not yet have the strength to resist her. Instead, I watched helplessly as my new friend disappeared behind an auburn mound of *ziromon*. By the time we met each other again properly, we were well on our way to becoming adults. We had already learnt our lessons. We were well aware of what was expected.

Sahana had long black hair and skin, the colour of honey caramel. She smelled of talcum powder and patchouli incense when she brushed past you in the school corridor. She had shy brown eyes that dipped the moment you looked at her. She liked reading and spoke very good English. She spent her free time dreaming and looking forward to the next time that her father would take her and her little brother to the cinema. She especially liked the martial arts movies. She liked the way that their lips moved and the way that the words followed afterwards. Nobody knew that she wanted to be just like Bruce Lee; not even her best friend, Darika. Nobody knew that the real reason she broke her wrist on the way home from school that day was because she tried to karate chop a tree at the edge of the playground.

I kept myself to myself most of the time. I liked to think of myself as the strong silent type. I was big boned and as strong as an ox, with a voice as deep as my father's. Of course, I was nowhere near as good looking as Frank. My brother was athletic, intelligent and handsome, while I was shy, mediocre and clumsy. I loved my brother and sisters with the ferocity of a mute lion. They would always come first. To comfort these teenage sensibilities, I began to read. I read any books that I could get my hands on. I kept my nose in a library book while my family and friends chattered on around me. I learnt how to disappear, how to dissolve into the pages, how to hide behind the letters and the lines.

None of the Creole girls paid me any attention. They had their favourites – the loud boys, the rude boys, *galan kolonn*. I of course, liked the look of the honey caramel beauty in the corner of the library. If I tilted the book at the right angle, I could watch her undetected for ages. She was the one I always had my eye on – the one who would make my life difficult – the one who would definitely set me apart from the rest. The one, I secretly witnessed breaking her wrist as she tried to karate chop the tree at the edge of the playground.

Chapter Seven

Tifi

'I need space to think.'

I stood up and grabbed the letters up from the table. Mother continued to sob into her sleeve.

'I need to go.'

She looked up, shrugged her shoulders and muttered, 'You do what you thinks' best.'

I ran upstairs and threw the letter along with the rest of his 'memories', back into the biscuit tin, clutched it all under my arm and ran back downstairs to the kitchen again.

I dabbed a quick kiss on her tear-smeared cheek. 'You'll be OK?' I asked, already unconvinced.

'I'll be fine,' she sniffed, 'Just go. Go home to your husband.'

'OK then, well, call me, if you need me,' I stammered.

She nodded and returned her face to her crossed arms. I looked over my shoulder as I closed the front door behind me. I didn't think it right to leave her, no matter what she said, but I had to get away. I needed time to breath. I drove home and parked up alongside Patrick's polished BMW five series in the driveway. The lights were on inside the house, his shadow moving from room to room. My mobile phone went off in my bag. The word 'MUM' flashed up on the screen. I let it ring. Five minutes later, Patrick's face peered out through the front window curtains. Then the front door opened and he stepped out into the late evening murk. Shoulders hunched, he pulled the neck of his jumper over the top of his head and jogged towards the car.

'Your mum just called. She wants to know if you got home safely. I said I wasn't sure as you're still sitting outside in the car.'

Rain poured down the window that separated us, his strong features melting and ebbing away before my very eyes.

'Do you want to come in and tell me what's going on?'

I felt for the familiar touch of my steering wheel. The dusty warmth of the heater reminded me that there had been happier times.

'OK, I'm coming in!'

He was opening the passenger door before I had the where with all to lock it. He sat down beside me. As if in protest the inside of the windscreen misted over, creating a makeshift cocoon from the rest of the world.

'Beth, please tell me what's going on. Why won't you talk to me?'

'Because I don't want to!'

His head fell forward and he let out a long sigh, so I decided that this was as good a time as any, to stun him with my news.

'I've just found out that my mother is not actually my mother after all and that,' I reached over into the back seat and grabbed the tin, 'this box contains the love letters that my real mother gave to my father, who, by the way, was also kind enough to inform me, actually died giving birth to me. So besides the fact that I've just found out that I'm biologically orphaned, I've just been told that I killed my real mother into the bargain.' The anger and hurt swelled and surged within me. 'And it gets better, because that means that both of my parents have lied to me for the last thirty-three years. I don't even know what I am; let alone who I am anymore. I mean, for all I know our marriage itself might not even be legal. In the last four weeks my life has fallen apart and all you've done is go on and on about how you're not happy with this and how you're not happy with that. That I'm losing the fucking plot. Well, now it looks as though you've hit the bloody jackpot doesn't it,' I dropped the metal box into his lap, 'so I hope you're fucking happy now!'

He gawked from my face to the object that had narrowly missed his testicles and back again. I let the horror of my day sink slowly into his brain before I allowed myself to cry.

'What are you going to do?' he asked.

'What can I do?'

He made to reach for my hand, but I managed to pull it away in time.

'Beth?'

He looked lost and almost fragile with his wet head of hair and sopping jumper. He shook his head morosely, 'I've been thinking,'

'Well whoopee do for you!'

'For God's sake, shut up and let me speak –'

I curled back defensively. 'What?'

He brushed his face, spraying rainwater all over my dashboard. 'I think it'll do us good to take advantage of this opportunity,' he searched for approval, 'give us some time to think about things, find out what we really want, decide where we're going.'

I was thinking, 'not now, not like this', but instead I shrugged and said, 'If that's what you want.'

He looked hopeful. 'I think it's what we need to do.'

My heart sank. 'Quite frankly, I don't give a shit what you think!'

He smiled uncomfortably, 'That's my point exactly.'

'Oh, fuck off!'

I jumped out of the car, marched into the house and ran up the stairs. This was the last thing I needed. His timing was lousy. If we were going to split, it shouldn't have been like this. I was so angry, so enraged, so upset and he couldn't stop thinking about himself for one tiny moment. He just couldn't help himself. I ranted under my breath while I grabbed a dusty suitcase from on top of the wardrobe and rammed it full of mismatching clothes and other useless possessions. He didn't come after me. Instead, as I swept back down the stairs, towards the front door, I caught a glimpse of him in the dining room, pouring himself a large glass of cheap whisky. I looked up at the hall wall, at the happy pictures of his expansive family and wondered whether he'd ever be able to understand.

'Kit?'

'Uh-huh.'

'Can I come over?'

'Yeah, of course. What's up?'

'I think I've just left Patrick.'

'Oh, OK.'

Kitty didn't say a word as she took my case and my coat from me in the hallway. Instead, she nodded at the living room door which, once pushed, revealed a coffee table, two glasses and an ice-cold bottle of Sauvignon Blanc. I slumped into her battered couch and concentrated my mind briefly on one of the photos on the wall - A blue-pink flamingo on a salt lake at dusk in eastern Spain. I'd always liked Kitty's house. It was warm and inviting and filled with odd pieces of furniture that she insisted on purchasing from

Charity shops, no visible evidence of IKEA anywhere. The walls were a reliable Magnolia colour that instantly reminded me of student days enjoyed in the last millennia. Kitty said that she liked the colour because it didn't detract the light from her pictures; images of other worlds, other people and other lives that covered all available space. We all find solace in something I suppose, and Kitty found hers in photography.

'So go on then, what happened?' she enquired finally.

'Revelations.'

'What?'

'Revelations, my dear.'

I explained the whole sordid story of my day again, this time tagging on that final conversation with Patrick. She listened and 'tut-tutted' at the correct intervals and as I finished, she drained the rest of her glass and astutely commented,

'Fecking hell!'

I laughed anxiously, 'I think I'm cracking up, Kit. I looked at myself in the rear view mirror just a minute ago and I didn't recognise myself. All those years I thought I'd inherited my mother's cheekbones, and the bridge of her perfect little nose. All those mannerisms that I copied from her that had become a part of who I thought I was. But it was all a pack of lies. It would appear, Kitty, that my life is a complete and utter bollocks.'

She smiled, 'Well look, hon, all I can say, like, is that you can stay here for as long as you want, you know, for as long as you need. I'll make up the sofa for you tonight and then I'll sort out the back room for you from tomorrow, if that's what you want.' She patted my leg, 'You just take as much time as you need like to think about what you're going to do and all. I mean, I don't know how much help I'm going to be, but I'm here for you, OK?'

'Thanks.'

'No worries.'

She leant over the armrest and pressed play on the CD machine.

'A bit of Moby alright for you?'

'Play?'

'Yeah.'

'OK.'

So, we sat quietly and listened, staring at the images around us, gradually emptying the bottle of wine.

Chapter Eight

Papa

Of course I remember.

You do not forget things like that, they stay with you forever.

And this is absolutely necessary?

Mr Nehru always dragged that one word over his palate.

'Ennggerlish.'

It always attained the desired effect.

'Today, I will be setting your end of year assignments. You will be working in pairs and you will both share the same marks. Each pair will have their own topic to investigate and report on. In Engerlish.'

The whole class moaned in unison.

Cheered by our response he continued, 'So as to ensure the rule of exam board impartiality, I have written down the names of all the students in this class and placed them in this cup.'

He held a chipped cup into the air that had 'World Cup 1966' written on the side. 'And in this cup,' he held up a plain one without any chip, 'I have written the topics that you will be writing together.'

He surveyed the room, obviously exhilarated by the power he could sometimes wield over a group of hormone filled delinquents.

'Is everything clear?' Are there any questions?'

He scanned the room, desperate to intimidate us further with his foreboding countenance.

'Good,' he drawled lecherously, 'then let us begin.'

He called out the names.

'Lucien and Marguerite, you will be writing a project on the fishing industry in Mauritius. Sanjay and Jacky, you will be writing a project on weather systems that affect the island. Hilda and Simone, you will tell me about the geography of the island.'

A lottery of groans or jubilation followed each reading. I bent down and fiddling with my shoelace, stole a glance at Sahana. I was encouraged to see that she was not whispering in conspiring tones with her friends but gazing out of the classroom window. I half listened to the murmur of names that floated across the room, caught for a moment in a fantasy that concerned her long black hair. A sharp prod in the ribs delivered me back to earth.

'George, glad to see you back with us.'

I felt the heat rise to my cheeks as Mr Nehru and my fellow classmates stared in my direction.

'You will be paired with...'

There was a moment of hesitation as Mr Nehru tried to extract his hand from within the cup in which he had lodged it. The eyes all returned to the front of the classroom and watched in glee as our teacher managed to disengage the cup and drop it unceremoniously to the floor. Half a dozen small pieces of paper fluttered like dying butterflies and the room exploded in laughter. Mr Nehru knelt down and scrabbled to pick up the pieces. I stole another glance at Sahana and met her gaze head on. I averted my eyes immediately and felt a shudder of electricity pass down my spine along with a familiar twitch of anticipation. Mr Nehru got to his feet, a bead of sweat trickling down the side of his face.

'George, you are paired with Simone.'

My stomach fell three feet to sit on the floor between my dusty leather shoes.

'But, Sir!' A whining tremolo flew across the room as he reached for the topic cup. 'I'm already paired with Hilda!'

Simone appeared to be close to tears as the class unleashed a cacophony of jeers. Exasperated, Mr Nehru grabbed at another name and read it aloud without any thought of the consequence that his flippant response would set in motion.

'Right you are then, Simone. George, you are paired with Sahana and you will be studying the sugar cane industry. Now who's left?'

Ayo!

A few hands went up and Mr Nehru sorted through the names on the table. No one could see that my stomach still sat on the floor between my leather shoes. No one noticed that I was too scared to turn around this time. Now I had someone's permission to talk to the honey caramel beauty in the corner, I did not know what to do. My back grew warmer as I imagined her behind me, waiting for me to turn around.

'George?' My desk companion, Pierre, grinned into my face, 'You don't have to make it so obvious that you don't want to work with the poor girl.' He nudged me in the ribs yet again, 'Where are your manners!'

I heard the muffled giggles of those in earshot and decided not to take the bait. I would wait and endure the lesson first, read a book, make sure everyone had left the classroom before I said anything – just in case I blushed and gave the game away.

She told me later that as the teacher had called out the names, a silky gown of perspiration had unfurled itself along her arms, legs and torso. She told me that she had not expected her incantation to work. She always recited the same silly rhyme when she wanted something to happen.

'Sahana and George, Sahana and George, Sahana and George.'

She had chanted it silently in her head as she gazed out of the classroom window. She had wanted to avoid looking at anyone, especially Darika, in case she read her thoughts or noticed the anguish in her face. When Mr Nehru read out her name, her stomach had fallen to the floor to rest between her Bata sandals. The horrific reality of what had happened raised its ugly head and chomped its teeth down on her fragile heart.

As our classmates scraped their chairs across the floor at the end of the lesson, we got up to do the same. Only then did we look at each other.

'Shall we meet in the library after school on Friday?' I asked.

'Péna Problem,' she replied.

'Trwa-z-er?'

I offered the contract.

'Dakor.'

She accepted.

We left the classroom and met up with our friends at the gates of the school. We did not say anything nice about our project partners to our friends. We did not say anything bad about each other either. We simply listened to the usual friendly banter as we walked our separate ways home.

That evening, I sat at the table, doodling her name on a piece of paper under the illusion that I was studying for my exams. Marie, who was about nine or ten at the time, sat cross-legged in the armchair, reading one of my discarded adventure comics. Juliet, then about eight, was happily combing and re-combing the yellow hair of her favourite doll. As the evening drew in, so the smell of starch and fried onions filled the room. Mama was preparing *rougay poisson salé sounouk* and *bouillon bred*, from a plant that she plucked from the hedge at the rear of the house. I looked through the front window and saw papa enter the square, exhausted from another long day at the factory. The air was thick with the reflected heat of the day and I watched as he pawed at his throat and slapped his lips together, quickening his steps towards a cold Phoenix beer and a good feed.

'They're going to promote that *kouyon*, Mahmood to foreman,' he said, as he stepped past me to kiss his daughters. 'God knows what will happen now.'

'Don't blaspheme, Claude!' Mama called from the kitchen.

'*Sori, mo koko.* And there have been more fires today; they say you can see the smoke rising over Port Louis.'

She came into the living room, her apron smeared with memories of other meals. 'I know, Madame Lasyet says that they've burnt down her favourite textile shop. She said she saw a gang of young Muslim boys hanging about near the market as well, this afternoon, said they were ready to fight anyone who came near them.'

Papa took off his shoes and shoved his gnarly feet into his well-worn sandals. 'Michel says he's thinking of leaving, going to Australia. His brother left nine months ago, says he can help find him work and a safe place to stay.'

'Now don't you go getting those thoughts in your head, Claude. This is our home and I'm not going to leave this country on account of no-one. Not even if *bann lapolis malbar* tell me to go.' She strode back out the room, back to her pots, a cloud of steam billowing in her wake.

'I know, my love. I was just thinking about it, that's all. It would be safer for the children.'

'I know it would, but I'll not allow *bann malbar* or *bann dimounn laskar*, tell me where I can or cannot live, even if it kills me. This is my country, the country where my parents were born. I will not leave it. And besides, where do you think we will get the money from? Not from your job, I'm sure.'

And that was when I truly understood that I would never be allowed to love her. Some things in life cannot change.

Chapter Nine

Tifi

Life went back to normal for a while. Well, as normal as it could be. I went back to the house a few times when Patrick was out, packed more of my things and moved into Kitty's back room. I visited the gym on nights when I knew he wouldn't be there until I became too paranoid of the knowing looks of our leotard clad instructors. I took up smoking pot again. Kitty insisted that it helped her creativity and warmed by the sweet aroma, the familiar meditation of licking and sticking fragile pieces of paper together, rolling and hoping to create the perfect spliff, I'd decided to join in.

I found it helped my newly acquired playstation skills as well as my ability not to think. Not to muse over the letters and the secrets they revealed. Not to imagine my father, knowing he was soon to die, sitting down and putting pen to paper. Not to remember my mother's expression as she opened her heart and faced her ultimate fears. Not to reflect that half of me was made up of someone I'd never known or would know. Not to picture Patrick sat alone in his study, sipping from a glass of cheap whisky, and certainly not to consider that I was completely out of my depth.

I didn't tell anyone at work about my mutating personal life and no one appeared to notice a change. It was generally understood that I just pushed paper around a desk and attended meetings with pointless agendas. Like most civil servants, I endured the daily nine to five grind to pay the mortgage and avoid having to get a proper job in the private sector where it was rumoured that employees weren't allowed lunch breaks. I started arriving later and leaving early and discovered that I could hide a multitude of sins by saying that I'd work from home in the afternoons.

I visited my mother occasionally. Usually the morning after a frantic 'phone call saying that she could hear groaning noises in the house. She said she'd rediscovered God at the back of the wardrobe in her bedroom. I stayed over once to ascertain exactly what it was she was talking about. I arrived at ten p.m., bypassed the TV, the comfort food, the eternally untidy living room, the grubby kitchen and went straight to bed. Perched on either side of the conjugal bed, we lay staring at the ceiling, her hair in rollers that never came out and me in a green velveteen pyjama set she'd kindly supplied. Nothing happened. I didn't hear any groaning, didn't smell the burnt toast signature of a poltergeist and didn't see anything float across the room. She said that I'd dropped off, that I wasn't being serious enough, and that I wasn't taking her seriously enough.

'I think it may be your father,' she said. 'I think he's in limbo because you won't spread his ashes.'

'Whatever you say, Mother. Now get some sleep.'

The following day, I arrived at the office at around half past two and had barely had time to take my coat off and make myself a cup of tea before I received the summons.

'Beth, Dan Patterson wants to see you in his office as soon as,' a colleague called as they passed by the kitchen on their way to the photocopy room.

I returned to my desk with my company issue mug and rifled through my bag for my lipstick. It took a while. After pushing paper, pens, rizlas, lighters, a calculator, translator machine, a plastic bag half filled with skunk, a note pad, various personal toiletries and my mobile phone covered in biscuit crumbs out of the way, I located my make up bag and extracted my 'daring' red lipstick. Once I was happy with its application, I made my way to Dan Patterson's office on the sixth floor.

The Director of Internal Communication, Dan's main responsibility was the writing of emails using the 'to: everybody' group address on the shared internal network. Rumour had it that he was shagging the head of accounts who in turn was secretly dating the Chairman, who was also having an affair with Dan's secretary. I tried to bear in mind all the juicy details as he opened the door and ushered me into his office. He waited for me to sit down before he pulled the Venetian blind shut and crossed the room to sit behind his absurdly large desk. He made a church and then a steeple with his fingers and examined the edge of the table in front of me.

'Elizabeth,' he said finally.

'Yes, that's me.'

He swivelled in his chair, and examined his computer screen for inspiration. I wondered what part of his extensive and expensive management training he could be calling on.

'Are you happy in your work?'

'Yes.'

He looked away again – stared out the window at a passing seagull.

'And how do you feel about your team?'

'OK.'

'And how do you consider your position within it?'

'Fine.'

He sighed, loosened his tie.

'You're not going to make this easy for me are you?'

'No, not if you don't get to the point, I won't.'

He grimaced, fiddled with his glasses.

'It has been brought to my attention that a number of your clients have been complaining about missed appointment and delays in payment.'

'Really?'

'A few of your colleagues have also reported a shift in your team sensibilities, which is now affecting morale in the whole group. There have also been a few reports concerning your behaviour towards certain members of the administrative staff.'

So the wolves had been out after all.

'I've no idea what you're talking about.'

'Well, there are testimonies from two of your colleagues.'

'Who?'

'I c-can't say,' he stuttered, 'you know that. It's confidential.'

'So what's going to happen?'

'We're in the process of deciding how to proceed.'

'You're not going to sack me are you?'

'Oh no, heavens no. But, I have spoken to HR and we are going to offer you a four week cooling off period while we decide what to do.'

He paused, checked his screen again, kept his eyes averted, 'with the recommendation that you, um, attend six sessions with a company appointed counsellor.'

'Pardon?'

'With a counsellor. The company health scheme will cover the costs.'

'Are you trying to tell me that I'm too nuts to work here?'

'Of course not. Of course you're not nuts, it's just that a counsellor will help you, you know, um, will help you get your priorities in, um, order. Help you work out your issues and, and hopefully guide you to be able to, um, work with other people successfully.'

'And if I decline?'

'Decline?'

'Yes, decline.'

'Then, y-yes, you may lose your current position, or at least, be transferred out of your team and onto a lower grade.'

'I see.'

Dan slumped into his chair exhausted.

'So, that's my choice, is it?'

'I'm afraid so,' he said, repositioning his glasses.

'OK, then,' I said, rising from the table, 'How about I take this four week cooling off period and I don't come back?'

He looked up, aghast, 'You'll have to work your notice if you've decided to leave. We can't pay you your last month's pay or any outstanding holiday pay and, and it, it will affect your pe-pension.'

'And what if I lodge a grievance procedure with HR, get my doctor to sign me off for four weeks with stress and inform my Union and my lawyer of the constructive dismissal elements of this meeting?'

There was no response.

'I thought so,' I said, holding it together and sauntering out of the door.

I decided to walk home. On the way, I found a park bench, swept a wet crisp packet aside and sat down. I rolled a joint, stuck it between my lips, savoured the reassuring crackle of burning paper, revelled in the naughty joy of the first drag. A small gaggle of school kids in crumpled uniforms passed by, sniggering as they inhaled the air that enveloped me. Neatly packaged white faces, without a care in the world.

'Hey lady! Give us a drag!'

I lifted my gaze, along with the middle finger of my left hand.

I didn't notice much after that. The days passed. I awoke when the front door slammed shut in the morning, fashioned a mould of my behind on the sofa and hardened the skin under the stamp of my thumb on the remote control. Kitty would wonder back into my life in the evenings, accompanied by a cup of tea and another toke.

'Like, what have you been up to today, Beth?' Kitty asked me one evening.

'Nothing much,' I replied, flicking through the TV channels.

'Do you want to come with me to the studio tomorrow?'

'Nah, it's OK. I'll only get in the way.'

'You won't, Beth. Seriously, I'd like you to come.'

'Maybe another time, if that's alright?'

She picked the empty cups up from the coffee table and placed them on the breakfast bar. 'Well, it's been over four weeks, now. Do you like, have any idea when you might be, you know, ready to join the human race again?'

'Sorry?'

She reached past me for the remote control and turned off the television.

'You heard me.'

I stared at the blank television screen, dived headlong into its darkness.

'Heh? Beth? Look, I'm just worried about you, that's all. It's been weeks since you moved in and you don't seem...are you alright?'

I felt her hand on my shoulder but was unable to recognise her attention.

'Heh? You can't carry on like this.'

I heard her voice, but was unable to listen.

'You've got to talk to me about it. Beth? Can you hear me? You have to start talking.'

I felt her take my hand in hers. I mustered something to say.

'He's left me with nothing.'

More words queued on my tongue, barred from escape by teeth and the unwillingness of my lips.

'Who has?'

'I'm too scared to look in the mirror.'

'Why?'

I slowly shook the thoughts from my head. 'I wake up in the morning and the first thing I want to do is shut my eyes again and disappear.'

'Oh, Beth.'

'I don't know what I'm supposed to think. I don't know what to eat, what to wear. I can't even look after myself properly. I mean look at me,' I tore at my jumper, 'I'm nothing.'

'You're not nothing.'

'I am. Why else would he have done this to me? Why would a father do this to his daughter?'

'I don't know, Beth. I really don't know.'

'I hate him!' I yanked at my unkempt hair, 'and now Patrick hates me. My mother hates me. God, even my work mates hate me. I'm shit. I'm nothing. I'm no-one.'

She hit my arm, 'Stop it.'

'I don't know what to do.'

We sat like that for a while. My head so crammed full of cotton wool that it was impossible to think, to put things into some kind of rational perspective. I knew I was losing the plot. As I grasped at the rope, it slipped through my fingers, encouraging me to drift further away from dry land.

'Look, I've got an idea,' Kitty said, pulling me to my feet and leading me through to the bathroom.

She turned on the shower. 'You need to get out of your pyjamas and into proper clothes. Get in there and have a good scrub. Use all of my smellies if you have to, I don't mind. Just take your time and make yourself feel clean.'

She shut the door behind her. Each small task had become Everest.

Kitty stood to attention in the living room, when I returned, brandishing a hairbrush in her hand, 'Come and sit here on this cushion.'

She pointed with the brush to the beanbag between her feet. I obliged - an automated response.

She combed the brush through my hair, 'What are we going to do with you, heh?'

'I don't know.'

'I never told you about my dad, did I?' she said, her voice soft, sapient. 'He left home when I was eight years old. There weren't any arguments, no screaming, no tears. Mum stood by as he dragged his bags down the stairs, and like, even opened the front door for him. I had no idea what was going on. I just stood there, with my thumb in my mouth, looking on as though it was all run of the mill stuff.' She placed her hand on my shoulder, 'Strange thing is I can't remember sensing any sadness between them. In fact, I'd say they appeared more relieved than anything else. Dad asked me to look after mum and I hadn't even bothered to take my thumb out of my mouth,' she chuckled, 'I told him that I would with it still firmly lodged in my mouth. Then he'd walked out the door and mum had shut the door and that was it. She told me to go upstairs and finish my homework and when dad still hadn't come home three nights later, I kind of knew that I'd never see him again. It was all as simple as that.'

I rolled forward off the beanbag and onto the floor, turning to face her.

'What I'm trying to say,' she continued, 'is that at least you know why your dad left you. It's not as though he wanted to go, is it?'

'I'm sorry. I didn't want to make it sound like...I know some people have it worse and -,'

'No, that's not what I meant. It's not that,' her face was calm, serene even, 'it's just you've got to find something to cling onto, you know. No matter how little or insignificant it may feel now, it'll make the difference later. He may have kept his secrets but, like, he never meant to leave you.'

'But that still doesn't help me know who I am.'

'You know who you are, Beth. You're the same person you were before he died. You're Beth Labelle. Beth the Beautiful. You're just having trouble recognising her at the moment. That's all. You'll find her again.'

'What makes you so sure?'

She reached over and tapped me on the top of the head with the brush handle. 'Cos, you're sat right in front of me, ye great idget!'

Chapter Ten

Papa

The moment?

It was quite simple really.

'What do you know about the sugar cane?' Sahana asked me from across the table. I could not keep my pupils focused on her. Our eyes were like magnets, one minute impossible to prise apart, the next impossible to make meet. I was pained by her proximity although I did not want to be anywhere else in the world. I knew that the situation called for a clearing of the air before we could ever hope to study together properly. I took a deep breath, raised my head and then let it drop again.

Ayo!

'Only what my mother told me about the British bringing the field labour from India,' I replied.

She could tell that I was uncomfortable in her presence. She thought that I wanted to be somewhere else, anywhere other than being trapped in a library on a Friday afternoon with her. Her gaze flickered over my face, along my shoulders and down my arms. Then she blushed and grabbed at a book on the table, opened it on a random page and started to read aloud.

The size of the sugar plantations on the island of Mauritius range from 10 hectares to 1000 hectares. The plantations will remain productive for a maximum of 10 years at which point they must be cleared and replanted to ensure continuing crops. The traditional harvest time is between June and September.

I lifted my head up from the notepad that I had been examining and finally caught her attention. I watched the red patch on the side of her cheek expand and flow down her neck, across the top of her chest and down beneath the fabric of her shirt.

'Are you sure you want me as your study partner?' she asked.

I took in her perfectly formed nose and travelled down across the light brush of her top lip until I reached the plump dark red lips. I watched as she articulated the question. My groin throbbed instinctively.

'Yes.'

The answer was sure, steady and clear.

'Really?'

Goosebumps flowed in a tide across her forearms.

'Since the moment I saw you.'

It came out of my mouth so naturally that I did not have time to stop it. It appeared to have the desired effect, if one had been expected – a smile that could light the sky over the oceans at night. I leant back in my chair, drank her in fully and let the corners of my mouth rise to mirror hers.

Sahana and I fell deeply in love over an English project in a library in the late autumn of 1969. Gradually, the deceit that our love elicited would come as naturally as had our affection.

Chapter Eleven

Tifi

A few days later, I actually managed to venture out of the house to buy two pints of milk from the Indian shop on the corner. My mother called that same afternoon and somehow I ended up agreeing to go to Church with her to commemorate the third month anniversary of my father's death. I hesitated on the steps up to the door, my apathy absorbed by the yellow pebble dash exterior of a council estate Catholic Church. Father Johnson, a tall, fat, red, balding priest, rolled up the aisle towards us. Behind him, magnificent gold painted tubes piped a flat key hymn. He held his hands out, all the while emitting an odd purring noise from the back of his throat.

'Ahhrrgghh, Mrs Labelle,' he took her mittened hands in his, 'and you've brought Elizabeth as well I see. How nice to see you.'

He didn't wait to see my half-hearted smile. Instead, he reversed us, steered my mother and me to sit beside him in the pews to his right, mumbling all the while, 'How are you? How are you? How are you?'

Beads of sweat appeared and spread along his hairy brow.

'I'm fine, Father,' my mother replied, 'It's Beth who needs your guidance.'

I instinctively calculated the distance between my feet and the chapel door.

'Ah, I see,' he said, failing to mask a wink, 'having trouble dealing with the death of your father? That is common, no matter how old you are. Losing a parent is one of the hardest trials that we mere mortals have to go through. You shouldn't feel embarrassed about it. Tell me child, what questions can I help you with?'

'None whatsoever thanks,' I replied, gathering my coat around me and attempting to slide away along the hard polished seat.

Feigning not to notice, my mother told him, 'George wrote a last will and testament asking her to spread his ashes in his homeland of Mauritius and she's refusing to go.'

'I'm not refusing,' I explained, 'I've simply no intention of going.'

She grabbed at Father Johnson's sleeve, 'I'm scared that his soul won't be able to rest if she doesn't do it.'

I rolled my eyes, 'She thinks that my dad is haunting her house.'

'Ah, I see,' the priest pondered theatrically, rubbing his chin and inadvertently pushing its flaps over his pendulous earlobes.

'It could happen though, couldn't it,' she said, still frantically gripping his robes.

'The Church doesn't believe in ghosts, mother.'

'What about the Holy Ghost?' She snapped back.

'You're not honestly telling me that I've got to perform this ridiculous errand because dad might come back and haunt me, for God's sake?'

Father Johnson coughed.

'Sorry.'

He accepted my apology with a curt nod, 'I'm not saying that I believe in ghosts, but sometimes we have to do things to help tame certain spirits within us.'

'And I don't see,' my mother added, 'what you find so ridiculous about performing your father's last wishes, God rest his soul.'

'Just like you didn't find it ridiculous to pretend to the entire world that you were my real mother for thirty years?'

The words rebounded off the now silent pipes, bounced within the crevasses of the pulpit, skated across the surface of the font, crashed against the alabaster ears of Mary and her saints and came to rest on a crown of thorns. Her fingers unfurled themselves from his sleeves, brushed the creases from her knitted skirt, repositioned her woolly hat and Father Johnson coughed.

'I'm sorry,' my mother said, rising from the pew, clasping her handbag to her belly and turning to leave.

The priest reached out and touched her back, 'Shelly, don't go. Wait for me in the vestibule. I'll just have a chat with Elizabeth and be along in a minute. There's a tea urn in the corridor. Why not make yourself a cup of tea? I won't be long.'

She nodded at the floor and shuffled away, along the pews, down the aisle and out of sight. He opened his mouth slowly, so I tried to cut him off at the chase, 'Before you say anything, I don't need any help.'

'I didn't say I would give you any.'

'Oh.'

'My main concern is your mother's welfare. Over the last four weeks, she has come to see me nine times. Nine times, Elizabeth and she's not even Catholic. I understand that you are coping with your father's death in your own way. That you have more or less lost your job, walked out on your marriage and that you're living out of a suitcase in the back room of a friend's house. Your mother is coping in her way, trying to exist in a world which she now feels has no meaning. You both have to deal with deep-seated issues and the bile of long harboured secrets. It's not an easy time for either of you but, at some point, you are going to have to face up to life and get on with it. There were three people in your family, each with their own reasons for thinking and behaving in the way that they did. Not all of these reasons necessarily revolved around you. Think about it. And while you're at it, remember your mother is all alone now. If she is unable to move on in her life because she believes his soul isn't at rest then that's something she's going to have to deal with. But, if you've got the power to help her and do not,' he beat solemnly at the middle of his chest with his fist, 'you have to seriously examine what kind of a person you really are deep inside.'

He emphasised every 'you', 'your' and 'you're'.

Shit.

I sat in a sulking silence as he suggested we bow our heads in prayer.

'Dear Lord, please give your child, Elizabeth, the strength to know and understand the importance of the task that you have brought to bear upon her. Bless her and help her to see how, by performing her father's final wish, she can give his soul rest and bring solace to her mother. And Lord, help her to look inside herself and find the courage to forgive those around her. Help her to see the world in a better light. Please protect her and her mother in their hour of need. We ask this in your name, our Lord. Amen.'

I was already standing when he opened his eyes. 'Well, I'd better be going,' I said, zipping up my coat, 'Thanks for everything. It's been great.' Then I trudged out into the frosty spring air and made my way back to Kitty's.

The first thing I saw when I opened the door was the mirror. It crept up on me as though it had been playing hide and seek all the while. It made me conscious of dry reddened cheeks and dark sunken eyes. It counted lines that I'd never seen before. I pulled my hair back up into a ponytail and turned my head to the left, to the right. My cheekbones and jaw line stood proud of my flesh. I shuddered and let my hair fall again. In a waking daze, I walked through the house, past a rug of crumbs on the carpet, a couple of empty packets of hobnobs, an abundance of empty cans of pop on the floor. My shoes squeaked on the sticky kitchen floor, my hand slid over surfaces sprinkled with fairy cake dust and smeared with marmalade. I even discovered a new ecosystem of vegetables and fruit with a bustling population of tiny little flies.

Driven by a pure instinctual urge, I took off my coat and rolled up my sleeves. The pink marigolds were under the kitchen sink alongside a bottle of bleach and a can of furniture polish. Three hours later, the house sparkled and giggled with glee. The washing machine purred in contentment. Even the carpet felt cheered by a good 'Shake n' Vaccing'. I took a shower in the gleaming bathroom, changed into some smart clothes that I'd actually ironed, checked my purse for my switch card and made my way on foot to the beauty salon/hairdressers on the corner of Leigh road and Thomas Street.

By the time I got back, Kitty was already in the kitchen, rolling a joint on the breadboard. 'What the hell's happened to you?' She asked.

'What do you mean?'

She licked the papers, 'The house? Your clothes? Heh, even your hair?'

'Don't you like it? I thought this was what you were waiting for.'

'Well, yeah, of course I was, I'm just surprised that's all, but, like, it's definitely good.'

'Good.'

I pulled a stool up to the breakfast bar. 'You working tomorrow?' I enquired.

'Well, you know, I was intending to. Why? What you thinking?'

'You fancy going on a little trip?'

'Like where?'

I shrugged, 'Mauritius?'

She poked the filter through the tighter end of the cone. 'Yeah, why not. I mean, I'm in need of some new material and stuff anyway and I've just got my new passport in the post. Have you got yours with you?'

'No, but it shouldn't be a problem to go back to the house this afternoon and pick it up before Patrick comes home from work.'

'That kind of settles it then,' she said, bringing the spliff up to her lips, lighting it and inhaling deeply. 'To Mauritius,' she wheezed.

'To Mauritius,' I replied, taking it from her. I held it to my lips for a fraction of a second, thought better of it, and much to Kitty's dismay, stubbed it out in the ashtray.

The following day, Kitty and I purchased the cheapest and earliest tickets to Mauritius that we could get our hands on and by way of the internet, located a reasonably priced apartment on the west coast of the island; all thanks to our flexible friends. Then I'd gone round to see my mother to pick up the casket. Her face had been a picture of maternal angst and misplaced pride as she passed him ceremoniously to me. She'd looked like some kind of fairy tale queen sending her offspring off on a quest from which she might never return.

'It's OK, mum, I'm just going to go over there, find the field, scatter the ashes and come home.'

I was filled with a new found optimism that everything was going to be alright; that somehow once those ashes were gone; my life would fall back into the same safe pattern; that we would all be allowed to get back on with our lives.

'Promise me you'll be careful. And call me. I'll worry myself sick if you don't,' she fretted.

'Mum,' I replied with a smile and all the confidence in the world. 'I'll only be gone ten days. What can happen to me in ten days?'

Part Two

Discovery

Chapter Twelve

Tifi

Sugar cane swayed in the wake of a tropical breeze. It stretched on for as far as the eye could see. My neck hurt, my legs felt as heavy as stone and my eyeballs itched with excessive air-drying. I hadn't slept a wink during the twelve hour journey from Heathrow and it showed. To make matters worse, as I made my way down the steps from the plane to Tierra firma, I felt a layer of sweat seep through to the surface of my skin. I stopped for a minute on the tarmac, put down my cabin bag and rubbed the blood along the veins of my legs. I looked up and noticed the sign on the top of the yellow building in front of us. It was framed by a clear blue sky and read, 'Welcome to Sir Seewoosagur Ramgoolam Airport, Welcome to Mauritius.'

'Security!' A cry from a police officer made me jump.

Click, click, click.

'No pictures, please. There are strict rules,' he panted as he approached, holding out his hand. 'I must ask you to take out the film and give it to me.'

'I'm a photographer, not a terrorist,' Kitty answered indignantly beside me.

I'm sure that you are not, but rules are rules and they must be obeyed, young lady.'

Within the first five minutes of our arrival, we already stood out from the crowd. I lowered my head and made like a turtle, denying my friendship with surprising ease. Kitty was so angry at having to hand over the camera that she didn't notice, or at least didn't comment on my unwillingness to get involved on her behalf. While she was made to wait at customs for its safe return, I scuttled off through passport control and arrivals and waited outside for her by the taxi rank. Fuming, she arrived an hour later, waving her passport at me and grumbling something about Guantanamo Bay. Eager to get on, I forgot everything that the travel agent had advised about taxis, and allowed a malnourished grinning man to yank the trolley out of our possession. While Kitty ranted incoherently at no one in particular, I followed along like a lemming, across the car park and past the more official looking drivers that were queuing at the gates outside. The man said he knew where we wanted to go and offered what appeared in my jet lagged state, to be a reasonable price. Then I sat down in the backseat of his little battered car and listened in resignation as our luggage was thrown into the boot.

The car swerved erratically in a vain attempt to avoid the potholes and helmet-less moped drivers that littered our path. Now and then, an antique bus played chicken with us from the other side of the road, belching dark clouds of noxious fumes in through the cars' open windows. Kitty tried to wind her window up but the handle fell off in her hand. The taxi driver looked over at her as she cradled the limp apparatus in her lap and informed us that, 'it is broken'. He took it from her and placed it in the glove compartment along with a smashed wing mirror, a severed windscreen wiper and a rusty car door handle. Then he laughed and proudly announced that his car was falling apart.

Small towns and villages appeared and disappeared just as quickly as we reached them. Half constructed concrete boxes with flat roofs and barred windows mingled amongst rows of concrete shops with painted signs celebrating Liverpool Football Club. Neat school children in blue pleated skirts and shorts waited at Zebra crossings, their satchels slung nonchalantly over their shoulders. The taxi driver waved to a group of smouldering young men who sat under a tree on the side of the road. Belonging in a Californian gangster movie rather than this Bollywood backdrop, they sported bandannas, woolly hats, cropped trousers and basketball tops. All they were missing was an UZI nine millimetre and some crack cocaine. They nodded coolly as we passed, and at the turn in the road, the scenery returned yet again to the sugar cane.

The taxi weaved its way through the little village of Flic en Flac, past a spar supermarket, a casino, a night-club and a sprawling Chinese restaurant; a line of old shanty houses and a couple of mangy stray dogs failing to blend in with their more modern surroundings. The beach and an expanse of clear blue water appeared along the right hand side of the road.

The taxi driver said, 'Is pretty beach, no?'

'I believe it is, yes,' Kitty replied, leaning over me to get a better view out of my window.

He slowed the car. The muted scent of curry leaves and salt drifted through the open window as we passed umpteen families picnicking in the shade of the trees that lined the sands. Many of the women were wearing saris and sat on cloths around camping stoves, preparing and cooking food for the minions of laughing children who ran back and forth across the grass and pine needles. The men sat and chatted amongst themselves, drinking from large bottles of Coca Cola, while others who were less fortunate were prised away by demanding offspring to play amongst the waves. Large brightly painted public buses also hid from the sun; garlands of flowers as well as posters and icons of Hindu gods hanging from their windows, along with placards that still impudently displayed the destinations that they should have been visiting elsewhere.

The taxi came to a halt outside a four-storey block of holiday apartments and as if by magic, a portly security guard waddled out of a side entrance, a beaming smile spread haphazardly across his face.

'*Madame Stephens*?' he asked, directing the question at our bags.

'*Oui*,' I replied

'*Ah. Bonjour et bienvenue á L'île Maurice*,' he said, jovially, one eye on me the other directed at Kitty, 'You must be very tired after your long journey. Please take your key, your apartment is on the fourth floor. I will help you with your luggage.'

'*Merci*.'

Moments later we're stood on our balcony admiring the view. Kitty opened her hand luggage and pulled out another camera, never one to miss an opportunity. The sun was still high in the sky, casting its glare over a line of jagged mountains that separated us from the mainland. In the other direction, I could just catch a glimpse of the sea over the tops of the trees.

'Let's choose bedrooms and get some rest,' she said, as her film came to an end.

She chose the room with the bunk-beds; I chose the room with the double bed. Both thankfully had air-conditioning. I took the small wooden casket out of my bag, placed it on the bedside table, lay down on the bed and closed my eyes. Within moments, I had a headache. I tried to ignore it, but it grew and grew into a relentless mushroom cloud of pressure. Resigned to having no rest, I stood up and the pain miraculously abated. I shuddered, staring at the little box that sat alongside my pillow. I lay down again and my temples complained instantly. I stood up and the pain immediately disappeared. There was nothing for it. Picking him up at arm's length, I took him into the living room, placed him on the sideboard, and covered him with a tablecloth that I found in a drawer. Then I scurried back to my room and strangely enough, fell soundly asleep.

It was dark by the time I finally woke up, half my body covered by a nylon sheet, the other covered in goose bumps from my overzealous programming of the air conditioning unit above the door. I slung on my dressing gown and trotted across cold floor tiles to Kitty's room and knocked on the door. Her bed hadn't even been slept in. I found her empty camera case on the dining room table along with a note saying that she'd gone looking for provisions.

Using the old fashioned finger dialling phone on the wall, I called home to let my mother know that we'd arrived safely, but there was no answer. Still holding the receiver, I toyed, for a split second, with the idea of phoning Patrick but decided that it'd be better if I went back to bed.

I lay back down on the bed, noticing the letter out of the corner of my eye. It was resting on top of my suitcase, gently glowing in the moonlight. I tried to relax and ignore it, but it begged me to open it one more time. I gave in once again and ended up reading and re-reading it several times, hypnotised by the phrases that clamoured from the pages; words that even in death my father couldn't bring himself to tell me.

We were not supposed to love each other... Her name was Sahana and she died bringing you into the world... we lost more than we bargained for...we had to run away, if only to keep you safe.

Where did his lies begin? Where did they end? He had been my one true constant in life, like the position of the pole star; something solid from which I could navigate my thoughts and feelings. But all the while he'd been playing me like a puppet, pulling my strings, just like he was now. Sending me five thousand miles across the globe to a country I knew nothing about, except for what little I'd managed to glean from the illicit cuttings I'd kept in a children's scrapbook. From beyond the grave, he expected me to scatter his ashes on his homeland with only the letters of a misguided teenager to guide me.

I thought about the little box – a small wooden casket with a bronze plaque that demanded my grief. I didn't want to let him have it. I didn't care for the little box or for the little person who resided in pieces within it. I was doing this for mother and to put an end to all the lies. I wanted this all finished as soon as possible. Out of the way and finished so that we could get on with our lives. In my mind, he'd ruined everything. He'd made me doubt. Just as I thought I was finally getting somewhere, he'd stripped me of knowing who I was yet again, having already conned me into thinking I was someone else throughout my childhood. What made things worse, was that he'd even deceived me into accepting an apology without knowing the full extent of his betrayal.

I felt myself starting to get upset again and in a futile attempt to try and calm my thoughts, I put the letter down and reached for the Jilly Cooper novel that I'd bought at Heathrow. But even she couldn't suppress the babble of memories from surfacing.

My father, taking me to my first Judo lesson when I was eight years old. Holding my hand with its glitter nail polished fingernails tightly in his massive bear claw. Dojo sounded like Dodo. Knowing that he was sitting behind me on the same long benches that we would jump off in the gym at school. Hah Jimmy! Sensing his anxiety as I took my first tumble. The way the white cotton pyjama top accentuated my brown skin. My Dew Doggy. Sat in the roof, looking out of the skylight. Pointing at stars that twinkled like my mother's eyes, his long strong arm guiding my gaze. The Great Bear. The Buckle. The Frying Pan. Mother preparing hot mugs of Ovaltine and passing them through the trapdoor of the loft. Waiting breathlessly for a shooting star. Wishing that I would grow as proud and strong as my father. Wishing that I would become as beautiful as my mother. Feeling different. Feeling loved. Feeling safe.

Happy memories broken by the immature squeal of juvenile voices that I'd thought I'd put away a long long time ago:

'Oi, Wagon Wheel!'

'Oi, Paky!'

'You stink of curry!'

'Whad'your mother do? Roll you in dog shit when you were born?'

Followed swiftly by the composed and condescending voices of adulthood, people who thought they had a God given right to pigeonhole me from birth:

'Where do you come from?'

'Nah, I mean, where do you REALLY come from?'

In a final act of surrender, I'd pulled my sheet off the bed, wrapped it around my shoulders and stepped out onto the balcony. The southern sky above was navy blue and crystal clear. A million and one stars curved their way across it, delineating the all-embracing arch of the Milky Way. The moon was full and low, resting lazily on top of the palm trees that lined the sea. I stood there for quite some time, hugging myself tightly, sinking and then swimming into the sky's wide expanse; the warmth of the night air enveloping my body as I listened to the gossip of whispering crickets and the croaks of lamenting toads, praying for rain and a respite from the desiccating heat of the day.

Chapter Thirteen

Papa

I know the letters off by heart. I cannot say how many times that I have read them. When I came to England, they helped me to get through the day, they helped me carry on. I know that it is pathetic, but these childish letters were all I had left. They were the only proof I had that she had existed. They were the only piece of her that I could leave to Elizabeth.

October 1969

My dearest George,

I decided to write you this letter because I wanted to be able to talk to you even when we were not studying together. I cannot stop thinking about you. Why does life have to be so difficult? I saw you in the corridor at school today and I could not say hello because I was with my friends and you were with yours. But my heart felt as though it was going to explode and all I wanted to do was run to you and touch you just to make sure that you were real. I spend most of my time looking forward to our next study session in the library and dreaming of a different world where we would be able to be together alone. We have been in the same class for as long as I can remember and I always knew I liked you, but I never thought that you would have any time for someone like me. If you did talk to a girl it was always Sara or one of her friends. I could not believe it when you looked into my eyes and told me that you felt the same way. I thought I would melt away. I thought you thought I was the boring Indian girl in the corner that none of your friends liked. I am so very glad that I was wrong.

Yours

S.

February 1970

My dearest George,

Thank you for your note. It made me so happy to receive it. I think of you always too. I have to be careful because it comes so easily and I was writing your name on a piece of paper and my brother came into my bedroom and nearly saw it. I had to scribble over it quickly so that he could not see. I am so happy to know that you feel the same way too. I do not think that I have ever felt this way for anyone else in my life. Sometimes, when I look at you in class, I am sure I can feel my heart move inside me. I see your face in nearly all of my dreams and find that some nights I cannot sleep because I wish to see you so much. I am in an eternity of discomfort. I know that we should have picked others, but there is nothing that we can do. We have to hope that our Gods know why we have to be as we are. I hope that these words do not scare you.

Yours

S.

May 1970

My dearest George,

Good news at last. My piano teacher has asked that I start going to my lesson from half past four until half past five on a Saturday instead of at five o'clock. I have not told my parents yet as I thought you might be able to meet me in the thirty minutes that there is left. I could pass the tabagie where you work on Saturday's on my way home from my lesson. There is a sugar cane field opposite that we could meet in and be alone. I know it is difficult for you to talk to me at school so I will wait on Saturday. I will be just inside the field at a quarter to six. Please be there if you can.

I love you.

S.

June 1970

My dearest George,

I feel more awake and more alive than ever before. I think this is the happiest that I have ever felt in my life. Does it get any better than this? Can it get any better than this? I know it is affecting my studies and my exams but I cannot help it. Each time I try to concentrate I think of you and everything is lost. I dream of a day when we can go to the same college and onto the same University or maybe even got to France or England like your brother. It would be nice to think that one day we could be forever together where no one could find us.

Love

S.

July 1970.

George,

As we sow, so shall we reap. The exams are over and in celebration my parents tell me that I am to be married in the spring. I do not know what to do. They tell me that they have found me a husband in India because father thinks that it is better that I have a proper Indian husband. I should have guessed that this would happen, but somehow I hoped that I would be allowed to go to college. But it would be too expensive to send me as well as my brother, especially since I am one day to be a wife anyway. We will be going to India in October to meet him and his family. I do not know what else to say.

S.

November 1970.

My dearest George,

The first thing that I thought of when we landed at the airport was how I was going to speak to you. I gave him the benefit of the doubt as we discussed and I tried desperately to break the bonds between us, but I could not. I met him. His name is Baba. He owns two clothing factories and is from Lucknow, where my grandparents are from. He was kind enough but I could tell that he did not really like me. I tried my best to be polite and to imagine spending the rest of my life with him but all I could see were the wrinkles on his forehead. I do not know what to do. My parents deserve a loving daughter, who will make the willing sacrifices in the name of the family. Marriage is a very important step in our faith. My parents smile at me with such pride and I now fear to look at them back in the eyes. I cannot think of a life without you.

Your

S.

Chapter Fourteen

Tifi

Our first full day on the island was a bit of a non-event. I spent most of my time getting things together: maps, a hire car, cash, directions etc., and Kitty spent most of the day on the beach poaching herself into a sickly shade of salmon pink and making friends with a suspect individual who had salt crystals for teeth.

'Heh, Beth, this is Lewis. We just met.'

He was sat beside her, already cosy on her beach towel, one of those ageless creatures with dark leathery skin, who could easily convince you that they were either twenty or fifty years old. Timelessly decorated with a thin line of black beard, this specimen had the added quality of looking as though he'd spent the best part of those years high on an ocean wave.

'He's got a boat that he says we can go out on if we want,' Kitty explained excitedly, 'What do you think? Do you think we've got time to go out on a boat while we're here? It'll be cool won't it? And we can maybe go diving as well, if we want to or, you know, snorkelling. It'd be cool wouldn't it?'

Two faces grinned up at me like Cheshire cats, turning me instantly into a strict mother in a sweet shop.

'Well, I don't know. We'll have to talk about it.'

'Péna problem, mo kamarad,' our new friend boomed, with a shockingly false Caribbean accent. 'I live here all year round, on me little boat over there,' he pointed to a small fishing yacht anchored a few hundred metres out to sea. 'I'm here every day. You wanna go out onto the waves with Captain Crayfish, you just come down here at sunset and I'll be waiting for you.'

Without thinking, I picked up Kitty's book and suntan lotion and put them in her bag, 'Thanks for the offer; I'm sure we'll think about it.'

'Thank you, Lewis,' Kitty replied, ceremoniously holding out her hand as she stood up to follow me back to the car, 'It's been a pleasure. I'm sure we'll see each other again soon.'

He laughed. 'Here in Mauritius we say goodbye and hello with a kiss, not a handshake,' he said, grabbing her by the shoulders and planting a sloppy kiss on each cheek. She staggered a second, taken off guard and as he lunged towards me, I turned aside just in the nick of time, leaving his gesture to float in the air between us.

He chuckled as he regained his balance, and directing an embarrassed smile at Kitty, said, *'Salam, zoli minn.* Until the next time we meet,' before he thankfully strolled off into the sunset.

'What was all that about?' Kitty huffed, cramming herself into our 850cc Japanese car.

'What?'

'You know damn well, what.'

I shrugged, 'I didn't like him.'

'Well, that was kind of obvious.'

'I'm sorry, I didn't mean to be. It's just that I don't think we've got time to be swanning about on boats with strange men. And besides,' I added with a sheepish grin, 'I've got bigger fish to fry here, than a sparkly toothed crayfish.'

Kitty hit me with her beach bag and half heartedly sulked for the rest of the day, even over dinner in a quiet fish restaurant we'd found off the main stretch. Our fellow diners had looked on in awe as I'd picked gently at a grilled Dorade, and she'd smashed a lobster to pieces with a hammer, spraying liquid and shell all over my plate.

'So, have you decided, you know, what we're going to do tomorrow then?' She asked, bringing the mallet down once again.

'Well, I've studied the map and checked it with as much information as I could from the love letter's Dad left and I think the field he was talking about is in an area called Quatre Bornes. I thought we could just head out there and have a look.'

'So you haven't like, got any kind of address or anything really concrete to go on, have you?'

'No,' I agreed, wiping lobster juice from my forehead, 'only some vague description of a place called Tabagie Jerome and a sugar cane field in Quatre Bornes on the way to Rose Hill.'

I knew it wasn't that good a plan, but what else could I do? With the resources at my disposal, all I could hope to do was point the car in the right direction and miraculously stumble across the field we were looking for. I reached into my bag, pulled out the map and passed it to Kitty for illustration.

After a few minutes silent study, she lifted her head and commented astutely, 'This place that you're looking for could be anywhere.'

'Yep.'

'You sure we don't need any help?'

I wasn't going to be fooled that easily. 'No. I think we'll be alright,' I told her.

She clattered her cutlery onto the plate, reached into her bag and brought out a box of cigarettes. 'Do you mind?'

'Of course not.'

She puffed the smoke into the atmosphere around us. 'What time do you want me ready and dressed then?'

'Ten o'clock?' I hesitated.

'In that case, we mustn't waste any time, should we?' she said, getting up from the table, 'I'll get the bill and we'll be off.'

It was obvious from the outset that Kitty hadn't understood the level of involvement that was going to be expected of her. It had taken time for the realisation to dawn that I'd dragged her five thousand miles across the world to help me locate a piece of agricultural land in which to dump some ash. I knew I'd be pissed off if I was in her shoes. But, at least in my defence, I'd never said that it was going to be a holiday. My actions were completely dictated by my dead father, who was sitting on a sideboard, covered in a tablecloth and waiting for me to do my duty by him. It was all I could do to remember to eat.

The following day and much to my dismay, I'd discovered that most of Quatre Bornes was infected with a noxious stench of petrol and exhaust fumes that forced us to drive with our windows closed. Sat in the car in the sweltering heat, we'd had to wait half an hour in a queue, to make it through the traffic lights and onto the main road into town. I pulled up outside a bus station and set about asking for directions. I asked a number of passers-by whether they knew of Tabagie Jerome. I tried the question in French first and then in English, and was met mostly with wide eyed stares or a tirade in Kreol that I didn't understand. In the end, one helpful soul had pointed to a modern building on the other side of the road and said, 'Ingerlish.'

I also realised at this point that Kitty was no longer beside me. Surveying the street scene, I caught a glimpse of her disappearing into the market, waving her camera and calling to a row of street vendors selling unidentifiable food from giant woks, to say 'cheese'. I sighed. I locked the car and made my way over to what turned out to be a bank, where all the clerks spoke English. However, after much irrelevant discussion, it was decided by one happily helpful clerk that, 'since you have a car, the best way of finding Tabagie Jerome is to drive around the housing estate and look to see if the name 'Jerome' is painted above any of the shop doorways.'

'If only I'd thought of that myself,' I replied as I thanked him.

This avenue of investigation exhausted, I returned to the car to find Kitty propped against the bonnet, popping small balls of some deep fried substance into her mouth.

'Chew! It's called gato-pima, like, chilli cakes in English,' she informed me, swiftly placing an offering on my tongue.

Suffice to say, I lost the power of normal speech for about five minutes, during which time Kitty and I made our way back to the queue at the traffic lights. I turned the car into the sprawling concrete estate that spread off to our right and we wound our way through narrow and severely pot holed streets, past three Hindu temples, two Catholic churches, a mosque and a giant bronze smiling Buddha. Kitty made me pull up outside each one so that she could take a picture. We'd both laughed aloud as we drove past a football pitch which advertised the combined merits of Manchester United, Everton and Preston North End in dripping white paint, before she made me turn the car around so that she could remember it on celluloid. Then we turned another corner and found ourselves back in the sugar cane, a magnificent volcanic mountain soaring into the sky on our right.

'What's that?'

'Corps de Guard Mountain.'

'Stop the car!'

Gradually we followed the narrow road through the fields until we reached and entered another built up area. The same hotchpotch of concrete box houses perched precariously on each side of the road, their grey masses dulling the picture postcard mountain behind them. I made Kitty lean out of the window to take her photos as we drove up and down the streets dodging well-dressed women carrying innumerable blue carrier bags. Each road appeared to be exactly the same as the last. No sugar cane here, just row upon row of symmetrical housing. In quiet defeat, I stopped the car outside an open fronted shop, allowing Kitty to hop out and buy us a couple of cans of pop.

'They haven't heard of Tabagie Jerome either,' she said, getting back into the car and passing me a can of 7Up. 'But, they reckon there's a lady who lives about a quarter of a mile down this road, who should be able to help us. Her name's Madam Lasyet, or something. They said she's lived around here for years.'

Gobsmacked, I faced my friend, unable to comprehend how she'd managed to find out so much in such a quick trip.

'What?'

'Nothing,' I said, starting up the engine. 'You say she lives about quarter of a mile down this road?'

'Yes. Number 36.'

'Okeley Dokeley.'

As instructed, I pulled up outside number thirty-six, a high walled house with a tall metal gate that protected pedestrians from the two carbon copy black and white dogs that circled nervously behind it. They announced our arrival, jumping up and slavering contentedly. A young girl, about fourteen or fifteen years old peered out of the front door, her tightly braided hair framing a suspicious frown.

'My name is Beth and this is my friend, Kitty,' I called to her.

She walked tentatively towards us.

'Parlez-vous Français?'

She relaxed a smidgeon, *'Oui, bien sur.'*

I explained our predicament and asked whether it was true that Madame Lasyet would be able to help us. All traces of human warmth drained from her face.

'Is she your mother?' I asked.

Her eyes flickered suspiciously from Kitty to me and back again.

'Look, it's really important,' I prompted, 'I promise I won't take more than ten minutes. I just need to know whether she knows where Tabagie Jerome is or at least, if she knows where it used to be.' The girl just stood there staring at us as though she'd had some kind of seizure and refused to speak. So, in desperation, and thanks to some exceptional forethought, I scribbled the 'phone number of our apartment on a piece of paper I found in my bag and passed it through the gate. 'Please take this,' I said, shaking the paper in her face, 'It's really important that you tell her that I'm George Labelle's daughter and that I've come to spread his ashes in the field opposite Tabagie Jerome. Please ask her if she remembers him. I've only got a short time to do this and I could do with all the help I can get.'

I looked towards Kitty for any other ideas, but she simply shrugged her shoulders and pulled a funny face.

'Doesn't look like we're going to get anywhere with this in a hurry,' I said, turning to go. For an exquisite moment, I'd been buoyed by the hope that I'd be able to sort everything out with the minimum of effort, but now it appeared that chance had been ill conceived.

'Wait!'

We looked round, to see the girl open the gate, swing a quick glance over her shoulder and shuffle her flip flopped feet through the dust to catch up with us. She bent down, picked up a dead lighter that happened to be lying beside my foot and held it out to me.

'Come back tomorrow,' she whispered, placing the lighter in my open hand. 'Just after three o'clock and I'll see what I can do.' Then she ran back behind the walls and closed the gates silently behind her.

Chapter Fifteen

Papa

Of course we knew that we might get into trouble.

As my schooling came to an end, I secured myself a permanent position at *La Boutik Jerome*, a male oasis on the weary road home from work. It provided solace for the lonely, the unwanted and the married men of the area.

La Boutik.

The letters J.E.R.O.M.E. were proudly daubed in black paint above the doorway and inside a single light bulb buzzed and flickered in its mooring on the corrugated tin roof, while a small wooden shelf held Matinee cigarettes and a few boxes of damp matches.

It was not much to look at but I enjoyed some of my happiest moments at Jerome's. It had started as a Saturday job, Jerome being a good friend of my father's and then as he had come to trust me, he had asked whether I could help out some evenings as well. You see, Jerome was a big man in the proper sense of the word and had trouble lifting and standing for long periods of time. The regulars used to joke that one of his ancestors must have been a Sumo wrestler, to which Jerome would always retort, 'My grandparents came from China you idiots. Any educated fool knows that Sumo are from Japan and not from China.'

He had a nervous habit of wiping his sweaty forehead every ten minutes or so with a yellowing handkerchief that he kept permanently in the breast pocket of his shirts. About twenty times a day, I would watch him waddle from the bar to the door and back again, sit down and wipe his brow, while he told stories about his experiences as a cook on a merchant frigate, as a chef for the Admiralty, and as a butler for a British Ambassador. And wherever Jerome went, Hercules, his ginger tom cat was soon to follow. A regular puss in boots, Hercules prowled the corners of the *boutik* hunting for juicy rats and cockroaches by night, and curled himself into his master's ample lap when he could, by day. Each evening, it fell to me to serve the regulars, while Jerome played host, and entertained his paying guests.

'So, one day, I open the living room door and you'll never guess what I saw.' Jerome eyed the room steadily, so that we all understood that this was the moment to lean forward for the punch line. 'I opened the door and there on the floor in front of me is the damn Chihuahua's head,' he nodded his head furiously, 'yes, yes, you heard me correctly, its head lying there in the middle of the rug and my bloody cat licking its paws and purring with satisfaction!'

The regulars erupted with canned laughter.

'What did you do?' asked one.

'What could I do?' he chuckled, 'I couldn't even find its body.' He wiped the tears from his plump cheeks, 'Ended up having to blame it on the guy next door and his bloody *chien mechant*.'

'Was he Hindu?' enquired Christian Lasyet.

'Who?' Jerome asked.

'The guy next door.'

'Yes, I think he was.'

'Good.'

Christian Lasyet was a bitter young man who drank in the *boutik* only once a week, usually on payday when he would get very drunk and start swearing about the state of the nation. Jerome and the others put up with his behaviour because Christian's father, a previous regular, had disappeared during the riots in 1968, leaving Christian to look after his mother and five younger siblings.

'What is it you've got against Hindu's, Christian?' I asked naively from behind the bar.

'I'll never trust a Hindu, George,' he said, spraying his venomous spittle across the room, 'They're the kind of people who pray at their temples and then come and sit in our Catholic churches for God's sake, to hedge their bets. They earn more money than us, they run the Government, they run the Police and they'd prefer to see me in the gutter begging to clean their shoes sooner that share their newfound power with us.'

'And how do you feel about the Chinese and the Muslims?' Mr Duvall asked, winking at Jerome as he said it.

'They're even worse, but as long as they keep out of my way, I'll keep out of theirs.'

Jerome laughed uncomfortably, 'Oh, thanks a lot, Christian.'

'You know what I mean.'

'Actually, no I don't, Christian' he replied, wiping his forehead nervously, 'and I'll kindly remind you that you can't go around saying things like that anymore and especially not here.'

'Why not? I'm only telling the truth,' Christian said, turning to face me, 'If I want to work, I have to work for an Indian. If I want to feed and clothe myself and my family, I have to buy from an Indian. If I am ill, I have to be looked after by or buy drugs from an Indian. And you don't think that they're not laughing at us? Those same people who came cap in hand for food when they arrived here? Now they run this country as though they invented it, as though we never existed before they were sent here. They build mosques, they leer over our women, and they ridicule our religion and our customs. And you laugh at me?' He slammed his glass down on the counter, 'Now pour me another drink!'

I picked up the bottle and stepped back from the counter.

'I said, pour me another drink!'

Jerome came forward and tried to heave Christian out of his seat, 'No more for you now Christian. I think it's time you were getting off home,' he said.

'I just want another drink.'

'I know, but it's getting late and your mother will be waiting.'

'Fuck her,' he stood up and spun round, flaying his arms, 'Fuck her and fuck you!'

'Christian!'

I ran out from behind the bar and moved in tandem with Jerome to usher him out of the door.

'That bitch has ruined my life and scared away the only woman I ever loved.'

'We know, we know,' I cajoled.

'What do you mean, we know?' He stopped in his tracks, 'I'm not a bloody child, not like you,' he spat,' And don't you think I haven't seen you, sneaking about in the fields. He'll find out sooner or later and then you'll be the one that gets done good and proper. Then we'll see who's crying and telling everyone that you can't ever trust a Hindu, you mark my words.'

I ducked in the glare of the headlights.

'What's he talking about, George?'

'I've no idea,' I replied, wiping my hands on my trousers and returning to the other side of the counter. I smiled and changed the subject, 'Now who needs a top up?'

Chapter Sixteen

Tifi

The dogs announced our arrival at the Lasyet household at three o'clock the following day. The young girl ran to the gates, holding her fingers to her lips, 'Quickly,' she whispered, 'before somebody sees you.'

She led Kitty and I through the house and into a dark bedroom. A thin ray of light shone through the curtains. It cast a shadow on an Egyptian mummy, laid out on an old wrought iron bed in the corner. The prerequisite odour of stale urine and lavender oil hung in the air like a wrecking ball. I recognised the small picture of a saint above the headboard. It was the same as the one embossed on the pendant in my father's cachet; the one I'd thought was a Saint Christopher. Apart from his staring face, there was no other decoration in the room.

The girl shook the inactive mass of bed linen and murmured softly at it in Kreol. The body stirred, a long flabby arm appearing from within the folds and waving her away. The girl took a few steps backwards, wrinkled her nose and walked out of the room. The bundle erupted again, and this time a weather beaten and wrinkly face came into view; a snow-white meringue sat on top of its head where its hair should have been. It propped itself up onto its audibly creaking elbows and allowed two sleep filled eyes to peer out at us grumpily. The girl appeared moments later with a steaming mug of liquid, placed it on the bedside table and then with some difficulty helped her grandmother to sit up in bed. When the old lady was satisfied, the girl left us, closing the door behind her.

Madame Lasyet slurped noisily from the cup that she cradled in her hands, her eyes darting around the room, taking in our unusual forms amongst the bare walls.

'Bien, vous êtes-la,' she yawned, 'I'm not usually allowed guests these days. My son forbids anyone but the doctor to see me. Apparently you made a convincing plea to my granddaughter, yesterday. I wonder what an old woman like me can possibly do to help someone like you.'

'I'm looking for a certain field on behalf of my father, George Labelle,' I explained.

'Ah, so the child was right,' she replied, sagely.

'You knew him?'

'Knew him, yes. I knew George Labelle and Frank and Marie and Juliet. I knew their mother and their father well. They lived in the square next to mine.' Her gaze returned to the mug in her hands, 'I wondered when someone would come.'

The room became stifling, the air thick and edible.

'Why?'

'Because that was a tragedy,' she said, taking a long loud sip from her cup.

My stomach lurched.

'That was a tragedy,' she repeated, 'One son murdered. One son disappeared. Madame Labelle never recovered. They put her away in one of those 'mental' homes,' she hissed, 'Mr Labelle went north with the girls, to be nearer to her and I never saw them again.'

'Murder?' I said, incredulously.

'Oh yes!' she said excitedly, 'Murdered in 1971...or was it 1972? Anyway, his body was found in the sugar cane. They never caught anyone for it though. Then George, the second son, he disappeared or maybe ran away. No one really knew for sure which one, although we all had our suspicions.' She stared at the ceiling above her bed, 'It's all gone now though. All disappeared after Claudette. They've built houses where we used to live; concrete ones that won't blow away in the wind. And the sugar cane. That is all gone too.' She shook her head slowly, 'My Christian used to know both of them. He was such a good boy until he met that woman, and then he changed too. They all change in the end. All boys change and leave their mothers to die.'

I took a step forward and grabbed at the iron frame of her bed. 'My father...was there ever any idea of why he disappeared?'

'Some say he was the one responsible, others said it was because of *bann malbar*. Either way, they say Madame Labelle's heart and mind died from the grief and the shame that he caused.'

'And your son, you say he knew them both, my father and my uncle. Would he know anymore?'

'My son will not help you. He doesn't like to help anybody, especially not strangers.'

'Are you sure?'

'I think I have told you enough already,' she said, visibly agitated, 'It is better that you leave now before he finds you here. You don't need to know anymore. Everything is gone now. There is nothing for your father to find. He is not welcome here anymore.'

'My father is dead.'

'Then you have no reason to be here.'

'I have to spread his ashes in the sugar cane field opposite Tabagie Jerome.'

'That is not my concern,' she replied, 'Cynthia!'

The door behind us opened too swiftly, 'Wi, grandmère?'

'I am tired.'

'Wi, grandmère,' Cynthia said, stepping forward to help her grandmother settle back down into her tomb. When the task was finished, she turned and asked with forced curiosity, 'Did you find what you were looking for?'

'Enough to be getting on with thank you,' I croaked in response.

Kitty drove back to the apartment, while I sat in the passenger seat, despondent and confused. This twist had not been part of the game plan. My uncle being murdered at the same time as my father suspiciously disappeared was not exactly what I wanted or needed to hear and poured over my already shattered senses like salt and malt vinegar.

'Don't let it confuse matters,' Kitty had suggested helpfully, 'let's stay on track, here. Find the field and go home. You don't need to know anymore.'

'I know, but what if –'

'Don't go there,' she said, 'it's just a mad old lady rambling on about a load of old nonsense. What good would it do, sending you here to find that out? I mean, it's your dad we're talking about here. Why would he send you here after all these years to find out from a complete stranger that he might have murdered his brother?'

Kitty had a point but it didn't detract from the fact, that ever since all these revelations had started, anything, in my mind, had become possible. I found myself in the unsettling position of not ever knowing what I was walking into from one day to the next.

'Have a little faith, for goodness sake, Beth. It's not all that bad,' Kitty said cheerily, pulling the car up alongside a beach bar near our apartment. 'Come on, I'll buy you drink.'

We sat on the sand and sipped margaritas as Kitty photographed a sunset of pinks, gold's and pastel blues, dissolving over the silver crackle of horizon.

'What's going on in your head?' she asked.

'What's not going on in my head would be a better question,' I replied.

'OK. Let me rephrase it then. Is there anything I can do to help you figure out what is going on in your head?'

'Wave a magic wand and find that field for me so that I can go home, would be a good start.'

'You really don't like it here?'

'It's not that I don't like it,' I explained, 'it's just that it's difficult to enjoy a country when you know you've come here to do something so specific and morbid. It's not like I'm on holiday. I've actually got a job to do.'

'It's hardly a job, Beth. You're laying your father's ashes to rest and I'm sure your dad didn't intend for you to spend your whole time worrying about locating a field for the purpose.'

'What are you getting at?'

'I'm saying, that I think it'll do you the world of good to fall in love with this place. I think that should be your top priority. Finally being invited to come here, to see firsthand the place where your parents grew up, should be like manna from heaven for you and yet you've not once suggested we go sightseeing or shopping at the markets. All you have done is moan on about a bloody field-.'

'Excuse me ladies.'

Our little chat was interrupted by a familiar Caribbean accent.

'Lewis, fancy seeing you here?' Kitty exclaimed as Lewis sat down beside her.

'What can I do when I sees two beautiful women sitting alone on the beach?' he explained, waving his order to the waitress, 'I must come over and see if you need any assistance.'

'Don't mind us, Lewis. Make yourself comfortable,' I told him.

Kitty grinned, 'Actually, maybe Lewis is just the man we need to sort out our dilemma.'

'What is that my dear?'

I nudged her in the ribs, but she continued, undeterred, 'Do you know anyone who would be able to locate a field for us?'

'A field?'

'Yes, a very specific sugar cane field, next to a Tabagie called Jerome, somewhere near Quatre Bornes?'

'I am sure I can try. I have friends who may be able to help. In fact,' he said, rubbing his bearded chin, 'I will be seeing one of them tomorrow afternoon.'

'Cool,' she said, smiling at me smugly, 'so, now there's no reason why we can't have the day off and do some sightseeing instead, is there?'

'I suppose not,' I conceded.

'But I will want something in return,' Lewis added, 'I will do you this favour and you will both agree to come over to me boat in the evening for a good Mauritian meal and maybe a ride out to the coral reef?'

Kitty turned to me, her eyes flashing with excitement, 'Any objections, Beth?'

'Well, from the looks of you, I don't think I've really got any choice in the matter, do I?'

'No, not really,' Kitty confirmed, still grinning.

Lewis looked confused, 'So, we have a deal?'

'Yes, Lewis. We most certainly do have a deal,' she replied.

Chapter Seventeen

Papa

'Mo kontan twa.'

'I love you too.'

'I love the way you dream that one day everything will be OK.'

'I love the way that you believe me.'

'It is so hard to leave you.'

'I know, it is very hard to let you go, but you must go, Sahana.'

'Salam.'

'Salam, mo disik dou.'

I know that I was not always there, but she told me enough so that I could imagine it happening.

Sahana told me that she met her husband on a rainy day. Baba Chandels was a rich, upright man, a heralded member of the New Delhi Chamber of Commerce, thirty-six years old and a bachelor. He was searching for a wife because his family and business associates had decided that it was time for him to get married.

He is himself a half man and the second half is his wife.

Baba smiled politely as Sahana poured him a cup of tea. The pictures her parents had given her had hinted at an older man, but in person, he looked far more haggard and worry-worn than she had been led to believe. He wore a dark green western suit with a yellow shirt, an orange kipper tie and brown leather sandals. His greying hair was swept back over the top of his head and held in place with pungent pomade.

She told me that the Hindu belief in *jati* and *dharma* was central to understanding the importance of marriage in the Hindu faith. Knowing one's place in society and understanding one's duty within the caste. Marriage was the thirteenth *samsara* of sixteen rituals that a person had to pass through in a lifetime. It fulfilled the three aims of a man's life; duty, children and sensual pleasure.

Once the tea pouring ceremony was over, Baba commenced the painful exchange of pleasantries with her parents. He sat perched nervously on the edge of the sofa, continually rubbing his paper like palms over one another so that the movement created a sound that reminded Sahana of the breeze that swept through the sheaves of the sugar cane.

'Are you quite alright, Sahana?' Mrs Sundaram had asked.

'Yes, mother, just feeling a little hot. It will go in a minute,' she'd replied.

Mr Sundaram whispered something to his wife, then said, 'Maybe you would like to stretch your legs, Sahana? You have been sitting down for such a long time. Mr Chandels, I suppose you have a courtyard where our daughter can get a breath of fresh air?'

‘Oh, yes,’ Baba replied, ‘we have a large garden at the rear of the house, which looks onto a small river. It is quite charming. Maybe the gardener should escort your daughter?’

Baba Chandels’s mother coughed, ‘I believe that in the circumstances, young Miss Sahana may wish to have someone a little more mature in attendance with her in the garden, just in case she encounters any difficulty in walking the distance.’

It took Baba a while to compute the hidden prompts in the conversation, sighing as he stood up and walked her out into the damp evening air.

The parents had compared their horoscopes and consulted their astrological charts. They agreed that Sahana and Baba would marry the following spring.

I know that she was resplendent on her wedding day. Silver thread, gold chains, rich red and cream silks, large black Egyptian eyes and dark crimson lips. Days of preparation had led to the sacred ceremony that was taking place in front of her. She would have had no trouble in maintaining the traditionally dour demeanour expected of a young Indian bride. She kept her eyes lowered to her hands and traced the henna patterns that scrawled across them.

First now, they bring to you in bridal procession this Surya, guiding her steps in circular motion. Return her now, O Agni, to her husband as rightful wife, with hope of children to come.

Under the heaviness of her eyelashes she saw her guests, people she didn’t know, nodding their heads judiciously. She looked at Baba. He was not there. His eyes transparent, declaring the void that there was between them.

I hold your heart in serving fellowship; your mind follows my mind. In my word, you rejoice with all your heart. You are joined to me by the Lord of all creatures.

She felt sick as he put the red powder in her hair. His parents gave her a piece of silk, the guests threw rose petals and everybody clapped. Her stomach gurgled as she fought the desire to retch. Her mother ran forward at the end, putting a caring arm around her and leading her away to the bathroom.

'Oh, Sahana, you have made your father and me so very happy. Everyone is saying that you are the most beautiful bride that they have ever seen. You are happy, no?'

Sahana felt the acrid juice erupt in the back of her throat and ran into the cubicle.

'Ah, do not worry, Sahana. It is normal. All girls are nervous on their wedding day and you are only seventeen,' Mrs Sundaram said, stroking her daughter's back, 'please do not cry. Tomorrow you will be a woman and all this bad feeling will be gone away.'

Sahana retched again but nothing came; her eyes brimming with tears, smearing the kohl that her mother had so lovingly applied that morning.

'Oh God, Mother. What am I going to do? How can I sleep with such a man?'

She felt the unfamiliar sting of her mother's hand.

'You will do as all women before you have done,' Mrs Sundaram said, her own tears softening the anger. 'Sahana, my dearest child, this is the way of the world. You should be happy. At least you will be able to return to Mauritius to set up your home. You only have to stay here a few more days and then we will all go home. You are lucky. Your husband respects you and will give you time to adjust and get used to the idea before he comes to live with you in the country of your parents. Most girls are not that fortunate.'

Who better to advise Sahana than a woman who had been wrenched away from her family and her homeland at eighteen years of age to look after a man she hardly knew? At least she would be coming home. Baba wanted to set up a factory in Mauritius and he had already bought a piece of land close to her family home. The marriage was good for her parents as well. It bestowed on them a firmer standing in both the worlds of commerce and public service. All she had to do was remain focused and she could get through this. It was time for her to grow up.

As the evening drew nearer and the sun died away out of the redden sky, Mr and Mrs Baba Chandels stood together in their bedroom.

'You needn't get undressed, my dear.'

Sahana paused, the top half of her Sari unravelled to the floor, uncovering her red bodice and narrow dimpled waist.

'You can sleep in the room next door. I have had a single bed made up for you to use, just through those doors.'

He pointed to what appeared at first glance to be a walk in wardrobe. Sahana looked at the door and then down at her pretty painted hands.

'Go on. It leads to your dressing room. I think you will find that it is big enough for you to sleep in.'

Sahana looked on as Baba stepped out of his pants and slithered under the crisp clean sheets of his own double bed.

'Go girl!' he said sternly, 'and don't worry about the sheets. I have left strict instructions that they are to be cleaned before anyone asks to see them. Your honour will remain intact. I will ensure that everyone assumes that you were very attentive on your first night.' He rolled over onto his side and plumped the pillow below his head, 'And turn the light out as you leave, won't you?'

She told me that she did not know whether she should jump for joy or cry out in despair as she closed the closet doors behind her. It did not really matter in the end. Either way, the tears had run down her cheeks until sunrise.

Chapter Eighteen

Tifi

Sitting on the veranda in my pyjamas, staring into day five, I couldn't shake the feeling that I was trapped in a maze of dead ends. I hadn't been able to sleep the night before, my thoughts spinning with conspiracy theories and accusations. In the early hours, I'd sought solace in a cheap bottle of red wine while Kitty was sleeping and discovered the telephone directory while creeping around the kitchen, searching drawers for the bottle opener. Pouring myself a drink, I flicked through the pages until I found the one containing surnames beginning with 'La'. There were ten entries for Labelle in the phonebook. Six lived in the north of the country and four in the centre. Of the six that lived in the north, one began with an initial 'M' and another two began with an initial 'J'. The first line of their addresses and their phone numbers were filed in a line. Marie and Juliet Labelle.

'-Beth, are you listening?'

Kitty stood in front of me, her hands on her hips.

'What?'

'Oh, you're hopeless,' she sighed, 'I said, I've been looking in the rough guide and Grand Baie looks like a good day out. There's plenty to do and see, you know, and it's near this little village called Peréybére where there's supposed to be a great beach.'

'Sounds great,' I replied, cradling my fragile red wine head in my hands. 'I'll get my stuff together.'

'I'll go and make breakfast.'

'Great.'

I skulked back into my room and pulled the ripped piece of paper out of my bag.

Labelle, J. 10 Rue L'Amrial Pasteur.........Goodlands 263 9919
Labelle, J. 5 Rue Johnston...............Pamplemousses 272 8433
Labelle, M. 342 Route Royale.................Peréybére 272 8267

It had all appeared tantalizingly within reach; so easily obtainable. If my father's sisters were still alive, they may know what had happened and know exactly where the field had been. I'd kicked myself for not thinking of it sooner. Who else would be able to help me put my father's story to rest, but his own family, or rather, my family? Wouldn't these people be the answer to my childhood prayers? They held the key to my past and my heritage and could fill the hole that gaped open inside me.

'Beth?'

I quickly rammed the paper back into the bag, 'Yes!'

The only obstacle was Kitty; how to get away without offending her.

'We've run out of milk, so I'm going to have to go to the shop. Do you need anything while I'm out?'

'No, I'm fine.'

She wanted to pull me in one direction. I wanted to go in another.

'Right, I won't be a minute.'

I waited to hear the door close, then un-scrunched the list and found the 'phone.

'*Alo*?' a high pitch voice answered within seconds.

I explained in French that I wanted to know whether Juliet Labelle lived at that number.

'*Mo pa pe konpran twa,*' replied the Kreol voice, '*ou ti kapav repete, siouple*?'

God, how I wished at that moment that I'd bothered to remember the Kreol phrases that my father had taught me as a child. I tried again, this time slowing my speech with short words.

'Sori. Mo pa pe konpran twa. Mo bizen alé. Salam.'

The 'phone died in my hand as Kitty walked in through the front door.

'Who was that on the phone?' she asked, sweeping past me and into the kitchen.

'No one, just me. I thought I'd try calling my mother again, but there was no answer.'

'Probably cos she'll still be in bed. It's six o'clock in the morning back in England, you idget!'

'Oh yeah, silly me.'

I refolded the paper, slid it carefully into the back pocket of my trousers. Moments later, Kitty joined me, brandishing two steaming mugs of vanilla scented tea, 'You sure you're alright, Beth?' she asked, handing one to me, 'You sure you want to go out today, you look a little peaky and you know, if you don't want to go all the way up to the north, we don't have to. There's plenty for us to see and do around here.'

'Kitty, how many times do I have to tell you that I'm fine. A day out at Grand Baie and Peréybére sounds absolutely great.'

'Well, if you're sure,' she said, examining her watch, 'we'd better drink up and get going.'

Kitty, Kitty, Kitty.

We picked up the motorway just past Quatre Bornes and then weaved our way through the city traffic of Port Louis until we reached the familiar sight of a two-lane stretch of road flanked by the sugar cane fields. We followed the signs to grand Baie and within no time found ourselves hunting for a parking space along a busy length of coastline. Small boutiques offering designer labels, jewellery and handcrafted boats jostled for attention along the main strip, their façades reflecting a perfect pale blue bay dotted with large and small yachts whose sails fluttered in the breeze. Needless to say, Kitty's camera had a field day.

We spent an hour or so looking in shop windows at things that we couldn't afford before taking a stroll along the bay, hopping on and off mounds of gnarly black volcanic rock. Once tired of that, Kitty suggested that we go on one of the semi-submersible boats and have a look at the coral reef, at which point I saw my perfect opportunity to get away.

'I can't go. I'm scared of the sea.'

'Since when?' Kitty demanded.

'Since always. Anyway, nobody's stopping you from going. I'll wait here for you, over there at that café. It's no big deal.'

'Suit yourself then, Beth Stephens,' she said with a scowl reminiscent of a teacher I once had at primary school. 'I'll be back in about two hours.'

I smiled and waving her goodbye, watched her clamber back over the rocks to the main road. Once she'd safely disappeared from view, I ran to the car; hurriedly un-scrunching the paper from my pocket as I went.

Twenty minutes later I was pulling the car up outside a tired looking bungalow in the main street in neighbouring Peréybére. Three tabby cats lay in the shade of a granite walled compound, the tips of their tails swaying gently in unison. High in the trees above, small birds twittered, carefully going about their business. I pushed the front gate open slightly, made a customary check for a rabid guard dog, and proceeded past an overgrown garden to the front door. The disappointing doorbell chime told me all I felt I needed to know about the occupier of this household. I waited an eternity for any sign of life and was about to give up and return to the car, when a dark shadow fell upon the inside of the glass door. One beady yellow eye peered out past an industrial strength security chain, while four crooked nicotine stained fingertips tapped on the side of the frame, the thick rasp of enforced inhalation echoing around me.

'Does Marie Labelle live here?' I asked, not sure whether I wanted an answer.

'Non!'

The door slammed shut in my face so I rapped my knuckles against it again. This time, the door opened a fraction wider, presenting the lopsided yellowing face of an elderly woman.

'Do you know if a Marie Labelle ever lived here?'

'Non!'

I managed to wedge my foot in the door before she slammed it.

'How about Juliet Labelle, have you ever heard of her? Do you know if a family called Labelle lives around here?'

Without a word, she rammed her full weight against the door, unceremoniously propelling me backwards and off her doorstep.

'Well, sod it, then!' I shouted.

Something or someone was trying and succeeding in making my life as difficult as possible. I looked up to the heavens and swore under my breath, before dusting myself down and pulling the sheet of addresses once again out of my pocket. There was one address in the north left to try.

Labelle, J. 5 Rue Johnston............ Pamplemousses 272 8433

I looked at my watch and much to my surprise, it was already well after 2 o'clock and it looked as though the third J. Labelle would have to wait for another day.

I made my way back to Grand Baie as fast as I could, but Kitty was already sat drinking cocktails in the café where we'd agreed to meet.

'Where have you been?' she fumed.

'Why? What's wrong?'

She looked me up and down incredulously.

'There weren't any trips out on the boat today. I was gone a total of fifteen minutes and when I came back, you'd gone, taken the car and left me here not knowing what to do, where you were or how I was going to get home. That's what's wrong!'

I sat down beside her and ordered an ice cold Coca Cola.

'So are you going to tell me where the fuck you've been?'

I took the piece of paper out of my back pocket. 'I've been trying to find my family,' I said with resignation.

She snatched the paper from me, snorting her derision, 'And have you?'

'No, not yet.'

I looked over the bay. It was exactly how I remembered it from the photos in my scrapbook. Picture postcard. A paradoxical cliché; a hint of soft white sand, stark black rocks, transparent water, a little surf, palm trees and coral.

‘So, how many of these have we got left to visit?’ she asked.

‘There’s only one left to try around here.’

‘And where’s that?’

‘Pamplemousses.’

It was still the people who grabbed my attention. Watching them walk past, women strolling arm in arm, men in a hurry. Beautiful women, slim women, all blessed with shining ebony skin and commanding smiles.

‘We pass Pamplemousses on the motorway back to Quatre Bornes, don’t we?’ Kitty confirmed.

‘Yes, but I’ll go tomorrow.’

‘Why?’ she sighed.

‘Because it’s obvious you’re not interested.’

She lowered her eyes. ‘Is that what you really think?’

I didn’t want to laden Kitty with excuses that she wouldn’t want to hear. ‘It’s not important.’

‘It is to me,’ she retorted.

‘Look, I’m sorry,’ I backtracked, ‘just ignore me. I’m having a tough time keeping it together, that’s all and I got the distinct impression that you’d rather be enjoying yourself.’

She sat and stared at me for a long while, her cheeks flashing a hot red that clashed with her hair. ‘You can be such a bloody pain in the arse sometimes, Beth.’

‘And so can you.’

‘Ok then, well, why don’t we just both shut up and drive back to the flat via Pamplemousse and get this over and done with, before this turns into a rumble.’

I felt the twinge of relief. ‘Thanks,’ I smiled.

‘For Christ’s sake, Beth, you don’t have to thank me.’

‘Sorry.’

‘And stop apologising for God’s sake.’

I shrugged, ‘Sorry.’

'Oh, for fuck's sake,' she replied, sighing and leading the way back to the car.

We sat in silence as I drove up and down and in and out of the narrow streets of Pamplemousses. The house we were looking for turned out to be a half built concrete box, just like the new homes that were springing up on the outskirts of Quatre Bornes. Cramped in between other similar boxes and painted lilac pink, it paraded a row of battered oil cans along a low breezeblock wall. A yapping Jack Russell terrier jumped up to greet us.

'*Res trankil, Yasper*!'

A soft feminine voice floated from the front window and the dog immediately sat itself down, its body rocking with the force of a furiously wagging tail. A minute woman followed the voice out through the front door, placed her hands on her hips and strained to see through our front windscreen.

'My God!' Kitty exclaimed, 'She looks just like your dad, only, you know, in miniature.'

She made a move for her camera and I placed a hand on her shoulder, 'Not yet,' I told her, stepping out of the car.

'Mademoiselle Juliet Labelle?'

She wore a yellow nylon dress, decorated with tiny pink flowers, over a Marks and Spencer's white vest and had my father's dark black eyes and familiar deep brow.

'I think I'm your niece. George's daughter. From England.'

Her attention flickered between me and the car and back again as Yasper began to growl.

'I don't know what you are talking about,' she said, reaching behind her for the door handle, 'I've never had a brother called George.'

I'd learnt by now, that I couldn't afford to give up too easily. 'Please mademoiselle, please remember. George. He ran away to live in England shortly after Frank died.'

'What do you know about Frank?'

'I know he's my father's brother and that he died around 1971.'

Her knees weakened as she reached out for the doorframe. 'I do not know who you are talking about,' she said, turning on her heals and ushering the dog through the door before her, 'Now please leave me alone or I shall call the police!'

And once again a door was slammed shut.

'What was all that about?' Kitty called from inside the car.

'I don't know.'

This scenario was becoming far too familiar. Nothing made sense. It was so obvious that she was Juliet, my father's sister and my aunt. What would compel a person to pretend that her own flesh and blood had never existed?

'Pass me my handbag, will you?'

Kitty held it out to me. I rummaged inside until I found the envelope of photograph's and picked out the one of Juliet in her first Holy Communion dress. Turning it over, I wrote the 'phone number to our apartment under my father's inscription.

'I'm going to leave you this,' I called out at the house. 'Please call me if you remember. I need to know what happened. I need to know the truth about my father.'

I propped the picture up against one of the tin cans and returned to the car.

'Do you want me to drive?' Kitty asked.

'Would you mind?'

'Not at all,' she smiled.

She drove me home through the traffic, past the people, the towns and the sugar cane. Submerged in doubt I wondered what could have happened. What had my father done? What had he done that had been so wrong, so bad that he'd never return and they'd never miss him? And why the hell did he think that it was a good idea to send me here when he knew I'd be compelled to find out?

Chapter Nineteen

Papa

You could be forgiven for believing that Frank had invented a cure for cancer, with all the fuss that was made when he returned from England.

Alé do!

Following father's instructions, Marie and Juliet decorated a huge paper banner to hang over the front door that declared to the entire world,

WELCOME HOME FROM ENGLAND FRANK!

It was obvious to me at least, that its purpose was not to remind Frank where he had been living over the last few years.

He was chewing gum as he walked through the arrivals gate and wearing a very wide pair of flared denim jeans. We all stood in our Sunday best, our shoes polished and our teeth gleaming. Mama strode towards him first and kissed him on both cheeks. Papa followed and shook his hand, the pride oozing through his fingertips. Then Marie and Juliet ran forward and flung their arms around his waist, burying their smiles in his brown suede jacket. When he looked up, Frank dipped his head at me and I nodded back at him.

We had a party in his honour that evening. I remember distinctly, that before the guests arrived, mama insisted that she *tir lizyé*, to get rid of any evil spirits that may have inadvertently travelled with Frank from England. He stood with a cheeky smirk on his face as she passed the salt above his head, chanting her spells and tossing the discarded crystals into a flaming pan of chilli's and onion peelings. We had just enough time to clear the air of the stench before the rest of the family arrived preened and excited. Mama had been preparing all day; *Roti, farata, diri blan, karipoulé, satini pom damour, zasar, gato-pima*. So, we all crammed ourselves around the table, drinking from pink plastic cups filled with Coca-Cola or Beer and talking through mouthfuls of food.

Hasn't he grown? Isn't he handsome? How was London? Did you see any of the royal family? Jeanette's been having trouble with her English; would you be able to help her? Did you bring anything from my cousin, Gerard? Was it cold and raining all the time? Did you meet any nice girls, *bann tifi zoli*?

Frank told them exactly what they wanted to hear. He told them that he had thrown a snowball that had accidentally hit the guardsman's box at Buckingham Palace and that the guard had not flinched. That, yes, he had seen his cousins now and then, and that yes, they were doing well in highly respected jobs in the City. That no, he did not like English girls because they were too easy but yes, he had met a nice girl whose parents were from a good Catholic Mauritian family. That no, he did not like the English food but yes, he had scored high marks in all of his exams and come top of his class.

He'd shared a room in his last year with a visiting French student who told of his first hand experiences during the Paris riots. It was the year of Apollo 13, the year Nixon started to pull troops out of Vietnam, the year Jimi Hendrix and Janis Joplin died and the year my brother chose to become aware of his rights. Frank returned to Mauritius the conquering hero, brimming with political ideas to spark a social revolution. At the same time as his privileged education gained him a respectable engineering job at the docks in Port Louis, the power of his convictions procured him a voice within the Mouvement Militant Mauricien, the new political party of Mauritian youth.

I had occasion once to listen to one of his rallying speeches, perspiring in standing room only at the back of a cramped warehouse. He was tall and proud, his voice steady, commanding our patois, claiming our language as his God given right. He talked about dreams, about opportunities, and about hope. He talked about all the things he had never needed to feel; of desperation, fear and frustration. He talked and men listened, became inspired, straightened their backs and cheered. He smiled and the faces before him applauded. He frowned and they growled their solidarity. He lifted his fist into the air and announced that the fight had begun and they raised their hands, a sea of drowning men, and agreed to be his soldiers.

'We must strive to achieve a balance. We must work together and work as Mauritians. We must show those people who believe that they have power that they do not have anything without the Mauritian people. They think that they can scare us, divide and conquer us, but they cannot. Not if we are strong. Not if we unite and demonstrate our power! '

He became their icon; a working class boy made good against all the odds. He was the epitome of what our little island needed to become, to survive and flourish in an evil world. In short, he was perfect.

His success made my failure all the more apparent.

I was still working for Jerome at the *boutik*, even though my impetus to do so had now married and moved on. I told my parents that I was awaiting inspiration while I sat and read my books behind the glass cabinets with the bottles of Pheonix beer. I was waiting for life to bite me. There was no real point in trying any harder than that. It was not as though it would be appreciated if I did; no one would care. I was doing exactly what everyone expected me to do, so there was no real reason for me to change. I knew that whatever I did would be second best; that Frank would have done it better than me given half the chance.

Or so I thought.

Chapter Twenty

Tifi

We met up with Lewis again at seven o'clock, on the beach in front of his boat. I followed as he and Kitty held hands and waded out into the tepid water. My skirt pulled up over my head, I'd kept my sandals on to protect my feet from the jagged coral and sea slugs that hid in the depths beneath me. Fish came all the way into the shallows here, forcing me to remember with every step that I was doing this for Kitty, that I was doing this to keep her happy.

As we neared the boat, I noticed a lantern swinging in mid air on the deck. Lewis called out to it and a shadowy figure appeared, holding the light above its head. It waved and Lewis and Kitty waved back.

'Beth, meet my good friend, Sandeep.'

A soft plump palm strangulated by a copper bracelet offered itself to me over the side of the boat.

'Pleased to meet you.'

'Pleased I'm sure,' I replied, yanked on board.

I looked around the deck for a towel.

'If it is a towel you are looking for,' Lewis said, pointing at a white box, 'there is one in a locker, but I do not know how long it has been there.'

I looked about and decided instead to rub my legs dry with my skirt.

'So you are from Mauritius?' the newest stranger asked.

'No, I'm British,' I replied curtly, keen to stem the conversation and follow the others inside.

'But this is not English, madam,' he said catching my arm, 'this is something else.'

About a foot shorter than me, I looked down at his wide open face. 'I assure you, I'm English,' I replied.

He stroked his fat face in confusion, running a trail of doubt along his jowls, 'I do not believe you, but if you say so –,'

'I say so,' I replied, shaking my arm free and hurrying through the door into the heart of the boat.

Inside Kitty and Lewis were already busy in the galley, preparing the feast. In a desperate attempt to widen the distance between myself and the prying questions of my unexpected guest, I tried to get involved, started stirring pots and slicing onions, but the space was far too small and I was unceremoniously turned away.

'Why don't you go and chat to Sandeep and let us get on with it, Beth,' my best friend insisted.

'No, it's OK; I'd like to help you guys.'

'But it's no trouble, Beth and you've had a long day. Just go and sit down and let us take care of everything.'

I raised my eyebrows at her but she didn't get the hint so resigned to my fate, I sat down at the table and waited uncomfortably while Sandeep's bulky frame hovered at my shoulder.

After a long moment he squatted down beside me and opened a cupboard that clinked with bottles, 'Would you like an aperitif?'

'Do you have any Martini?'

'I think there's a bottle in here somewhere,' he said, disappearing into the depths, his ample bottom stuck up in the air, calling out to be shot.

'So, are you a friend of Lewis's?' I asked inanely to fill the space.

'What?' he said, clambering out again, 'Lewis? Oh, yes, we have been friends a long time. We have helped each other many times over the years. In fact, that is why I am here, because he came to see me today to ask for some help with your problem and I thought it best that I meet you.'

'Great!' I replied through clenched teeth, taking a glass of Martini from his outstretched arm. 'It was my friend's idea that we ask for help actually.'

'Well,' he said, with a grin,' it was a good thing she did since I am in the property business and will hopefully be able to run a search on this sugar cane field for you, tomorrow.'

Kitty and Lewis barged through the door, brandishing cutlery, and an array of condiments and set about laying the table.

'You like spicy food?' Lewis asked, pushing my glass aside to make room for his table mat.

'The spicier the better.'

He flashed his crystal teeth, 'Oh, good, that means you are going to enjoy this.'

'Beth?' Kitty slid herself along the bench to sit next to me, 'Lewis has just been telling me that he's actually from France.'

'Is that so?'

Her face sparkled with the naivety of a teenager in love.

'Yes, he stepped out onto a boat in Marseilles ten years ago and ended up here.'

'So, you're not Mauritian either then, Lewis?' I asked.

'God, no,' he replied, 'although, sometimes I wish I was. It definitely makes me life more easy.'

Intrigued, I asked, 'So, if you're French, then shouldn't that mean that you're called Louis or something, instead of Lewis?'

'Ah, I am always being asked that,' he replied, laughing, 'Me father was an English teacher and being born a boy, he realised he cannot be calling me Alice, so he called me Lewis, after Lewis Carroll instead.'

I suppressed an overwhelming urge to scream, 'liar, liar, pants on fire,' and took another sip from my Martini. Sandeep made himself comfortable opposite me and opened the bottle of wine on the table. Within minutes our host was ladling a clear noodle soup into willow patterned bowls and sprinkling teaspoons of chopped chilli on top. *Click, click, click;* a group photo and the meal was underway. The steam from the soup misted over Sandeep's glasses and he took them off to wipe them as he turned to me and asked, 'Would you mind telling me why you are looking for this particular field?'

And caught off guard, I fell into his astonishingly aquamarine eyes, 'My father sent me to find it.'

'So, it is your father who is from Mauritius after all,' he said with satisfaction, 'And your mother?'

I glanced at Kitty once again for support, 'I'd rather-,'

'Who'd like some more?' she responded faithfully, standing up and holding the ladle under Sandeep's nose and inducing him to say, 'Yes, yes, that would be very nice.'

'I thought your real mother was from Mauritius too?' Lewis piped up, lifting his face from his spoon, 'Is not that what you said, Kitty? That this is her first visit to Mauritius and that she is adopted in England but that her real mother is Mauritian and died in childbirth?'

Kitty sat down, the ladle still in her hand as an uncomfortable silence ate at the tablecloth and the curtains around us. Lewis looked up from his dish and asked, 'Have I said something wrong?'

'No. It's OK, Lewis. You haven't said anything wrong,' I informed him, 'it's just difficult for me to talk about it, that's all. It's still very raw.'

'Then it is me who should be sorry,' Sandeep said, filling my wine glass, 'I should not have asked such a personal question. It was impolite of me. I ask you to please accept my apology.'

I have no idea why, but his words made me blush. There was something unsettling about this fat little man, something that made me relax and feel anxious at the very same time; something that meant that I couldn't locate the words to reply. Thankfully Lewis took this as his cue to stand up and declare, 'Now I will get ready to serve the main course.'

He disappeared into the galley, quickly returning with a bubbling deep iron pan, brimming with a thick crimson sauce and broken chicken bones; a salivating aroma of cinnamon, cardamom and curry leaves, floating in his wake. As he served it up on plates with sticky clumps of white rice, Kitty set about imprinting the image before us onto film. *Click, click, click.*

'You like it?' Sandeep asked, through a mouthful of food.

'Mmmm,' I replied, 'My father used to cook this for me sometimes, when I lived at home.'

'Ahh, so, you do know some things about Mauritius.'

'About the food, yes, I know a little bit, but not much else really. I kept a scrapbook when I was a kid, and that's about all I've had to go on before I came here. It's not quite the same thing as being here and tasting everything first hand.'

Lewis looked over, fascinated, 'Have you heard of sega music?'

'Yeah, when I lived at home, my father used to play it now and then. I'd get to listen to one song by a guy called...*tea friar*?'

Sandeep laughed, '*Ti-frer*, yes, he is very famous. And what about seggae? Have you ever heard of that?'

'Can't say that I have, no.'

Sandeep nudged his companion, 'Lewis, have you got any?'

'I've got some Kaya.'

'Well, put it on, put it on. We could do with some music.'

Lewis placed a tape in a battered cassette recorder on the sideboard and pressed play. As the sound drifted towards me, I was hit with the strangest sensation, I imagine it's how an amnesiac must feel when the mist clears. I heard the rhythmic beat of a ravanne, the tapping of wood on tightly drawn skin and was instantly transported into my father's arms, enveloped in the desired warmth of belonging.

'Do you like it?' Sandeep asked, getting up from his chair to notch the volume up a few extra degrees.

I nodded my head to the beat, 'Yes, it's good. It reminds me of the music I listened to a long time ago, but of course, this stuff is more modern.'

'Yes, it is called seggae because it is a mix of sega and reggae. It was invented by the man who is singing, whose name was Kaya.' He said, returning to the table and replenishing our glasses. 'It is a sad story because Kaya was a Creole man who wanted to smoke marijuana and make music, but of course, the police do not like this type of person. He was arrested and died in custody which made a lot of people, especially the Creoles, very angry.'

'Yes,' Lewis added, 'there were riots in Port Louis after he died that were so bad that the government had to declare a state of emergency. It was very, very bad time for Mauritius.'

'How awful,' Kitty commented, while ripping chicken from a bone, 'you know, I don't remember hearing anything in the news about that.'

Sandeep put down his spoon, 'When diplomats come here, they describe Mauritius as the 'Rainbow Nation'; all flowers and colours and harmony, with many different types of people all living together happily under one sky. But this image in the most part is for the tourists and the visitors who stay in their rich hotels and never wander away from the beach. They keep them in their hotels and tell them lies so that they do not try and see the real island. They even dress up as colonials for them. They take them on trips to markets and museums where people will take their money and smile at them. The real Mauritius is a very different country where Hindus, Catholics, Muslims, Tamils, Whites and Chinese all live together and trade together but are sadly actually divided against one another.'

'How are they divided?' I asked.

'Well, let me think...do you like football?'

'I do,' Kitty replied, 'I'm a Saint's fan.'

'Good,' Sandeep smiled, 'I support Manchester United.'

'That figures,' Kitty groaned.

Sandeep cocked his head with a quizzical glance but didn't comment and continued, 'We used to have two football teams here in Mauritius, Sunrise and Fire Brigade. Sunrise was Hindu and Fire Brigade was the Catholic team. The government got rid of them because of the racial tensions they caused and now that the teams are regional, the differences still exist but no one watches the football anymore.' He paused thoughtfully while he enjoyed another spoonful of food. 'Then, there was the time the Egyptian football team played the Mauritius national team.'

'I remember that,' Lewis said with a grin, 'The Muslims screamed so loudly for the visiting team to win that there was nearly more riots, this time between Mauritian Muslims and the rest of the Mauritius supporters.'

I slouched back into the bench as the pieces of my puzzle slowly began to take shape.

'And then,' Sandeep went on, 'there was the time the Government wasted some fifty-eight million rupees taking bank notes out of circulation because Tamil's did not like the fact that Hindi words were put above Tamil ones on the new bank notes. There were so many complaints that they feared it would end in violence again.'

'This happened a long time ago though, didn't it,' Kitty enquired hopefully.

'Unfortunately, not that long ago, something happens often enough. It is like a cycle. Tensions build and then tensions are released.'

'But why here? I don't understand. This is a paradise island.'

Sandeep pushed his chair back and stretched out his legs, 'Because the West brought all these people here for different reasons and when they did not need them anymore, they left them to fend for themselves.' He took a sip from his glass, 'Since 1968, everyone lives in Mauritius but they choose not to be Mauritian. The majority of people like to distance themselves from their neighbour. For example, those who do not call themselves Indian or Creole, call themselves Hindu, Muslim or Catholic. I suppose it is human nature but the problem here is that the country is so small and no one has a full claim to the island so only the powerful survive. It is bound to explode now and then.'

Lewis stood up from the table, holding the empty pan in his hands, 'It is the same when I arrive here, it takes a little time to get used to. You have to look around you next time you go out. Look at the names in the newspapers. Look at the people and see where they work and what they are doing. You will realise that it is staring you in the face.' He smiled at me with his salt crystal teeth, 'Now who wants pudding?'

It was raining when I managed to scramble off the boat in the early hours of the morning, leaving my best friend in the capable clutches of her lover. Sandeep kindly offered to escort me to shore, slung over his shoulder in a fireman's lift. We staggered to the bottom of my apartment block and dripping wet and a little worse for wear, we said goodnight and parted. The waddling guard and his flea bitten dog stepped out of the shadows and watched me escalate the stairs to my door, where once safely locked away inside, I took off my clothes and draped my contented nakedness onto the settee. I watched the goose bumps ripple across my satisfied belly and out along my arms, toward my hands. I stared at them a long while, then sat up and picked up the 'phone.

'Hello?'

'Patrick?'

'Hi, Beth,' he answered.

I couldn't think of anything to say.

'Beth? Are you alright?'

'Yeah, I'm fine.'

'Good...where are you?'

'Away.'

'In Mauritius?'

'Yep.'

'And you're doing OK?'

'I'm doing fine. Kitty's here.'

'Oh, good.'
The silence unfurled and made itself comfortable.
'Well, I'll be going then.'
'OK.'
'Goodnight.'
'Beth?'
'Yes?'
'It's been good to hear your voice again.'
I thought about it.
'Same here.'
The hint of a smile.
'Goodnight then and take care.'
'Goodnight.'

Chapter Twenty One

Papa

Sahana's brother escorted her to the cinema every week. I waited for the martial arts movies to be sure I caught her. Sitting in the moth eaten, smoke filled stall, I usually watched the back of her head for a full ninety minutes. Now and then, a gang of kids would disturb my concentration – pulling the hair of some unsuspecting Muslim, Creole or Hindu girl. They never touched Sahana, though. Everyone understood that she was untouchable; the married daughter of Detective Chief Inspector R. Sundaram.

The light from the film flickered around us, casting shadows that danced in forbidden places – along the nape of her neck, its nudity betrayed by a tightly drawn plait, the few hairs that could not be tamed, lightly caressing the side of her face. Or the arched lift of her shoulders as she fought the desire to join in with her hero; karate kick to the chest, a slicing blow to the side of the face. Or the silver glow of the screen along the rise of her cheek, glittering from her long curled eyelashes.

I would have to shift my position from time to time, to release the strain. I held my popcorn box firmly in place on my lap. No one noticed. No one knew. I made sure that I always sat behind her. It gave me time to follow her in and be out before she could notice me. It was my little secret.

But it was Sahana who held a darker secret in her heart.

The labourers who worked on a two storey house in Quatre Bornes, on behalf of Chandels Textiles Ltd, toiled six days a week to finish the construction in time for the following summer. Ragged blue overalls clinging to the sweat patch that seeped like oil across their weary backs. Every hour or so, they took a ten minute break to replenish their dry mouths with a bottle of cold beer. Every day at about three o'clock they watched a ghost like creature drag her sandals along the dirt track that would one day be her driveway and survey the progress on her future concrete cage.

Baba was due to visit Mauritius during the first week of August. There was a factory in Phoenix that he wanted to buy and since the house was still not ready, he had conceded to stay at the Sundaram family home for three whole days.

'That is great news, no?' Mr Sundaram had told his daughter.

'Yes it is, Father,' she had replied politely.

'It is a pity that your house will not be ready, but it might work in our favour anyway. It will be a good opportunity for me to discuss another very interesting business proposition with him, if he is living in our home.' Detective Chief Inspector R. Sundaram scratched his greying head nervously, 'Sahana, you do understand that you must promise to do everything you can to make him amenable to the idea of helping me?'

'I will do my best, Father.'

'Good girl. This marriage has been good for us as a family. I have made a number of influential friends already as a direct result of our connections to Chandels Textiles.

You could help to make your family very, very rich. Is that not good news, no?'

'I am happy to make you so happy, Father.'

'Good girl.'

Sahana's husband walked through the arrival gates wearing the same brown suit and the same dour expression that he had worn on the day that they first met, eleven months previously. He offered his wife the quickest of cursory glances before proceeding to shake the hand of his beaming father-in-law.

'Welcome again to Mauritius, Baba. It is an honour to receive you and to invite you to our home. I know that my daughter especially has been looking forward to seeing her husband and showing him all the preparations that have already been made in his absence.'

Baba simply grunted and started pushing his luggage trolley towards the exit.

'Our car is not parked too far away,' Sahana's father said skipping alongside him, 'here, you must be tired, let me take your trolley for you.'

Baba yielded it immediately and yawned.

'Sahana has been preparing you a feast all day,' Sahana's father went on, 'She has been very eager to celebrate your arrival and we are hoping that you must be very hungry after your long journey from India.'

Baba shook his head slowly, 'On the contrary, they fed me very well on the plane. It should not be necessary for me to eat again today. I do not want to become a fat Indian, after all. A cup of tea should be more than sufficient to revive me in time for my business meeting at six o'clock.'

Sahana watched her parents and noticed the way that her mother was able to control the hot flush of her cheeks, so as not to bring further embarrassment upon her husband. If she cared, she too would have been embarrassed; but she did not. Ever since her baby brother had been born eight years previously she had had to learn that she was no longer special. Now she understood that his birth actually meant that she had become nothing more than a vehicle by which her family could be wealthy and powerful. Having begun her life so coveted and privileged, a bright and interesting future ahead of her, she now found herself tagged and branded and sold into nothing.

That evening Baba did not dine with the Sundaram's. He left the house at half past five and did not return home until three o'clock in the morning. Sahana had waited up for him, as instructed, and as she opened the door he had barged past her, coated in a noxious cloak of other people's fumes, – tobacco, alcohol, sex and perfume – his pomaded hair scrawled across his forehead, his eyes rimmed with a band of raw pink flesh.

Sahana hissed, 'You're drunk!'

And he wheeled around and brought his hand up to meet her face. She clasped the sides of her head, screaming soundlessly with the agony of the blow.

'You can sleep here on the sofa,' he growled.

She did not reply.

'I never wanted you anyway!' he spat.

She did not cry.

'Just keep out of my fucking way.'

She did not say a word. She kept her eyes on him and waited. Waited and watched. Waited and watched until she saw his feet stagger up the stairs to her bedroom, before she crept into her brother's room and curled up on his floor.

The next day her father said he wanted to talk to her. Apparently Baba had left very early that morning for a meeting and her father had not had a chance to see him before he left. Detective Chief Inspector R. Sundaram had therefore left instructions with his wife that Sahana was to visit him at his office that afternoon.

'I do not want to know what happened between you and your husband last night,' he said as she entered the room. 'Let's get that straight from the start.'

She stood in front of his vast wooden desk holding her hands behind her back. Pictures behind his head portrayed a dignified and powerful man. Certificates that hung from the wall in a diagonal line told of a man who knew his job. The stacks of paper that sat in his in-tray testified to how busy he must be.

'Sit down child, sit down,' he ordered, his features softening, 'I need to ask you a question.'

She pulled up a chair, 'Yes, Father.'

'Tell me Sahana,' he tapped his fingertips on the table, 'are you happy?'

She did not reply, deciding instead to upset him with her po-faced expression.

'Well, you should be happy!' he said in agitation. 'Do you have any idea of how important your husband is?'

She shrugged.

'Well, you should do!' He gasped.

The word 'should', she thought to herself, covered a multitude of sins.

'When you married earlier this year, a few colleagues and I invested a large sum of money into Chandels Textiles. A large sum of money,' he repeated, once again drumming his fingertips on his desk, 'all on my word that Baba would be opening another factory in Mauritius.'

A few more building blocks fell into place.

'Do you understand what I am telling you, Sahana?'

'Yes, Father.'

'And what is that?'

'You are telling me,' she replied, 'that if Baba suddenly decides that he doesn't want to open a factory here, if he decides that he would rather take his wife back to India and give up the whole project, then you and your colleagues would lose a lot of money.' She smiled, 'Am I correct?'

He looked her straight in the eye, 'Yes.'

'So, it does not look good that Baba and I do not like each other.' she added.

His line of vision did not alter, 'No it does not.'

'So,' she continued, 'it does not matter what he does to me.'

He finally faltered, 'Yes, I mean, No, I mean...' he sighed heavily, 'If you left Baba for any reason it would make it difficult for him to open the factory because he needs your passport.'

She stared at her father, 'You agreed to allow him to marry me because he needed my passport?'

'His family wants him to open the factory,' he said shaking his head, 'Textiles and fashion will be the new wealth of Mauritius.' He looked at his daughter imploringly, 'Sahana, please understand, we have to keep ahead of the game if we want to get rich.'

'And why do we want to get rich?'

'Do not ask stupid questions, child. You know full well that it is our duty as Hindu's to be wealthy so that we can look after our families and our communities.'

'I am sorry, Father.'

'It would do you good to remember that your ancestors worked their way out of a system that kept them down at heal for centuries.'

'Yes, Father,' she replied, bowing her head.

'And I will not allow anything to destroy what they have achieved. I will not allow my family to be ridiculed and poor,' he concluded, rubbing his chin, 'Do you understand me, Sahana?'

'I understand you, Father,' she replied, still examining her Bata sandals.

'Good,' he said shuffling some papers, 'Now I have important things to attend to and I cannot waste any more time with chitter chatter. So you can run along now, that's it, like a good girl.'

Chapter Twenty Two

Tifi

I'm a detective, wearing a long trench coat. I'm investigating a bloody murder in the middle of a wide expanse of desert. It's night time and countless bodies cover the ground; freshly slaughtered, hacked to pieces and pulled apart. The bodies are of men, women and children, of every colour, creed, race and religion. Their blood is of the same hue and flows together as one river. The sky above is clear and calm. I'm here to seek out clues, to find out why these people are dead; to determine a possible reason. I kneel over each corpse and examine the wounds. I have to ease my fingers into them, in an attempt to feel the shape of the instrument that has caused the laceration. The flesh gives way like soft sponge as my probing ultimately meets the hardness of the white bone that supports it.

Drifting silently towards me I can see the sugar cane. It's moving in uniform lines, upright and strong, just like a marching army. They circle the scene and my feet sink into the soil as I try to move. I look down and see a lake of dark blood sweep around my feet and ankles, covering my legs up to the calf. The cane is sucking the blood up through its stalks, like milkshake through a straw. I bring my palms up and notice that they now drip with the thick sticky fluid. I stretch my hands out and touch one of the canes nearest to me, marking each one of its segments with a smear from my fingertips. I count twelve. The cane begins to shake violently, its leaves now cutting and slicing at my face. I try to push it away, but the leaves have wrapped themselves around my body, strapping my arms firmly against my sides. I can no longer move. I call out and there is no one near to hear.

I awoke with a jolt. Not a good way to start any day, so, to recuperate, once washed and dressed, I retired to the balcony with some sweet vanilla tea and my Jilly Cooper novel. I leant back in my chair, put my feet up on the rail and absorbed the short lived human silence.

'Beth!'

I looked over the rails and saw Sandeep's rosy face beaming up at me from the car park.

'Have you any plans for today?' he called.

'Not yet, why?'

'I am going to run that check and wondered whether you might like to come along. I have a meeting first, but then I am free for the rest of the day.'

I wondered naively for a moment whether Kitty would miss me.

'Then, I thought,' he went on, 'I could maybe take you for something to eat and show you a little bit of our nation's capital.'

I peered down at him, the princess to a green eyed Rumpelstiltskin. 'OK.'

'Great. When will you be ready?'

'Give me five minutes and I'm all yours.'

I left a note for Kitty, grabbed my bag and skipped down the steps to his chariot, a black pickup truck with flaming sides.

'Climb aboard,' he said cheerily, helping me in.

'So, we're off to Port Louis?'

'Yes, my office is in the centre. I have my meeting there for about half an hour and then we can do the search, or,' he said with a wink, 'I am thinking, we can leave the search with my assistant, Rajesh, while we go out sightseeing instead?'

'The second option sounds fine to me. Just as long as I get the information I need, I'll be happy with whatever we do.'

'Great.'

We rolled into the capital twenty minutes later, having battled through the traffic, the pedestrians and cyclists until we reached a modern complex of towering buildings, tiled terraces and fancy shops facing onto the waterfront.

'This is Caudan Waterfront,' Sandeep informed me with pride.

'Very nice.'

'My office is a five minutes' walk from here, but it is easier to park here and walk than it is to try and find a place nearer,' he explained, leading the way.

Roads and pavements bubbled with moving bodies; workers, traders, tourists, sailors, policemen and children. Prancing like Billy goats from curb to gutter, we took our lives into our hands to move a few precious metres. Tricky vendors bartered hot goods on every street corner. Market stall holders haggled with passers-by for cheap electrical goods with batteries included. Lofty office blocks and western style chain stores flanked both sides of each street. The noise was deafening as human cries and calls, car horns and revving engines mingled together in the leaden air.

Sandeep hurried forward, trotted up some marble steps and held open an immense glass door, 'Welcome to my offices, Mrs Stephens.'

Air conditioning immediately hit and greeted my melting torso.

'We are on the eighth floor. I always try to climb the stairs but we can use the lift if you prefer.'

I wiped the sweat and grime from my forehead, 'The lift will be fine, thank you.'

Sandeep's smile exploded into laughter as he ushered me past a bevy of Japanese businessmen and into a waiting lift. 'I keep forgetting how new this must all be for you.'

'Yeah, you can say that again. In England, we're lucky to get two weeks tepid sunshine a year. This heat takes some getting used to.'

He cocked his head to one side, 'Even when your skin was made for it?'

I held out my hand and examined the dark brown layer that I'd begun to forget, 'This stuff's just cosmetic,' I explained, 'I've lived in England too long.'

He nodded a pretend gesture of comprehension as the lift doors opened out onto a red carpeted corridor and into a plush reception area where an immaculately dressed youth stood underneath a sign that read 'R.S.S.C. & Co Ltd.'

'Alain,' Sandeep said, stepping forward, 'this is my friend and very important client, Mrs Stephens. Can I be assured that you will look after her while I am in my meeting and make sure that she is comfortable and well refreshed?'

'Yes, sir.'

'Good. And can you tell Rajesh to come out as soon as he can and ask Mrs Stephens for the information he needs to run the land search that I spoke to him about yesterday?'

'Yes, sir.'

'Good,' Sandeep said, returning his attention to me, 'I should not be too long. If you need anything, just ask Alain. There are some magazines over there on the table and the bathrooms-,'

'Sandeep, I'll be fine. Now go on or you'll be late.'

'OK,' he smiled.

Rajesh, a small ferrety looking gentleman in his late forties, came by a few minutes later and took away as much information as I could give him about the whereabouts of the field. Then Alain kindly made me a cup of coffee which I took over to the vast feature window that looked out over the city. Port Louis stretched out to the sea, past the clinically scrubbed buildings of Caudan Waterfront, the jostling market stalls, garden parks, bus stations and traffic queues. In places, you could even be forgiven for liking it to London, its diversity so obviously apparent from the rooftops and tips of innumerable mosques, temples, pagodas and churches that were interspersed among it all; the kind of skyline my mother would have adored.

'We are lucky to have such a fine view,' Sandeep said, grinning beside me.

I clasped my hands to my chest. 'That was a quick meeting.'

'Thirty five minutes and forty seconds to be precise, so not very quick. In fact, it was reasonably tardy.'

'Don't worry,' I said stepping away from the window, 'I didn't notice.'

'That is good. Did Rajesh see you about the information?'

'Yes, he did.'

'Great. So now we can eat.'

Out into the busy streets below, he masterfully led me through thickets of arms and legs until we reached a grease smudged glass stand, filled with fancy Tupperware.

'Dé!' Sandeep shouted at the man behind the counter.

'Avec Kari, Misyé?'

'Non.'

'Pima?'

'Wi.'

I regarded the tightly wrapped yellow package with fear as it was held out to me, Sandeep ordering, 'Eat! Eat!' through crumb laden lips. Tentatively, I nibbled a corner of the flat bread and finding it quite palatable, proceeded to devour it in one mouthful. Only once it had gone down did I feel the flame of chilli paste hit the back of my throat, my eyes watering in the back draft of the eternal fires of hell.

'It is good, no?' he grinned.

'Oh, yes, very good,' I croaked through the tears.

'Come along then,' he said, taking my arm, 'now I will show you some more of my city.'

He talked as we walked. He talked about the weather, about people and about the geography of the island. He talked about his business, about how successful he was and about his grandfather, the man who'd financed his rise to eminence. He talked as he guided me through parks, down narrow streets, across busy roads and into bustling markets where he explained the multitude of uses for the array of herbs, spices, plants and vegetables sold around us. I was lulled into a sense of security by the cadence of his voice; the particular way in which he ordered his words that made me aware of how much I'd missed male company. He led me into an austere building, a dusty museum crammed with glass boxes and the aroma of dead moths.

'The Dodo,' he proclaimed, standing aside the central exhibit. 'Our oldest ancestor.'

It was bigger than I thought it would be, fatter too and I felt an immediate and overwhelming affinity with the creature, stuffed and sat on a plinth.

'You know of course, about the Dodo,' he said.

'Yes.'

'Your parents must have told you all about it.'

'No,' I said circling the case, 'I read about them at school.'

He cocked his head to one side, his seemingly habitual gesture, 'Your parents did not tell you?'

'My father never told me anything about Mauritius.'

'And you mother?'

'My real mother or my biological mother?'

'Your Mauritian mother.'

'I never knew her.'

He sighed, 'Ahh yes, I remember, I am sorry.'

I peered into a neighbouring display that held similarly unfortunate specimens. 'Don't be. It's not as though you can do anything about it.'

We danced around each other, between the information boards and placards.

'What was your father's name?' he asked.

'George. George Labelle.'

'And your mother's?'

I looked up, 'She was called Sahana.'

Sandeep shook his head, 'That does not make sense,' he said, perplexed. 'Are you sure that was her name?'

'As sure as I can be,' I replied, 'It's what my father said her name was in the letter he left me when he died. Why? What's wrong?'

'Nothing's wrong, it is just those names belong to a Catholic man and a Hindu woman,' he explained, uncomfortably, 'It would have been impossible.'

'Well, not that impossible it would seem,' I said smiling.

'I suppose not,' he agreed unconvincingly.

We walked out into the glare of the sun and back amongst the busy streets of Port Louis.

'Does your father's family know that you are here?' he asked as we waited at the traffic lights.

'I've been trying to locate them, but it's been a lot harder than I thought it would be. There's this one woman I met yesterday who is his spitting image. I'd have sworn that she was one of my relatives, but she refused to talk to me, said that she'd never heard of my father, even though they shared the same surname and she looked just like him. It was all a bit strange, as though I'd really upset her by asking, but so much so that I knew she must have been lying.'

'From what you have told me already, her reaction may not be all that strange,' he said thoughtfully, stepping from the pavement. 'Your father never told you about his family, your mother or your home until he died.' He looked me dead in the eyes, 'What kind of a man would do that to his child unless he had something terrible to hide?'

I stopped moving and found myself floundering upstream in a sweeping current of brown bodies, a teaming river of familiar physiognomy; Dark cocoa skin, ebony eyeballs with small yellow stains, walnut cheeks splattered with freckles, tiny pinched noses and black crimson lips. 'What do you mean?'

'I mean that you should be careful while you are here,' he replied, taking my hand and leading me across the road. 'You may uncover things that you do not want to know or comprehend. Mauritius is a strange enough place for those of us who live here. It will be an even stranger place for you, especially when you do not know or understand what you could be walking into.'

I stepped onto the pavement and pulled my hand away. 'What are you saying?'

'I am saying that you should be careful, Beth. From what you have told me already, there may be people on this island who will not be happy to know that you are here, especially since you are the daughter of a Creole man and a Hindu woman.'

'Don't be daft.'

'I am not being daft,' he retorted. 'This is not Europe. Your land is a very, very long way away. Things are very different here. People do not tolerate that sort of thing.'

I was dumbfounded and at the same time oddly relieved that someone had finally articulated the undercurrent of anxiety that I'd felt since this all began. 'It could be that bad?'

'Yes, it might be that bad.'

I thought about what Madame Lasyet had said a few days before, unpalatable words that had seared into the soft tissue of my brain; one son murdered, one son disappeared. I mulled over the same reoccurring fears and concerns; a grief that had driven a mother mad; a dreadful truth that would have kept a man silent for the rest of his life; a strange and ominous request in dribbled blue ink.

Ambling aimlessly over old ground, I asked Sandeep to call ahead to the office and check whether the land search had been completed. Turning his mobile on for the first time that day, it was with some consternation that he discovered he'd received a number of missed calls from Rajesh.

'What is it, Rajesh?' he yelled down the phone.

I didn't understand what else was said, as he continued the heated exchange in Kreol.

'I have to go back to the office,' Sandeep flustered, sliding the mobile back into his pocket. 'Something has come up that is very urgent.'

'Oh, OK.'

'I give you some money to take a taxi home,' he said, pulling his wallet out of his jacket.

I placed my hand on his to stop him. ‘It’s OK, Sandeep. I’ll get a bus home.’

‘You cannot travel by bus.’

‘Why not? It will be an experience,’ I said with a smile.

He relaxed slightly, ‘If you insist. I am sorry to have to rush off like this but-,’

‘What about the land search?’

‘I will bring it to your apartment this evening,’ he called over his shoulder.’ If you are not in, I will leave it with Lewis.’

And then he was gone, sucked back into the current of bodies that surged along the streets.

Chapter Twenty Three

Papa

Then everything changed forever.

Old women and children retold the stories of face painted Creoles hiding out in the mountains. They spoke of how the violence was triggered when a group of Muslim boys burnt a Creole girl with a cigarette as she watched a movie at the cinema. An eleven year old boy in the square next to ours, described the moment that an Indian man had crept out of the sugar cane wielding a pistol. The man had lifted his finger to his mouth as he moved past the boy and into the bushes on the other side of the road. Terrified whispers told of bodies lying in the roads of Port Louis, of sabres cutting babies' heads off, of rape and robbery. Men locked up their daughters and wives. Chinese shop owners watched on as looters passed goods from their windows. Indian shop owners looked on as their shops burnt to the ground in the light of the setting sun.

I listened to the tales of woe from the comfort of the *boutik*. I watched as the protestors passed in the street outside the door. I saw the police holding their batons and pointing their guns into the air. I heard the odd bang, recognised the earthen smell of burning in the electric atmosphere. I even experienced the same spine tingling nervousness of the moment, the same sensation that provoked the destruction, hate and paranoia that spun on around me.

I was lifting an empty crate out into the road when I saw her. She was running towards me, clutching a black jacket around her shoulders, the orange flame of her skirts lapping against her dark brown legs. I moved out into her path. She did not see me, her eyes glazed, panicking like a goat before the lion. They darted back and forth, between the road and the sugar cane, taking in the pedestrians who shuffled past her, searching for an avenue of escape. I stood my ground. She tried to skip out of the way. I grabbed her arms. She screamed and tried to pull away. I recoiled but my grip remained firm.

'Sahana, it's me!'

She lifted her gaze, her arms still rigid; a yellow patch of skin along her cheekbone. She weakened slightly as the orange flecks of her pupils contracted and focused.

'Hide me!'

I spotted the opening to the path through the field. People passed along in the street with no more than a flicker of interest, before scurrying on about their business. I pulled her across the street and into the sugar cane, its rough leaves scratching our skin, forewarning us to go no further, but we ran on until we found the clearing; the place where we had found each other as children.

I held her close, wrapped her warm and tight in my arms and kissed the top of her head. I felt her sob against me, into my chest. I did not want to let her go. I wanted to protect her tiny frame within my massive embrace. The world around us was in chaos. It would not understand the purity of that moment as I held her to me. She was all that I wanted in the entire world. No one else deserved her as much as I did. No one could ever love her more.

She pushed herself away, to stand before me, her features naked, denying her secrets. I placed my thumb on her bruised cheekbone and smearing grime in its wake, wiped away the tears. She looked so sad, so lost, so imploring. She grabbed my hand and rested the whole side of her face in my palm. She was so small and fragile that I could have crushed her beneath my fingers. I think that is why she did it. To show me how breakable she could be. She took the same hand in her tiny nimble ones and pulled it down to rest on her breast, her left hand holding me there. I heard my breath quicken, felt the uneasy thud of familiarity, and her gaze was transformed, unwavering, commanding, resolute, her large brown eyes deriding me, stripping me to the bone. The warmth spread as she placed the palm of her right hand there, cupping me. Her eyes steady, powerful, shredding me to pieces, disabling me completely. I grew beneath her touch, straining, wishing that I could do something more than just stand there and let her do this to me when she was not mine to touch in this way.

Her fingertips found me. The heat cracked through my abdomen, up through my stomach, thumped at my kidneys and punched a hole through my back. She let go of my hand and held onto my arm to steady me. My cheeks flushed like red coals. The sugar cane whispered around us, shaking their leaves in annoyance, hiding us, colluding in treason. She pressed me into the ground, the earth hard and unforgiving under my back. Sharp black rocks cut into skin, rubbed and scratched, straining to bleed. The sun shone on above, searing my eyes, creating shadows and echoes of movement around me.

Warm skin touched my thighs, whilst fabric played and tickled my chest. I gave way willingly to the weight and listened as the cane applauded the moment she gasped. A jolt, a painful interlude, prompted me to consider events that would have conspired against her. I tried to read her but her face rode black and featureless above me, wild tentacles suffocating in the close air. I heard her breathe out as she lowered herself. I heard her catch words in the back of her throat. I felt the frenzied grip carrying me away to a land of no return. My stomach burnt up through my chest, a fireball of blood twisting my insides, concentric circles rippling out...

And it was over. I lay embarrassingly exposed on the ground, a rock in each palm, hidden by unfurling fingers while she brushed herself down and pulled her hair back, away from her face, licked her thumb and rubbed away the dirt from her cheekbone. Still dizzy, I lifted my hips and covered myself, the cane swirling around me, condemning me, berating me.

'I must go,' she said.

And then she was gone; a wisp of burnt orange fabric caught flying in the midst of the sugar cane.

Chapter Twenty Four

Tifi

'And where have you been?'

I opened the apartment door to find Kitty sat at the dining table, camera in one hand, cigarette in the other.

'Out,' I replied.

'With Sandeep?'

'Yep.'

She giggled like a schoolgirl, 'Did you have a nice time?'

'Yep.'

I flipped off my sandals and lay down on the sofa.

'That good, heh?'

'Sod off!'

'Heh! No need to be like that grumpy pants. I'm just asking, that's all,' she said, standing up from the table. 'I only got back myself a few minutes ago because I wanted to let you know that Lewis is taking me out to dinner in Tamarin tonight and like, I doubt I'll be back again 'til morning.' She walked towards me and ruffled my hair, 'You don't mind do you?'

'Why would I mind?'

'I don't know. I was just asking to be polite.'

‘Well, there’s no need,’ I told her, ‘Go on, bugger off and enjoy yourself without me. I could do with some peace and quiet anyway.’

‘Suit yourself,’ she replied, gathering her bag and coat and flouncing out of the door, ‘and be sure not to do anything I wouldn’t do.’

‘Well, that doesn’t leave much now, does it,’ I called after her, as the door slammed shut.

I closed my eyes and felt my body sink into the cushions, pulled down by the weight of my thoughts and memories; ten tonne trucks of emotional matter driving headlong into a collision course. It’s funny what peculiar and irrelevant recollections the human brain can toss out when you don’t want to think. I actually believe that my subconscious mind must be a morbidly obese ‘Trisha’ addict who gets off on flicking through my catalogue of reminiscence, ripping apart every seam of my life and directing my craving synapses towards a bucket of ice cream.

I caught a glimpse of Patrick, in his starched jet-black mod suit the day we were married and recalled the cream sixties shift dress that I’d worn and the way my hair had been sculpted into a stylish black bob. It reminded me of the vows we had written and recited on the parquet floor of a dance school on Leigh road and of the makeshift aisle we’d created between the plastic chairs, so that we could sashay down it to the tune of ‘Be My Baby’ by The Ronettes.

I remembered arriving home at the end of my first year at University, my mother standing on the station platform waiting to greet me, a paper tissue in her hand. She’d asked me a hundred and one questions about how I was, how I’d done in my exams, how much money I’d managed to fritter away over the last term. She’d fretted over my health and my eating habits, and then thrown in a few derogatory remarks about boys and too much partying for good measure.

I heard my father shout, 'Heh, Elizabeth, is that you?' from his greenhouse and ran round to find him surrounded by ceramic pots, bags of compost, trays of seedlings and trailing vines.

'Have a look at this!' he'd declared, holding up a pot and gently prodding at a small green bud that dangled from a fragile stem. 'Our first pima,' he'd stated with pride, 'I grew this from one of the seeds of the chillies that I bought from our Indian friends on the corner. When it is grown I will make you something special, Elizabeth. I will make you a *chatini, chatini coco*, or *archards*, yes that is it, I think I will make you *achards, un pot d'achards de legumes*.'

I jumped. The 'phone was ringing.

'Yes?' I asked groggily, holding the receiver like a baby with a dirty nappy.

'Vous êtes bien la fille de Georges?'

A soft feminine voice.

'Yes, I am Beth Labelle,' I replied.

'Tell me, is he well?'

'No, he's dead.'

I heard a gasp caught on the end of a line.

'When?'

'A few months ago, the 20th January.'

'How?'

'Cancer.'

Sadness seeped through the handset.

'Same as Papa,' she sighed.

'Juliet?'

'Yes.'

I sat up as my internal hamster returned to its wheel. 'What made you change your mind?'

'The photo.'

'Why?'

'It is difficult. There was something about it, something that started me thinking,' she replied. 'I don't remember George being hit. From what I can recall, we all had a wonderful day and no one got into any trouble. That party, the one after the service, was actually one of my fondest childhood memories.'

'The inscription?'

'Yes, the inscription on the back of that photo you left. It's been bothering me ever since you came.'

A stagnant pause as we figured out what to say next.

'Do you want to meet me?' she asked, finally.

'I'd like to.'

'How about tomorrow?'

'Where?'

'Have you heard of the botanical gardens in Pamplemousses?'

'Yes.'

'Meet me there at the entrance, at, let's say, two o'clock?'

'No problem.'

'Good. Well, until tomorrow, Elizabeth.'

'Until tomorrow, Juliet.'

I replaced the handset and walked over to the balcony. I looked out over the trees, towards the setting sun. I could feel answers on their way; pieces coming together. The climbing roller coaster of the last three months was about to peak, about to cough out the secrets of my hidden past.

And as if on cue, I heard the scrunch of tires on tarmac and gravel and looked down to see Sandeep descend from his truck, an A4 manila envelope tucked tightly under his arm.

'It is not exactly what you are hoping to find out, Beth,' he said, passing me the envelope under the glare of the security lighting.

'Come in, come in,' I told him, 'Whatever it is, it's an answer, Sandeep. That's all I'm looking for.'

'I would not be too sure,' he replied, rubbing his hands nervously and following me through to the kitchen.

'I'm going to put the kettle on. Would you like a cup of tea?'

'Have you anything stronger?'

'Yeah, yeah,' I said, waving at the fridge, 'There's a cold bottle of white wine in there and a glass on the side. Help yourself.'

'Thanks.'

'Did you get everything sorted out at the office this afternoon?' I asked, filling the kettle.

'Y-yes, thanks.'

'Nothing too serious, I hope.'

'No, not at all. These things never are.'

I lit the flame under the gas burner, picked up the envelope and tore along the edge. I pulled out two pieces of paper.

The first sheet informed me that the plot of agricultural land that was annexed to the commercial property once owned by a Jerome Tong, on the district border of Quatre Bornes and Rose Hill, had been decommissioned in 1980. The land had then been sold onto property developers and now formed part of the Stanley housing estate.

'So, the field doesn't exist anymore?'

'No,' Sandeep said, glumly. 'I am sorry.'

'Well, I suppose that's nobody's fault.'

He wiped the sweat from his cheeks. 'Read the other sheet.'

It was a computer printout of a newspaper article from the Mauritius Times dated 20th November 1971.

YOUNG MAN'S BODY FOUND

The body of Frank Labelle was found late last Friday evening in the province of Rose Hill. Labelle, 21, had been missing for four days when his body was discovered by a group of children in a sugar cane field on one of the main roads into Rose Hill. The family of the deceased has been informed and a formal identification took place yesterday afternoon at the central mortuary in Curepipe. Police are now awaiting an autopsy report to ascertain the formal cause of death, although preliminary forensic reports suggest that evidence of foul play is unlikely. A well-known Creole rights activist and vocal member of the Mouvement Militant Mauricien, the death of Mr Labelle has come as a great shock to those who knew him. One friend and acquaintance, Jerome Tong, the owner of the bar located in front of the field where the body was discovered, recalled Mr Labelle as *'an upstanding member of our local Catholic community and an honour to have known.'*

The MMM has been at the centre of a wave of neo-Marxist rallies of late and is to blame in the most part for the rise in localised cases of civil disobedience throughout the country. Mr Labelle was last seen at a trade union rally at the Port Louis docks last Monday afternoon, where he spoke to a gathering of around 50 young workers. The alarm was raised as to his disappearance after he failed to return to his family home in Quatre Bornes the following morning. As is procedure, the police would welcome any information that may aid them in their inquiries.

'Shit!'

I felt the cogs of the roller coaster slowly clunk, clunk, clunk, as they finally reached their zenith.

'I am thinking that you might react in this way.'

'How did you find it?'

'It was Rajesh,' Sandeep replied. 'He ran a check on the internet after he completed the land search.'

'It was that easy?'

'Apparently, yes.'

'Fuck!'

The kettle began to whistle beside me. I turned off the gas, 'Can you pour me a glass of that wine?'

'Yes, of course.'

We adjourned to the living room and the comfort of the sofa.

'So, what do you think?' Sandeep asked, handing me my glass.

'I don't know. I'm pretty stunned really. The old lady the other day, Madame Lasyet, told me that one son had been murdered, but I hadn't at any point thought it would be in the same field that I was looking for.'

'And your father disappeared at about the same time, didn't he?'

'Yes, that's what she said.'

'So, it looks like you might have found your answer.'

It wasn't the answer I wanted to hear.

'What? That my father killed his brother and that is why he ran away?'

'It would seem to be a logical conclusion.'

'I can't say it hasn't crossed my mind, but it doesn't explain Sahana or the fact that this article suggests that it might have been suicide.'

'He may have tried to cover it up to look like suicide and then murdered Sahana too.'

I threw him a sideways glare. 'I think you're getting a little carried away.'

'It is only a suggestion,' he shrugged.

The fact of the matter was that I'd been thinking exactly the same thing but I wasn't about to admit it to a near stranger. 'I know and thanks, but if you'd known my father you'd know that there's no way he could have been a serial killer. Anyway, I received a phone call just before you arrived. Juliet, my father's sister, I mean, my aunt called and I'm going to meet her tomorrow. She'll hopefully be able to shed some more light on what happened and then I'll be able to decide what to do.'

'Juliet, you say, the lady from the other day, the one who refused to speak to you?'

'Yeah. She rang and apologised. I don't know why she lied but I'm sure she'll tell me when I speak to her.'

'You are not going alone, are you?'

'Why?'

'I just do not think it is safe. You should take someone with you.'

I looked at him squarely, careful not to hurt his feelings. 'I'll be fine. Besides, I think it'd be better if I went on my own.'

He didn't look too convinced, 'Well, if you are sure.'

'I'm quite sure.'

We sat and talked some more about other things, draining our drinks and calming the teetering roller coaster carriage inside.

'Where is Kitty?'

'She's gone out with Lewis for the evening.'

Sandeep nodded his head as though he should have known. 'I do not think it is very good you being left alone so much.'

I laughed. 'Well, there's not too much I can do about that really, especially where Kitty's love life is concerned.'

'Do you think she is in love with him?'

'I don't know. I hope not.'

'Why is that?' he asked, a smile stretching across his plump face, 'Are you jealous?'

'God, no,' I chuckled nervously, 'I'm a married woman, I'll have you remember.'

'But you do not miss your husband.'

His questions kept catching me off balance.

'I do.'

'You sound as though you are trying to convince me.'

'I don't need to convince anybody. Besides, it's none of your business.'

He grinned as he stood up and made his way over to the front door. 'You know, Elizabeth, some day it might be.'

'What do you mean?'

'Now,' he said, opening the door and stepping out into the mosquito filled stairway, 'that is none of your business.'

I watched as the door closed behind him, utterly bemused, anxious and alone.

Chapter Twenty Five

Papa

Then one day at work, I looked up from behind the bar to see my older, more respectable brother standing in the doorway.

'Frank, my boy,' Jerome yelled, striding forward to take him in his arms, 'long time no see. How are you?'

'I am fine, Jerome. I just came by to see how you are doing and to check up on my little brother, make sure that he is not getting up to any mischief.'

Jerome's hearty laugh resounded off the corrugated roofing, 'Ha, Ha, George, did you hear that, your brother has come to wipe your nose!'

I feigned a smile and returned to cleaning the glasses behind the counter. There were a few other regulars in the bar, that day and Jerome ushered Frank over to meet them.

'This is Frank Labelle, my friends, our George's older brother and the more good looking of the two, if I do say so myself,' he chuckled.

'Ah, the young activist, no less,' replied one man, 'you must make your father proud with what you have achieved.'

'Yes,' piped up another. 'I've heard that you are quite good, even though you are a bit young to be preaching the riot act.'

'I don't preach the riot act, sir. I simply state what is in my heart.'

'Ha! another wise head on silly young shoulder, I see,' Jerome interjected. 'Tell me Frank, more importantly, what do you want to drink?'

Frank turned and looked at me, 'George,' he called, 'can you bring me a beer?'

'Péna problem,' I replied, bringing it over to their table, 'would you like anything else?'

'No, no, this is fine,' he smiled. 'You get back to your work.'

I returned to my place behind the bar while the men chatted and laughed along with Frank. He was their shining example, the image of the young virile men they dreamt that they used to be; free to fight for principles instead of having to worry about feeding the women and children. The very fact that he walked upon the earth confirmed my status as a coward and made it all the harder to love him. For me, he was not just Frank; he was the know-it-all who proved how useless and insignificant I was.

When the crates were tidied away and the doors and blinds locked up for the evening, I took his arm and led him out into the warm night air and out into the middle of the road to avoid the inevitable pot holes and vicious dogs that hid in the sugar cane.

'Tell me little brother, are you happy with your life?' he slurred, maintaining his balance against me.

'As happy as any normal man can be, I suppose,' I replied.

'And you are satisfied with your work?'

'Yes, Frank. It suits my needs for the moment.'

'And what needs are they, little brother?'

'To earn enough money to pay my keep while I decide what I am going to do with the rest of my life.'

'And how long are you planning to take to decide, my brother?'

'As long as I need.'

His body shuddered beside me, laughter boiling away inside of him. 'And what of love, George? When will you decide to fall in love?'

I paused, unsure of where he was leading me.

'When will you fall in love, George?' he demanded, 'When will you decide to take a good Creole wife?'

'I will fall in love when the feeling takes me,' I told him.

'So, there is no one already?' he sniggered. 'There is no secret love which you hold in your heart?'

I pushed him away to stand on his own two feet; watched him wobble and dance in the moonlight.

'Why are you so angry, brother?' he sang, 'Have I said something to upset you?'

I marched past him, unwilling to be drawn into his little game, my stomach tied up in knots. Seconds later, I heard his body crumple and fall and turned to see him scrabbling in the dirt on all fours. I reluctantly returned to his side.

'Louise has broken with me,' he sobbed as I pulled him to his feet. 'She says that her father will not allow her to be married to a man like me.'

I held him up under my arm, dragged his uncoordinated feet along beneath him. 'She says that I am too dangerous and that I will not make a good father. She says she wants a stable husband, one who puts his wife and child before his politics.'

'How are you dangerous?' I asked, bewildered.

'They are going to ban the party. The government wants us destroyed. We have started winning seats now and they are frightened. Some have even been saying that they are planning to arrest us. That they are even planning to arrest Paul.'

'So, Louise is afraid that they may arrest you too?'

'Yes.'

'But that is understandable isn't it? You would not want her to be married to a man who may go into prison for his beliefs.'

'She is my woman, she should stand by me!'

'Frank, when it comes to women, life is not that simple.'

He yanked himself away from me, 'And what would you know about it, you queer!'

'I am not queer!'

His eyes flared in the darkness, 'So why does nobody ever see you with any women then? And why are you always hanging around in that bar with that fat Chinese tart? You might as well have a big number six tattooed on your forehead for God's sake.'

'Frank, do you honestly think that I am a homosexual?'

'Why not? I'm not the only one. If you weren't my brother, I would have flogged you by now. Come to think of it, it is probably because you are my brother that no one has done it already.'

'I assure you, Frank, that I am not a homosexual,' I said, panicking, 'I am in love with a woman. I have been for a very long time.'

'Who?'

'I cannot tell you.'

'God damn it you lying bastard, who is she?'

'I told you, I cannot say.'

'Why not? Has she got three heads and a penis?'

'No.'

'Tell me!'

'I cannot because she is already married!'

He stood back, staggered to keep his balance as a wicked grin arched under his flaming glare, 'You sly old dog, George.' He reached his arm around my shoulders, hopped along beside me until he regained his stature. 'So, you can tell me her name though, can't you? You can trust your older brother to keep your little secret.'

I shook my head, 'No way. It would be more than my life is worth for anyone to find out who she is.'

'So it is worse than just being married isn't it?' he mumbled pensively. 'She is not an Indian is she?'

I refused to respond.

'She is isn't she?'

'Look,' I said, stopping short and looking my brother straight in the eye. 'Leave it alone!'

'OK, OK,' he apologised, lowering his arm, 'I was only playing, that's all. My lips are sealed. I will not tell anyone.'

'Good,' I said, 'I do not want any trouble.'

'Do not worry little brother. I tell you, your secret is safe with me.'

Chapter Twenty Six

Tifi

Juliet was already waiting at the gates when I arrived at the gardens a little after half past one; her frizzy hair pulled back tight in a bun, a touch of red lipstick on her lips. She was standing taller than she had been the other day, a good twenty centimetres straighter than the person who'd hidden nervously in the doorway. She'd also dressed for the occasion in a homemade twin set and fake pearls, accessorised by a matching black patent handbag and shoes; her Sunday best in an effort to impress.

'*Il faut m'excuser*, if I appeared rude when you came by the other day,' she said, handing me the photograph. 'It's just that I was unaware that George had a child.'

Familiar features manipulated an oval face blessed with dark almond eyes, smudged with ink and encircled with a chocolate sprinkling of freckles.

'I would never have believed it,' she added, 'if I hadn't seen you with my own eyes. It's amazing. I can see him just by looking at you.'

I smiled within. 'I could easily have said the same thing about you.'

The park stretched on in front of us; a map of carefully tendered trees and perfectly levelled green grass delineated by a looping tarmac path. Famous names pointed the way to the giant tortoises and the stag park; HM Queen Mother Avenue, Thomas-Huxley Avenue, a path simply called Shrimati-Indira Gandhi.

'Why did you say that you didn't have a brother called George?'

She hesitated for a moment. 'I don't know.'

We strolled on past a group of chattering school children half-heartedly listening to their guide as she described the origins and roots of the fish poison tree.

'You have to understand,' she continued, 'when George left, he went without telling anyone where he was going or why he was going, at a time when we needed him most. Papa decided that it would be easier to forget he ever existed than to think about why he never contacted us.'

We approached a pond teaming with green and crimson tea trays in preparation for what I assumed would be an amphibian dinner party.

'Is this your first visit to the gardens?'

'It's my first visit to the island.'

Her smile was warm and compassionate. 'You see those red flowers over there, floating on the water lily leaves?' She pointed at the middle of the nearest tea tray where a tea cup had been replaced by a clenched red fist with petals for fingers. 'When those flowers first open up they are white and within one day, when they close, they become red.'

I peered down into the water, fighting the urge to try my weight out on one of the larger leathery leaves. 'It's funny,' I agreed, 'how quickly some things can change.' I moved nearer to the edge, the side of my sandal tempting me to slip in. 'I only came to Mauritius because he asked me to spread his ashes here. I was supposed to find this field, a sugar cane field opposite a tabagie owned by a man called Jerome, lay him to rest and then go home.'

'You mean Jerome's *boutik*?' she asked.

'I suppose so.' I said examining a weed that had managed to squeeze itself through the concrete. 'Either way, it doesn't exist anymore. They've built a housing estate over the land now.'

'Yes, I know. That place has been gone for a very long time.'

The sadness in her voice was almost tangible; evidence of a longing, a hardship far greater than my own. I turned to face her. 'Are you sure you don't know why he left?'

Her gaze flickered away and looked out over the pond at a gathering of noisy French tourists. 'I've no idea,' she replied, 'I was assuming that you were about to tell me.'

And that was the moment that it finally dawned that there would never be any easy explanations. Instead of finding answers, I'd unwittingly discovered more questions, as well as a kindred spirit who was obviously in desperate need of the same closure I was seeking. I reached over and instinctively took hold of her hand. It was soft and pliable. I could feel her bones through the skin. I asked her tentatively, 'My father ran away shortly after your brother Frank died, didn't he?'

Her attention swooped in like an owl. 'It was at about the same time as Frank was murdered, yes.'

That word again.

'I thought it was suicide.'

'Who told you that?'

'I read it in a newspaper article. It said that the police believed that there was no evidence of foul play.'

She clicked her tongue and sneered. 'What, with a stone across the back of the head?'

Wheeling away from the water's edge, she marched back into the shade of the palm trees. My stomach lurched painfully after her. 'The article didn't explain how he died.'

'Well, now you know,' she replied with indignation. 'Frank was murdered and someone tried to cover it up. A few days later and we realised that George had run away and you can imagine what everyone was saying about it.' She came to an abrupt halt by another water feature, a monument to commemorate the life of a forgotten citizen of the Empire. 'And to make matters worse he never even called, he never wrote to us to tell us he was OK. What were we supposed to think? Mama and papa didn't know what to do. And it killed mama, the poor woman just fell apart.'

'And you're sure George had nothing to do with the death?'

'Mama and papa said that George would never have done that to his brother,' she said, slouching down on a bench between the two stone pillars, 'that even he wasn't capable of such an evil act.'

Two children ran up to us, a boy and a girl of about six or seven years old. They grinned and skipped onto the main concrete statue, waving their hands through the fountain, splashing each other and giggling happily before squealing off again through the trees.

I sat down alongside Juliet. 'How are you so sure that Frank was murdered?'

'Papa told me,' she explained, reaching into her bag and pulling out a handkerchief. 'He was the one who had to identify the body. He said he knew enough about corpses from his time in the war to know that the knife marks in his arms were made long after he'd died. The police refused to believe him and reiterated their opinion that Frank had cut himself while standing up and that the wound on the back of his head was caused when he fell on the rocks. The judge in the end decided to shelve the case file with an open verdict. No one wanted to believe our story and in the end we had to content ourselves with this one small concession.'

In the shade, the burning heat of the sun was exchanged for the sharp bites of mosquitoes and busy red ants. I reached down and scratched my bare ankles, cursing myself for not having put my new insect repellent spray in my bag that morning. 'And what about Sahana? What do you know about her?' I asked.

'Who?'

'His girlfriend Sahana,' I said, rubbing my legs, 'they were very close.'

Juliet shook her head, 'I wouldn't know about George being close to anyone and especially not to someone called Sahana. That's a Hindu name.'

'So you didn't know anyone by the same name?'

'The only person I know of with that name was Sahana Sundaram. Her father was the detective in charge of the investigation into Frank's death. I can't think of anyone else.'

I stood up from the bench and stamped my feet on the ground in an effort to shake off the ants. 'That must be her then,' I said. 'She's the reason he ran away.'

'He ran away because of Sahana Sundaram?'

I stopped stamping. 'No, he ran away with Sahana because she was pregnant with me!'

She allowed herself a moment of stunned silence before she said incredulously, 'George and Sahana?'

'Yes. That's what he told me in the letter he left me in his will. They used to meet in secret in the same field where Frank's body was found.'

She lifted her head, glaringly unconvinced, 'And he didn't tell you any of this himself before he died?'

'Juliet, I've only just found out that my mother actually adopted me when I was a year old.'

'Bondyé Ségner!'

Defeated, I sat back down beside her, 'Exactement!'

I told her how I'd discovered the truth about my Mauritian heritage and revealed the lengths that I'd been forced to go to, to perform my father's final wish. I told her about my conversation with Madame Lasyet and how I'd found out about Frank. She listened intently all the while and at times I was sure that I recognised the familiar twinkle of my father in her dark brown eyes.

'Your father was a young bull of a man from what I can remember,' she said, picking uncomfortably at her fingers. 'He could be really kind and helpful if he wanted to be, but usually he was fairly brusque and guarded. He was a mass of contradictions tightly bundled into a muscled and cumbersome body. He always kept a part of himself hidden away, as though he was protecting a valuable secret and was frightened of what people would do if they knew about it.'

She looked down and examined the trail of red ants that encircled our bench.

'Yes. Go on,' I prompted, eager to hear more.

'There's not that much more to tell you about him really. Maybe it's because I was so young when I knew him,' she said pensively. 'I remember papa saying that he was a very sickly child. He took a long time to learn how to read and everything. He just kept himself to himself really.'

'And Frank, what was he like?'

Her face naturally lit up. 'Oh, Frank was completely different. He was the proverbial blue eyed boy, except, of course, his were brown. He was handsome, athletic, intelligent and funny and the girls all used to fall at his feet, especially after he came back from England.'

'He lived in England?'

'Yes, he studied there for about three years. He came back here like a superstar, all western and modern and fashionable. I remember Marie and I used to fight all the time over borrowing his clothes.'

'And did they get on, Frank and George?'

'As far as I am aware, yes, they got on well together. I was only eleven when it all happened but my memories of my family before that time are all happy ones.'

'And Marie? Does she live close by?'

'Oh, no,' she said, shaking her head. 'Marie lives in La Réunion now. She moved over there back in 1980 when she got married to Pierre. She's got four boys, Matthew, Mark, Luke and John, just like in the bible. We write to each other often enough and sometimes she'll call me on the telephone when she has something really important to say. I could call her this evening if you want and tell her that I have met you.'

'Would you?'

'Of course. She'll probably remember other things as well. I can ask her for you.'

'Thank you, Juliet.'

She looked at me without smiling. 'It's the least I can do. We're family after all.'

She stood up and I followed her on our continued journey through the theatre of foliage; where overweight palm trees squatted alongside curtains of giant bamboo and reptiles with stage fright took flight across the knitted grass. She started to talk as though she was dreaming.

'When Frank died, it was like a light had gone out in our lives. The world stopped turning and a part of all of us curled up inside and died. It was so horrible that I can still picture it all clearly in my head. I can remember that day as if it were yesterday. I can remember seeing the policeman arriving at the front door, his cap in his hands. I can remember watching him speak to mama and then watching and sensing the horror as she fell on her knees in the doorway. I can still remember Marie screaming and running past me into the square, in search of papa, screaming for a telephone, screaming for God. Mama just lay there on the floor, shaking and wailing and I didn't know what to do.' Tears welled, teetered and rolled down her cheeks. 'I didn't know what to do. I was so frightened I wet myself. And George, he wasn't anywhere to be found. No one knew where he was. The neighbours came out of their houses and stared at us. Nobody knew what to do.' She pulled another clean handkerchief out of her bag. 'Mama never recovered. Dr Baglobin had papa sign the papers after about two months and then she was taken away and put into a home.' She unravelled the soft fabric with delicate fingers and dabbed at her nose. 'She never left. She never saw the light of day again. She died in there eight years ago.'

I swallowed hard, pushing back the emotion that threatened to surge up through my throat and into my head. I tried to remain focused. 'And you never married?'

She bit her lip, betraying her heartache. 'I couldn't. I was the youngest and someone had to look after papa.'

'And you never saw or heard of my father ever again?'

'I can't even remember him being at the funeral,' she said with bitterness. 'The police asked all kinds of questions. They asked everyone who knew him and nobody knew where he'd gone. He'd simply vanished into thin air.'

We were walking again, through what appeared to be an herb garden, the scent of camphor and sandalwood drifting covertly around me as I tried to absorb the magnitude of everything that she explained.

'That Sahana I told you about earlier,' she said, sniffing and wiping her nose.

'Yes?'

'She's still alive.'

I caught a brief sniff of cinnamon or it could have been nutmeg.

'She's not dead. As far as I'm aware, she's alive and well and living in Quatre Bornes with her family.'

Eucalyptus cooled the air that passed through my lungs.

I stopped walking. 'Sahana?'

'Yes, Sahana Sundaram, the one you think may be your mother.'

I reached into my handbag and carefully brought out the envelope that I'd carried with me ever since the skeletons had started to crawl out of my cupboards.

Her name was Sahana and she died bringing you into the world. In not succumbing to the wishes of others, we lost more than we bargained for and when we discovered that you were inside her, we had to run away, if only to keep you safe. We came to England to start a new life. We were young and full of hope and fear and we did what we had to do to give you a proper start in life. Then God decided to take my Sahana from me and left me all alone to look after you.

'That doesn't make sense. Sahana died giving birth to me. Why would he tell me that if it hadn't happened?'

I handed the letter to Juliet. She took her time reading through the passages, translating the messages that were written between the lines.

'My English is not as good as it used to be' she said placing it back into my open hand. 'But I think I understand most of it and it would appear that your father has lived under a delusion of his own making for quite some time.'

My mouth went dry. This had now become farcical. I'd lost one parent, then found out I'd lost another one I didn't even know I had and then after all that, discovered that she wasn't actually dead but alive and well and living on a tropical paradise in the middle of the Indian ocean. The image of one mother, my real mother, immediately popped into my head. Her creased pink face as she told me that she was scared that she was going to lose me. Her dry hands and bony fingers with their chipped pink nail varnish and gold sovereign rings. Stabbed with guilt I realised finally that I needed her. I needed her to take me in her arms and tell me everything was going to be alright; swear that she'd deliver me from this strange place and take me back to the world where I belonged.

Chapter Twenty Seven

Papa

Five days later Frank disappeared – vanished into thin air. There was talk that he was laying low somewhere safe, waiting for the arrests to finish. A few more astute rumours claimed that he had fallen in love with another girl and was probably making hay while the sun was shining. Either way, his disappearance was nothing to really worry about. He could have gone to Rodrigues or La Reunion for anyone knew.

What was certain was that he would turn up when the heat finally died down; stroll back into our lives and greet us all as the great man of courage, the Labelle Cavalier. I tried to reassure mama that this was exactly how it would happen. One day, talking in the kitchen, she squeezed her apron between her inflated fingers and prayed to Mary that I was right. Her nails black with the dirt of peelings, she swept curling hairs away from her eyes, uncovering worry lines that had never existed there three days before. I remembered wondering whether deep inside she wished that it was me who had disappeared instead; that maybe the lines would not have been so deep and indelible if I had gone away in his place.

That was the day that the boy knocked at the door. He stood on the front step, a young Hindu boy of no more than nine or ten years old, holding out a piece of grubby paper with my name on it. I took it from him and he sprinted away across the square, kicking up dust clouds as he went.

Meet me at 24 Avenue Rochefort, Candos, as soon as you can – S.

I thrust the note in my pocket and reached for my coat. Calling over my shoulder I told mama that Jerome needed me at the *boutik* and then I ran to catch a bus.

The house was brand new and smelled of freshly set concrete and creosoted garden fences. A manicured lawn, trimmed shrubs and a fairy tale path circled away to the side of the building, past a brightly painted shrine to a favourite many handed god. I spotted the ruffle of her skirts before she saw me; hiding away from the window, behind black trestle grills. This was Sahana's stately home. *Lakaz Chandels.*

On reaching the front door, I straightened my back and tried to appear professional, mature, and normal. It opened gradually allowing a flurry of perfumes to escape and greet me with a familiar mixture of patchouli, talcum powder and henna shampoo.

'Vini vit!'

I followed her into an expansive lobby then she ushered me along a polished corridor towards the rear of the house, past landscape watercolours, antique furniture, ornate golden ornaments and a carpeted stairway. We arrived at the kitchen by way of two elaborately carved swinging doors. It stretched out beyond us, a vision of culinary opulence; marble tops, hanging copper pots and pans, a fridge, a chest freezer and a stove big enough to cook a cow in.

'Mama would love this room,' I thought out loud.

'Well, she can have it if she wants,' Sahana replied pulling up a stool and placing herself delicately upon it.

'What are you talking about?'

She smiled uncomfortably and patted the seat next to hers. 'Come, sit down.'

I did as I was told. She knew I always would.

'George, darling,' she said reaching out for my hand, 'we're in trouble. Serious trouble.'

As our skin met, a bolt of blue, a lick of electricity shot up my arm. 'What is it, Sahana?'

She drew my hand across her and placed it on her hardened belly. She did not say a word.

'Are you sick?'

She laughed without laughter in her eyes. 'I suppose I am, in a way.'

The panic started to rise. 'What is it?'

She held my hand with her hands, gently pressing the palm against the rounded surface of her stomach. She stared into my soul with eyes like those of a deer caught in the sight of a gun. And then I understood.

I whipped my hand away. 'You are pregnant?'

Her face was calm, resigned. 'Yes.'

I did not understand. 'What has that got to do with me?'

She sighed, her demeanour evolving as we spoke from young girl into mother. 'I am pregnant with your child, George.'

The words winded me like a punch, expelling the air from my lungs. I did not respond for a long while as I regained some composure.

'How do you know it is mine?'

She folded her arms across her stomach. 'Because you are the only man that I have ever slept with.'

'And what about your husband?' I asked incredulously.

She blushed. 'He has no use for someone like me.'

My thoughts were confused and chaotic. 'Sahana, for Christ's sake, what is going on?'

She tightened the grip on her narrow waist. 'I have never had sex with my husband because he has never wanted to have sex with me.' Her body started shake, I could not tell whether it was from fear or anger. 'When you caught me and took me into the sugar cane I realised that I wanted you to have it. If I was going to have to lose it, I did not want it taken by someone who did not care for me or who had won me in a game. I wanted to decide how and by whom.' She looked at me, her eyes brimming with tears. 'So I chose you.'

'So, when we...in the sugar cane...that was the first for you too?'

She nodded. 'Yes.'

We sat in silence for a while in her brand new kitchen, a wall clock ticking away the seconds as the news took its time to sink in. I stared at her sandaled feet, her perfectly manicured toenails with their pink glittering nail varnish and wondered whether this was the bite that life had planned for me all along.

'What do you want to do?' I asked glancing up at her.

Her features were glazed now and as cold as ice. 'We have to go away.'

'Are you sure?'

'Yes.'

'And you are sure that there is no way that you can pretend that it is his.'

Her laughter was hoarse. 'George, the baby is already three months gone.'

I tried to smile but failed miserably. 'Where do you want to go?'

'England,' she answered resolute.

'England?'

'Yes.'

'But I do not have the money to go to England.'

She pulled an envelope from the waist band of her skirts. 'We already have tickets and money. All you need is your passport.'

'You have already bought the tickets?'

'George, I am going to have to go either way, with or without you.'

'Why is there such hurry?'

She sighed again. 'Baba called two days ago. He will be arriving tomorrow for a business meeting and I cannot allow him to see me like this.' She looked at me imploringly. 'George, if he finds me like this, he will kill me. If Baba finds out I have slept with another man and am carrying a Creole man's baby he will kill me and the baby and then, most probably, come after you. And if he does not, my father most certainly will. Now do you understand?'

'So we have to go?'

'Yes.'

'And I have to go back to my house and get my passport right now?'

'Yes,' she said sliding carefully off her stool.

I rose to join her, stepped forward and drew her body into mine. She allowed herself to relax into me. I stroked the top of her head and planted a kiss on the parted line of her hair. She moved away.

'Take some money now. Go and get your things and then get a taxi to the airport,' she said, slipping a few paper notes into my trouser pocket. 'I will be waiting for you there in two hours time. Our plane is due to leave just after ten o'clock.'

'I will have to leave a message for my parents,' I told her.

'No!' she snapped. 'We cannot tell anyone where or why we are going. It would be far too dangerous.' She sensed that I was not convinced. 'George, do you want your baby to survive?'

'Yes, of course,' I replied.

'Then do not tell anyone.'

She walked to the back door and opened it slightly to peer outside.

'It is clear, so you had better go now.'

I did not move.

'Please hurry.'

'Sahana?'

She turned around. 'Yes, George. What is it?'

'Have I ever told you how much I love you?'

The smile I had been waiting for finally dawned. 'Do not tell me now, George. Tell me when we get to England.'

Chapter Twenty Eight

Tifi

I dropped Juliet at her door and drove home to the apartment. She said she'd call me over the next day or so with news of Marie and the whereabouts of Sahana Sundaram. Unsurprisingly, Kitty wasn't at home when I got in; a scribbled note informing me that she was having a diving lesson with Lewis and wouldn't be back until later that evening. I decided to take a shower. I propped my weary body against the cold tiled wall and closed my eyes to the world. I heard the rain on the window, the rapid machine gun fire of a torrential downpour during a flash thunderstorm and found myself as a seven year old again, running into the living room; seeking solace between the tree trunks of his legs.

'The sudden storm lasts not three hours,' he'd said from behind his newspaper.

'What's that supposed to mean, Daddy?'

'Exactly what it says, child,' he explained without lowering the paper. 'If you are not expecting the storm when it comes along, the best thing to do is keep your head down and wait it out.'

'Can I wait the storm out with you, Daddy?'

'Of course you can.'

I scrambled across the carpet to take my place between his size fourteen shoes and with ever watchful eyes peered up between the pages of the newspaper at my wise old dad.

'Can you read me, Daddy?'

He looked down his nose at me and smiled, folding his newspaper away. He hooked his bear claws under my already outstretched arms and lifted me up onto his lap. 'Of course I can read you, Elizabeth.'

'What do I say?' I asked excitedly.

'Your face says that you are a very intelligent girl and smart and as bright as a button.'

'Really?'

He pressed one of his sausage fingers against the tip of my nose. 'Yes.'

'And do you like reading me, Daddy?'

'Of course.'

'Why?'

'Because I helped to write you, Elizabeth. Just like you helped to write me.'

The lamplight shone off his polished forehead, hallowing the brain that I most admired in the world. He was smiling, but not with his eyes. He was smiling with his teeth, the same way that he warned that the English smiled. His eyes were sad, filled with longing. I suppose I'd always known.

Once again it was the 'phone that brought me back to earth. I heard it ringing through the bathroom door. It rang for ages before it finally stopped. Then it started again. When it struck up a third time I knew that it had to be urgent. I stepped out of the shower and threw on a towel. Tottering across the room, I slipped on the tiled floor and knocked my shin against the corner of the coffee table. The 'phone kept on ringing.

I lifted the receiver, expecting at least to hear the voice of someone I knew.

'Elizabeth Stephens?'

But it was a man's voice and one that I didn't recognise.

'Yes, speaking.'

'Elizabeth Stephens. If you know what is good for you, you will get on the next plane home to the United Kingdom and never come back to Mauritius.'

Then the 'phone went dead in my water wrinkled palm.

I dialled the first number that came into my head.

'Patrick?' I pressed the handset hard against my face to stop my hand from trembling. 'That wasn't you buggering about was it?'

'What? Beth? Is that you?'

'Just tell me alright! Did you just ring me at the apartment?'

'Beth, calm down. I'm at work. In fact I'm in a meeting. I'm not sure what's going on but no, I didn't ring you. Look, I've got to go. Stay where you are. Your number's on my screen. I'll ring you back when I can.'

The line went dead again.

I pulled a chair out from under the dining table and sat down. Water dripped from my hair, *plip, plip,* to the floor. I focused on the small pool that gathered at my feet. A wall was being built between me and the real world; a black hole of information that fed the hounds on my tail. My mind drew a complete blank. If it wasn't Patrick, I'd no idea who the hell that had been on the 'phone.

There was a quiet knock at the door. I rose to open it.

'Sandeep?'

A pair of startled green eyes lowered themselves to my exposed cleavage. 'Hello, Beth. The others asked me to come and get you. We are going to have a pizza and thought that you might like to join us.'

'Isn't Kitty coming home first?'

He shrugged, at pains to lift his gaze. 'I do not think so.'

'Oh, for fucks sake!'

I slammed the door and marched into my bedroom, diving under the protection of the softened sheets.

Why were all these things happening to me? What had I done that was so wrong? Why did it feel as though I was being punished by every living breathing human being around me for simply existing and trying to get along?

In the end it always came back down to this; Elizabeth versus the universe – alone. Like some fancy flying superhero whose powers have been stolen; psychedelic clinging Lycra and a camel's foot – enduring the ridiculous and the insurmountable with no sidekick in sight. A pathetic 'Billy no mates', stood on the last foot of the plank, starring into the abyss and crying for my mummy. No one wanted to play with me because I had something worse than nits, something that I couldn't scrub away, a powerful cloak that couldn't be taken off.

The sound of jeering laughter filled my senses. A family day out to the zoo. Father and I standing by the monkey cages, watching them swing to and fro on their branches of bars. My hand as always encased in his. My wrist and arm, a thin sinewy thread that links me to him.

'Oi, mister, it looks as though a couple of your monkeys have gone and escaped!'

We turn in unison, his shadow enveloping me. A group of school children, teenagers, a guide and a teacher.

'Higgins, shut up!'

The teacher reprimands but cannot remove his smirk.

My father's hand unleashes my arm and clamps down on my shoulder.

Another voice calls out. 'Maybe you should send them back to where they came from!'

The group titters. The guide shifts his gaze to his muddy wellies.

'Now that's enough class,' the teacher tries half heartedly again.

I feel the clamp on my shoulder tighten and pull me round. 'Come along, Beth. Just ignore them.'

Even the monkeys have stopped swinging. They stare through their branches of bars. I can feel their pity. We walk along and leave them. Carry on, in a dead straight line until we reach the reptiles.

'Daddy?'

'Hmm?'

'What did they mean?'

'About what?'

'About sending us back to where we came from?'

His hand slips from my shoulder, becomes a shovel in the square of my back.

'It doesn't matter, Beth. Some people are just ignorant.'

I stop in my tracks, refuse to let him push me further and looking up I witness yet again the soft water resting on his bottom eyelash.

'Heh, you two! Why the hell did you run off? How was I supposed to find you?' Mother pants into frame, two ice creams creeping down her fingers. 'I've been looking all over the place for you. I thought you said you'd wait by the chimps?'

Her expectant expression melts with the 99 flakes.

'I need to go to the toilet,' my father answers solemnly.

'But what about your cone?'

'You eat it,' he replies over his immense shoulder.

I take my ice cream from her sticky grasp and paint on a clown's mouth. She looks down at me with that same exasperated face.

'What did you do this time?' she asks.

'Nothing,' I reply, through a mouthful. 'Those people said that we should be sent back to where we came from.'

'What people?' she looks around flustered and red cheeked. 'Where are they?'

'I don't know. They've gone now.'

'Oh for Christ's sake!' she says turning on the spot.

I tug on her sleeve. 'So where is it? Where do I need to get sent back too?'

She stops moving, throws her liquefied cornet to the floor. 'Nowhere, Beth. You're not being sent back anywhere. This is your home now, whether they like it or not!'

A gentle wave of self-pity prompted me to return to the living room. I lifted the cloth and uncovered him. Passing my hand over the smooth polished surface of his lid, I caught the hidden textures on my fingertips. An antique grain, warm, rich and forgiving, reminding me of how jealous I was because he could still be touched while he lay in pieces.

I lifted him up level with my eyes. 'What did you do, Dad? What happened here that was bigger than me? What did you do that I wouldn't have understood? What did you do that was so bad that you'd been too scared to tell me? Why did you feel you had to lie to me? Why did you carry it all on your own for all those years?'

I reached back and sat down on the arm rest of the sofa, waiting for an answer that would never come. Searching for excuses, I remembered that some behavioural patterns pass through generations; that the cast off emotion from a physical act two hundred years ago could still adversely affect your life today. Sitting in that room with my father in my hands, I wondered whether his great-grandfather had had a brother who was handsome and strong while he was quiet and shy. I wondered how many secrets it was possible for a parent to keep from a child, in the knowledge that it's impossible to forgive that which you don't understand. They'd even written it into religious texts. Thou shalt obey your parents, their word is sacred. It was nonsense; emotional blackmail providing all weak human beings with an opportunity to spread their curse for millennia to come. Looking down at my father I realised that parents were not Gods. My father was not a God. My father was a weak man, a proud man, a fearful man who acted of his own accord and had to pay the consequences for himself.

'That's it, Dad,' I told him, placing him back on the side. 'I've decided what I'm going to do. I'm going back to my real mother, patch things up with Patrick and put things back to how they used to be before any of this. This isn't my problem. It never was. In two days I am taking you back to England and I'll spread your ashes there. The rest of it can go to hell!'

Chapter Twenty Nine

Papa

I crept through the front door and scurried across the living room into the girl's bedroom. I walked up to the cupboard, opened the drawer and found Frank's passport underneath a bundle of photographs. I thanked God that it was still there. I did not have the heart or the courage to tell her that I did not have one. I took his travel bag down from on top of the wardrobe and filled it with clothes. I placed the passport and the photos in the side pocket, then patted the notes in my own back pocket.

Marie opened the door. *'Ki été?* What are you doing in here?'

'It's a secret.'

She looked over her shoulder and closed the door. 'For Frank?' she whispered.

'Yes, for Frank.'

She tiptoed closer to me. 'Can I help?'

'No.'

She looked hurt. 'Why not?'

'Because it is too dangerous for little girls.'

Her lower lip began to tremble. 'I will tell.'

I had to think quickly. 'You cannot tell anyone. Otherwise Frank will be in danger too.'

'Where is he?'

'Somewhere very secret.'

'Is he safe?'

'Of course he is.'

She walked over to the bed, pulled the bag towards her and reached for the zip. 'Can I come with you? I want to see if he's alright.'

I wrenched the bag away. 'I have already told you that it is too dangerous.'

She climbed up onto the bed and started to swing her feet. 'What are you up to?'

'Nothing.'

She grinned. 'You are. I can tell. You are up to something.'

'You are right,' I said with a sigh. 'I am doing something very dangerous for Frank and no one must find out. I have to take this bag to him because it contains something very secret. If mama and papa found out they would be very angry and so would the police.'

'What is it?'

'Dynamite.'

'Really?'

'Yes. So you have to promise not to tell.'

She shook her head. 'I won't tell anyone, George. I promise.'

'That is good. Now, I have to go now. I am already going to be late.' I opened the bedroom window and checked outside. 'You be good, Marie and make sure you look after your little sister while I am away.'

'Are you going to climb out of the window?'

'Yes. I cannot let mama or papa know that I am here.'

She jumped off the bed. 'Wait a minute!' She rifled through the drawer of her bedside table. 'Here, take this,' she said, handing me a small blue Père Laval pendant, her rosary beads and a prayer card. 'Give them to Frank, he may need them.'

I took them from her and placed them in the bag. 'I promise I will make sure that he gets them. Now I really must be going.'

I dropped the bag carefully to the ground on the other side of the window and swung my leg out over the ledge.

'You will tell him I love him, won't you, George? You will tell him that we all love him and miss him lots and lots,' she said.

I climbed out of the window and put my finger to my lips. 'I promise that I will tell him. Now you must promise not to tell anyone that you have seen me.'

She pretended to lock her mouth and throw away the key.

'Goodbye, Marie.'

'Mmmm Mmm,' she replied with a giggle, and closed the grate behind me.

Chapter Thirty

Tifi

I put on some clothes and went for a walk. I turned left out onto a silent road that wound away into the night time and into the sugar cane. I closed down my fear and allowed my body to lead me. I followed myself deeper and deeper into the field, away from the lights and the evidence of human existence. The cane stood taller than me on both sides, its arms shaking out to greet me and protect me. Natural shields to take away my perspective, reduce me in size, and help me appreciate my significance.

I didn't notice the rain at first. It was only when it began to roll down my eyelids that I realised the sugar cane was clapping around me. I tilted my head back and tasted the warm droplets in my mouth. I devoured the pure scent of moist soil and wet plants in the air. I heard a car race past nearby, and the playful splash of puddles. I felt the cold mud squelch between my toes, coating my flip flops. I reached the road and on the opposite side noticed a dilapidated orange brick bus shelter. I would have continued walking right past it if I hadn't caught a whiff of an old friend in a cloud of smoke trapped by the rain. I stepped into the shelter in the hope of remaking his acquaintance.

'Ki manyer?'

A Creole man with a wise and weathered face squinted through the dense fog of his pipe.

I shrugged and took my place beside him. *'Ki manyer?'*

He nodded his head very slowly. *'Korek,'* he said, passing me the pipe.

I inhaled the sweet tasting, throat burning smoke and held it tight in my chest. I waited until my head started to swim before blowing it out. The old man looked at me expectantly.

'Merci,' I said cautiously, handing back the pipe.

The sides of his lips moved. I could hardly describe it as a smile. *'Padkwa,'* he muttered lazily, his hazy gaze returning to the sheet of water that hung before us.

For all the rain and darkness the sky outside our shelter was surprisingly light, a silvery moonlight that stroked our skin and glittered on our eyelashes. He was wearing a hat, a pork pie at an angle to cover one ear, a brown short sleeved shirt and a pair of dark brown cords. His feet sat comfortably in regulation issue brown leather sandals.

Thankfully there are a few situations in life where explanations are not required to make yourself understood. This was one of them; sitting in a bus shelter with an old Mauritian man and a pipe packed with marijuana. We sat side by side and stared out at the rain, my clothes slowly drying in the warmth of his soul. I could have sat there for an eternity without any need to utter a single word; with someone who I could just be with. He nodded as though in agreement, repacked the pipe, placed it between his lips and expanded his lungs.

'Do you read?' he asked, allowing the smoke to escape over the words.

'A bit,' I replied.

He bent himself in two, reached under his section of the bench, pulled out a carrier bag and lifted it onto his lap. Still with the pipe between his lips, he rummaged inside it, thrusting his hand through what I assumed must be the possessions of his entire life and triumphantly extracting a tattered looking paperback book.

'Have you read this book?'

I looked at the title and shook my head.

'Paul and Virginie by Bernardin de St Pierre,' he sighed, passing it to me with shaking hands. 'You should read it.'

I took it from him and flicked through the softened pages. 'Thank you.'

He nodded again, his lips curling up around the pipe he held between his teeth. I turned to the first page and managed to read a few lines through the murk.

'It is a story of love,' he muttered, 'of star-crossed lovers here on the island of Mauritius.'

'There appear to be many of those around here,' I replied, closing the book and settling back into the bench.

His voice drifted into the space around us. 'He tries to save her and she refuses to be saved because her principles outweigh her desire for love and happiness. She decides that it is better to die with her honour intact than to allow him to undress her and save her life.' He spoke carefully and slowly, pouring over the meaning of each and every word. 'Sometimes people do the strangest things, make the strangest choices, and believe in the oddest of ideas.'

Sitting in the bus shelter in the middle of the rain, my brain tuned into a long lost radio station and understood everything the old man was trying to tell me. I didn't speak Kreol and he didn't speak English but we communicated anyway. I discovered that there was no need for language. Somehow it was like we were speaking in tongues.

'No one can tell you why they did what they did. All you can hang your spirits on is that they did it for a reason, that somewhere there is an answer, as there is for every mathematical equation. That's the best that any of us can do.'

I made myself comfortable against the wall and closed my eyes as he chattered on, his voice becoming my blanket, his melody of words my pillow. It didn't matter anymore whether there was any sense in what he said, or any sense in the world around me. I drifted into a peaceful sleep and finally enjoyed those dreams of little consequence.

I awoke to the sound of a car horn. Or a bus horn to be more correct. The rain had stopped and the sun was rising, the sky pink with its foreboding message of the day. The wise old man was no longer beside me. There was only a battered looking paperback book in his place. I peeled my face away from the brickwork and peered through sleepy eyes at a stunned bus conductor standing on the lower step of the bus.

'Kot to alé?'

I yawned and wiped the saliva from my chin. 'Flic en Flac?'

He turned his back and exchanged a few heated words with the driver, then facing me once again, rolled his eyes and asked, 'Vous êtes perdue madame?'

I nodded and picked up the book. 'Oui. Yes, that's right. I am lost.'

I looked down the length of the bus and saw the faces in the window; Men and women on their way to work staring at the strange foreigner in the bus shelter. I felt the sting of their hate and disgust through the glass.

'We will drop you just outside Flic en Flac and then you will have to walk,' the bus conductor told me, stepping up into the bus to allow me to pass. He handed me a pink ticket from his machine as I stumbled past and flopped myself down into the first available seat. Everyone stared. All eyes bored into the back of my neck. I sensed it right from the start. That somehow my behaviour had shamed them all on their way to work, that my existence among them was wrong and dirty. So, I hid in the lines of the story the old man had left me; in words, this time French, that could transport me away.

I strolled back to the apartment by way of the beach, rinsing my red painted feet in the gentle waves that lapped the shore, my neck still bent to the pages of the book. I took my time since there was no need to rush. Whether it was Kitty, my father's box or another phone call, I deduced that whatever awaited me was not going to be good.

I wasn't to be disappointed.

'And where the fuck have you been?' Kitty stood in the middle of the living room, her hands on her hips in a gunslinger pose. 'We've been worried sick!'

I'd managed to duck through the door and close it before her tirade began.

'We ran home last night from the restaurant after Sandeep told us that you went fucking ballistic at him on the doorstep for no apparent reason. And when we got here the door was wide open and you hadn't left a fucking note or anything. What the hell was I supposed to think?'

I walked into the kitchen, shook the kettle then turned the gas on underneath it. She followed hot on my heels. 'And to make matters worse, Patrick's been ringing every fucking hour on the hour shouting off about this and that about you calling him in the middle of a meeting, that something was really wrong. I don't know how many times he called wanting to know what's going on. And your mum called as well because Patrick had called her. And you know what she's like. I've had to spend hours just trying to get her to calm down. I've been up all night not knowing what the hell to do. We were about to ring the police and everything. You've worried Lewis and me fucking sick all bloody night.'

There's only one thing worse than having a best friend who turns into your mother. It's having a best friend who turns their new lover into your father.

'Beth? Answer me! Where have you been?' she ranted on. 'You didn't leave a note, you didn't ring, you didn't tell me where you were going. I can't believe you did this to me.'

Lewis stood in the doorway, his arms now around Kitty's bare mid drift, shaking his head in agreement.

'You can't just up and leave like that. I came all the way here for you. I can't believe you'd treat me like this. It's just not fair.'

I laughed.

'This isn't funny, Beth. It's deadly serious. I thought we came here together.'

I took the whistling kettle off the heat. 'Did we now?'

In the corner of my eye I noticed her giving Lewis one of those knowing looks, the ones I'm sure I've given Patrick over the years when Kitty was passed out on our sofa or in need of a few quid to help pay her rent. She rubbed his hands away and moved out of his embrace. 'I want to help.'

I felt the pressure build in my throat. 'Do you? Do you really?'

'I'm your best friend God damn it. If I don't who will?'

I picked a mug up off the draining board. 'I don't know, Kitty.'

She took another step towards me. 'What's happened?'

'It doesn't matter.'

'Of course it matters.'

'No it doesn't. It hasn't mattered since you fucked off three days ago with lover boy over there, so why should it matter now?' Her shoulders fell, a reaction that only served to pour fuel on my fire. 'There's shit going on here that you have no bloody idea about. Stuff that's happened, that if you'd actually been a friend you'd fucking know about already. So before you start giving it the big 'I AM', Kitty, maybe you should shut your gob and your legs for five minutes and actually talk to me as though I actually meant something to you instead of treating me like a fucking reason to bugger off and get yourself laid!'

You could've heard a pin drop forty miles away in the silence that followed as her guilt and my shame met and waltzed around the angry space between us. We stared each other out with daggers that seared through the air, piercing and shredding our friendship apart. Weeks of built up frustration that had simmered silently under the surface spat up through the vents of an impending volcano, my tea actually going cold in the time it took Lewis to realise that it was best if he went home and left us to it. Kitty paced the tiled floor in the living room as he gathered his things and closed the door quietly behind him. I could hear her mumbling angrily, psyching herself up for the counter attack.

I decided to take the initiative and calm things down. 'I'm going to have a shower and clean up before we discuss this any further.'

I marched straight through to the bathroom, not waiting to hear her response.

She was gone by the time I got out. She'd packed her suitcase and taken her passport and tickets with her.

'Shit.'

I'd gone too far; leaving a part of me horrified and a part of me glad. I stood in the middle of the living room for quite some time; my mind utterly blank and numb. I tried to cheer myself by remembering that I only had two days left to go before I went home. It didn't work. His casket watched me from the sideboard.

'No, I'm not doing it!' I shouted.

I stamped my foot.

'No, no, no, no!'

It didn't silence him either, so I decided to go back to bed.

Chapter Thirty One

Papa

We Mauritians are a forgotten people. Our endeavours have never been appreciated even though the wealth of the world has been borne on our shoulders. People in the western world sit in their warm cosy homes with no real worries about war, famine or poverty because of me and mine. The great cities of America, France, Britain, Holland, Portugal and Spain all have the blood of my ancestors on their hands, even though they do not wish to remember it. Their privileges, their power and their standing in the world came about by the subjugation of my people, of Sahana's people, of Jerome's people, of all the non white races around the globe.

We Creoles are a special case because we allow others to treat us in this way. We believe that we do not deserve any better. We play down our importance in the world today. I do not know why we do not shout loud and proud about what we can achieve. Maybe it is because no one wants to hear that we have the tools to teach the world a thing or two. We are Hitler's nightmare. We are the mixed bloods. We are born of generations of Africans, Indians, Sri Lankans, Malagasy, Chinese and Europeans. Our blood runs together and proves that man can love his brother, even though we ourselves forget it. Our very existence on this earth proves that there are no logical reasons to hate and hurt our fellow man.

We already love each other even when we are not aware of it. Each and every day we prepare, cook and eat *farata, karipoulé, biriani, mein frite, sauce creole, poisson salé, dal-pouri, lentilles, bred, rougay* with rice and potatoes. Our cultures absorbed and digested through our stomachs, providing us with fuel to stay alive. We put in our mouths that which we cannot accept with our eyes. Our heart. Mauritius.

I loved Sahana. It was as simple as that. I followed her half way across the globe, to keep her safe and provide our unborn child with a future. Because I loved her. I believed that it would be better being a foreigner in a foreign country than one in your own land. Because I loved her. I believed in the strength of our family, in forging our own way of life. Because I loved her. I did it all because I loved her.

We arrived in England and settled in Southampton. The council gave Sahana a flat because she was pregnant. I worked to pay our way, for cash in hand, for pennies and handouts to help feed my family. I brought home just enough to live off. It was hard but I was happy. For the first time in my life I had something to work towards that was mine. All mine. I made friends with our neighbours, people from all walks and avenues of life. I helped out where I could, did my bit for a growing exiled community. All the while I was respectful of the local people who opened their towns to us and gave us an opportunity to live our lives as we wanted. I thanked them for their smiling teeth and generous subsidies. I never took them for granted.

My daughter, Elizabeth was born into a sterile world of pink faces and cultural liberty and even when it rained outside my child could always muster a smile. The nurses in the maternity ward joked that there was no chance of them getting our black mop headed baby mixed up with anyone else's. She stood out like a black swan in a pond of ugly ducklings. While Sahana tossed and turned uncomfortably in her bed, our daughter, Elizabeth, slept on peacefully in her cot. Strong arms and legs encased in rolls of healthy fat, tiny puckered lips, a button nose and her tiny eyelids practically permanently closed.

I was proud and petrified and I remember thinking, 'so this is what it feels like to be a man.'

I sat down beside the plastic box and placed my hand on my baby. She was the image of her mother even then. I carefully stroked the downy whispers of hair on her soft head and traced the line of her cheek. I prised apart her clenched fist and placed my little finger within her grasp. Her minute fingers hardly reached all the way around it. I marvelled at her neediness. I wondered whether I would be a good enough father to help her through. Then she squeezed and I understood her power. I understood in that brief moment that she was mine no matter what happened.

Or, moreover, that I was now hers forever.

The next four weeks were the happiest four weeks of my entire meagre life. I had a wide eyed grin plastered on my face every second of the day. Nothing could get me down and as if in recompense I earned more money than I had ever done before. Everyone that I met wanted to know how the little one was doing. They wanted to see pictures. They wanted to know how Sahana was coping. They offered help and friendship and a home to us all. And one day I came home and Sahana was gone. The only sign to show that she had even existed: a broken pink lipstick lying on the top of the electric heater. And Elizabeth of course; sitting in her pushchair in the middle of the room, asleep and thankfully oblivious.

I rolled up my sleeves and knuckled down to the task in hand. I took Elizabeth everywhere with me, even when I had to work. I would not allow anyone else to look after her. It caused a few problems but I did not care. I found jobs where her pram was not an issue. I even did some taxi work for a while and strapped her in the front seat as a passenger. But it was not long before the authorities caught up with me. When the social services tried to take her away from me, I gathered our things together and set out to find another home. I went willingly without food to feed and clothe her. I always made sure that she was warm and safe at night, all the while constantly running from a lethal game of cat and mouse, terrified that she would be taken from me. That was when we found Shelly, the angel who saved me from a fate far worse than death. She saved me as a man and as a father to my child. If God had not sent her to help me I may well have lost the only thing that has made my life worth living.

My daughter. Elizabeth.

Chapter Thirty Two

Tifi

I wasn't sure how long I'd been asleep when the 'phone started ringing once again. My stomach lurched inside me, insisting that I sit up immediately and take heed of the noise. A horrible sensation took hold of my heart and caused my skin to prickle out with goose bumps and heat. I tried to ignore it but this time the ring was solely focused on calling me, of making me listen. I hid my head under the pillow and scrunched up my eyes but it wouldn't go away. The screeching wouldn't cease until I picked it up.

'Hello?' I spoke cautiously into the handset.

'Beth?'

I breathed an audible sigh of relief. It was Patrick.

'Beth, is that you?'

'Yes,' I laughed, 'Hello Patrick.'

'Are you alright? I've been worried sick.'

'Yes, I'm alright now. I'm absolutely fine now.'

'Are you sure?'

'Yes,' I said trying to control my smile. 'There's nothing to worry about. Just me being stupid, that's all.'

'Are you absolutely sure? You don't sound too convincing.'

'Yes, Patrick.'

He chuckled nervously down the line. 'So what happened then? What was all that about last night?'

'Nothing. Just Kitty making mountains out of mole hills. I went for a walk and got lost, that's all. Nothing bad happened and as you can hear, I'm home and safe now.'

'And the first 'phone call. What was all that about?'

'Nothing. Just a prank call, that's all. Just someone mucking about on the line.'

'Beth?'

'Yes, Patrick.'

'Are you telling me the truth?'

'Yes, Patrick.'

I could tell he wasn't convinced. 'Do you want me to come out?'

'No, no, there's no need for that. I'll be home in a few days so there's no real point in wasting your money coming out here.'

'You'll be coming home?'

'Yes.'

His voice sounded hopeful. 'Here?'

I looked at the floor. 'I don't know yet.'

He made sure that I became aware of his uncomfortable pause. 'I popped in to see your mother last night. She's in a right mess. You couldn't just call her could you? Just let her know that you're thinking of her and that you're alright.'

'I will, I promise.'

'I think she'd appreciate it, that's all.'

'Message received and understood, Patrick.'

'OK, well, good.'

We talked some more, about the trip, about the weather. Nothing important. I cuddled into the receiver and hugged his voice and for the first time in months, we actually spoke to each other without arguing; both of us listening and not telling.

‘I’d better be going. Lunch is nearly over,’ he said.

‘OK. Have a good day.’

‘I’ll try to and you remember that I’ll be keeping my mobile on and with me all day. If you need to talk, just call me, OK?’

‘OK.’

He definitely thought about it before he said it. ‘Love you.’

‘OK, then, well thanks for calling, take care, speak soon, bye.’

I replaced the receiver and walked out onto the veranda.

Only the year before, Patrick and I had travelled to Valencia for our wedding anniversary; for two days of palm trees, expensive wine and seafood. We’d laughed all weekend, our eyes bright with the excitement of our future together. There’d been such clarity in our dreams that it had been impossible for me to imagine a life without him. Now standing here alone, watching the palm trees sway in the breeze, listening to the laughter of the beachcombers, it was all I could do to picture him beside me, smiling with a glass of champagne in his hand.

Someone banged on the door.

I opened it to see the rather plump and perspiring security guard bent double and holding his throat.

‘Madame, you must come quickly,’ he said, straining to gulp more oxygen into his lungs. ‘There has been an accident.’

Chapter Thirty Three

Papa

I talked about it only once with Shelly; queuing outside the registry office on our wedding day, standing in the car park under an umbrella, the ground beneath us a soft mulch of dead leaves. 20th October 1973.

'You do love me, don't you, George?'

'Of course.'

I wore a borrowed brown tuxedo. She wore a pink frilly dress that she had made and designed herself.

'You'll never leave me?'

'Never.'

We waited nervously outside in the rain as married people emerged from the grey granite building; happy mouths spitting paper confetti and rice.

'You'll never take Elizabeth away from me?'

'Never.'

A black limousine drove away with a waving couple, leaving a cheering group of mitten clad friends.

'You promise that you'll never go looking for her?'

'For who?'

I met her blue grey eyes. They were as resilient as stone and as deep as the ocean. 'For her. Elizabeth's mother,' she said.

I pictured my daughter's brown Mauritian eyes; black brown with orange speckles. 'But what if Elizabeth wants to meet her?'

Shelly looked away. 'Do you think she'll get the chance?'

I did not know how best to respond.

'You know you've never told me why she left,' she continued.

'You never asked.'

'That doesn't mean I never wanted to know.'

We had known each other little over a year. She had invited me to lodge in her home and our friendship had grown from there. Shelly had fussed over Elizabeth from the word go. And my daughter being the way she is had giggled and smiled and slept her way into Shelly's heart. I watched them together so many times, content that I had found someone for my daughter, thankful that my daughter had the opportunity to enjoy the kind of love a mother could give. While Elizabeth played on around us, Shelly and I became gently entwined, like an old blended whisky; our histories assumed and assimilated without a second thought. We fell into a comforting and comfortable rhythm where everything simply felt right. There did not appear to be a need for passion, for burning heat or fireworks. We kept each other warm at night and fought off our demons together. We created a bond strong enough to withstand every eventuality. We came to understand each other without ever finding a need to explain.

'The truth is I do not know why she left,' I told her.

She still refused to face me.

'Will you go after her?'

There had never been a question in my mind of going back to Mauritius which is where I assumed she would be. 'I will never go back to Mauritius.'

'You haven't answered my question.'

Another newly married couple walked out of the registry office doors, holding hands, swooning into each other's embrace.

'What about when you want to return to see your family?' she asked.

I thought about my family everyday; whether they were happy and healthy, whether they were coping, whether they missed me, but the more time passed the more remote the possibility of conciliation became. Even back then I knew I would never return. 'That will never happen.'

'What if she comes here looking for Elizabeth and decides she wants to take her daughter home?' she persisted.

I traced my black finger down the length of her spine, so that her shoulders rose and fell like a heavy swell. 'Then she cannot have her.'

This woman had sacrificed so much for my daughter and me. She had deflected the stares and the taunts we received. She had fought her corner for us and was willing to give the essence of her identity to help us stay. I knew I had to do the right thing by her. 'Shelly, after today you are my family. You will be Elizabeth's mother. You have no need to worry.' The wind ruffled her hair and she pulled her pink jacket tighter about her. 'I promise that I will never tell Elizabeth about her. While I live on this earth, I promise that Elizabeth will be yours.'

She turned to me with the saddest eyes I think I have ever seen. 'Would you do that for me?'

'If we tell her, she will want to find her mother. We cannot tell her if you want her to be yours.'

She nodded solemnly. 'And you'll never allow nothing to come between us as a family?'

I pulled her to me, felt her closer than skin. 'Shelly, you are my family now. Your happiness and that of my daughter are the most important thing to me.'

'And you'll never leave me?'

I kissed her forehead. 'I will never leave you. From this day we have a new beginning, just you, me and Elizabeth. We are not going anywhere.'

But I did leave her. I left her alone to deal with it all.

Chapter Thirty Four

Tifi

Kitty was lying in her bikini on the soft stretch of sand; her body in the recovery position, her skin paler than milk, her lips blue. Lewis stood close by, hiding under the casuarina trees.

'Has someone called an ambulance?' I asked.

'There's one on the way, Madame,' the guard replied, his eyes popping red from the exertion of coming to get me.

'Lewis, what happened? What have you done to her?'

He came forward, tentative like a naughty schoolboy. 'It was not my fault.'

'What have you done?'

A small group of onlookers was already taking shape nearby; a nervous babble of chatter to heighten my panic.

'She insisted we dive,' Lewis replied at length. 'I told her to wear something on her feet but she did not want to and that is why it stings her.'

'What are you talking about?'

'The stonefish.'

'The what?'

'The stonefish,' he said, moving closer. 'It is one of the most poisonous animals in the world. She must have stepped on it or brushed against it. Either way, she probably would not have seen it, as it is so well camouflaged.'

I looked at the guard, who nodded his head. 'It usually lies at the bottom of the sea, Madame,' he explained with renewed animation. 'It can stay there for hours at a time awaiting it prey. It can wait an eternity and then,' he clapped his hands together, 'without warning it strikes.'

The sound of the siren blared out behind us.

'Jesus Christ, Lewis, is she going to be alright?'

He didn't respond.

'Lewis, for God's sake, tell me she's going to be alright?'

The paramedics arrived and distracted my attention. Without exchanging a word, they checked Kitty's neck, her pulse and examined the soles of her feet before lifting her onto a stretcher. I followed them through the parting crowd to the ambulance. Inside, they extracted a needle from the base of her foot and stemmed the bleeding with cotton pads. They injected her, plugged her up to the heart monitor and strapped her in, then invited me to climb up beside her and sit next to the machine that beeped her constant rhythm.

'I will meet you there,' Lewis called out as they closed the doors.

Enclosed in a sunless rumbling carriage, surrounded by plastic tubes, blanket laden shelves, machines and apparatus, I prayed to God that she would be alright. I placed my hand lightly upon hers, sick with fear that she'd wake up and scream that she hated me. I wondered how she'd like to capture this moment; whether she'd have to use a flash because it was so dark in here. I knew she wouldn't like the red blanket because it clashed with her hair and washed out her skin. I looked around for her camera. A chill descended along the full length of my spine as I tried to remember the last time I ever saw her without it. I couldn't recall a time when it wasn't near, that she couldn't just reach over and grab it when she needed it.

She'd explained it to me once, a long time ago, in a train on our way to Ho Chi Min city.

'When I look through the lens, I immediately see the world from a different perspective. I'm like an eagle with telescopic eyes, searching out my prey, the image that's gonna make me miss a heartbeat. It's like a meditation. It helps me think. I adjust the zoom, *click click*. Check for light, *click*. Centre the image, *click*. Take a deep breath and hold as the camera makes its final calculations. Press the button fully. Then listen.' She'd held the camera out towards me so that I could hear the film stretch itself against the cog. 'And like, there you have it,' she'd grinned. 'A simple trick of the light. My reminder of man's manipulation of the world. What I like to call a truly positive negative image.'

The same tune kept playing at the back of my mind. That somehow this was my entire fault; that it was all to do with me. I'd been the one responsible for bringing her here. I'd been the one responsible for hurting her feelings and pushing her away. It'd make sense that I'd been the one responsible for leading her into danger.

Kitty was still out cold when we arrived in the emergency ward. The paramedics pushed her through on a trolley as nurses ran back and forth, shouting orders, pulling on rubber gloves, eager to insert and extract various multi coloured needles. A male nurse raced over with a clip board and tick boxes.

Does she have any heart problems? Do you know if she is taking any form of prescriptive or non prescriptive medication? Do you know if she is allergic to penicillin? Do you know if she is diabetic? Do you know if she is pregnant? Do you know if she has consumed any alcohol in the last twenty four hours? Do you know if she has been taking any illegal drugs or substances?

After nearly ten years of friendship the best answer that I could give was a pathetic, 'I don't think so.'

I gave the nurse a copy of our travel insurance documents that I'd thankfully kept in my bag and details of Kitty's next of kin; her mother in London. I asked whether we could delay contact until we knew what was happening, so as not to worry her unnecessarily. The nurse agreed with my decision, saying that under the circumstances, 'these things can go either way.'

I watched on helplessly as another nurse lowered Kitty's inert leg into a bucket of hot water. A young white man, far too young to be a doctor came up and introduced himself with a South African accent as Doctor Folds. He set about extracting three vials of blood from her arm.

'Do you know what happened?'

I shook my head. 'I've no idea. A security guard came and got me and said that there'd been an accident. That's really all I know for certain.'

He smiled and shook the vials. 'Well, not to worry, I'm sure we'll soon find out.'

He went away and I pulled up a chair and sat down. The ceiling fan whirred noisily above me, adding to the clattering chaos in my head. Another nurse hurried over with a hospital night gown and slipped it around Kitty's shoulders. Then Dr Folds returned with two orderlies in blue overalls and told me that that they were taking her away to another ward to run an ultrasound to check for fragments.

He put on his best doctor demeanour. 'It would be better from now on if you waited in reception.'

I waited until she'd been wheeled away before I pushed through the swing doors and into the waiting area. I came face to face with Lewis and Sandeep.

'How is she?' Lewis asked, jumping up from his seat to greet me. 'Will she be OK?'

'How the hell should I know?' I replied, barging past them and marching out into the fresh air of the accident and emergency car park. It was raining again. I stopped just outside the doors and let the small bombs of warm water hit my face and warm my skin. 'God give me strength.'

I felt a hand on my shoulder and turned around.

'I am sure she will be well again,' Sandeep said, so close I could feel the words on my cheeks.

I looked into his eyes. 'Why are you here?'

'Lewis needed a lift and besides,' he searched for the correct words, 'I thought that you might need a friend.'

I shrugged his hand away and took a step backwards. 'Thanks, but I'm sure I'll be OK on my own.'

'You do not look OK, as you say. You look like you have the trouble of the world on your shoulders.'

I looked away briefly, across the car park at the palms that gathered before the sugar cane. 'Have you ever known anyone be stung by a stonefish before?'

He was thoughtful for a moment. 'No,' he replied, 'but then I only know Lewis who is a diver.' He took his glasses off and rubbed the rain water off with his shirt. 'Lewis is a very good friend of mine,' he said pulling me back to his turquoise eyes. 'I do not think that anything sinister has happened here. It was just an accident.'

I felt the heat begin to rise. 'How can you be sure?'

He pushed his glasses back onto his nose. 'I have known him for ten years and in that time he has proved to be a very loyal and caring friend. He is definitely not the type of man who would do this to the woman he loved.'

I laughed. 'Loved! He hardly knows her.'

'Why do you not trust him?'

'It's not just him. I can't afford to trust anyone, Sandeep.'

'What are you talking about?'

'It's like you said, if you remember correctly, about me having to be careful.'

He leant back, 'What has happened?'

'Yesterday, after I got back from meeting Juliet, just before you knocked on the door, someone called my apartment and threatened to hurt me if I didn't leave the island.'

His eyes flashed behind his glasses like emeralds under torch light. 'Why did you not tell me?'

'Because I don't know you Sandeep. The only person here, who I really know is flat out in some strange poison fish induced coma and she wasn't available to comment last night because she was too busy canoodling with Lewis.'

'And that is why you argued this morning?'

'Yes.'

His regard narrowed. 'And you think that the telephone call is linked to your father in some way?'

'Yes.'

'Have you told anyone else?'

'What about?'

'The telephone call.'

His urgency unsettled me. 'Only Patrick and I told him that it was a prank call.'

'Right.'

'So?'

He looked at his feet. 'So I do not know what you should do.'

I let out a sigh of desperation. 'Great.'

The doors behind us slid open and Dr Folds, the too young doctor stepped out onto the porch, a lit cigarette dangling from his bottom lip.

I pushed past Sandeep, drawn to the scent of the smoke. 'Is it bad, doctor?'

He took a few seconds to recognise me and then nodded. 'It looks like it might be quite serious.' He found a dry piece of wall to sit down on. 'I've done a bit of diving myself in my time but I've never seen anyone effected this badly by a sting.'

'Do you know when she might wake up?'

He blew smoke into the drizzle. 'I can't possibly say. She might wake up in the next five minutes or at anytime over the next week. She's had a bad reaction that's all that we know for certain.'

'But she'll be OK, won't she?'

He smiled that same medical smile as before. 'We are doing all that we can. The anti-venom should be arriving shortly from Port Louis and once we've administered that and received the results of the blood tests we should be in a better position to know what will happen.'

'So you're absolutely sure that there's no evidence of foul play?'

The doctor looked confused and uncomfortable. 'I couldn't possibly tell you any more about her condition until we get the test results back.' He stood up and stubbed his half smoked cigarette into the nearest flowerpot. 'Best thing is to try not to worry. Your friend is in safe hands here. We'll take good care of her and get her back on her feet as soon as we can.' He looked at his watch. 'Now if you'll please excuse me I have other patients to attend to.'

He hurried back through the doors and I made to follow him but Sandeep gripped my shoulder and held me back.

'Why did you say that?' he snapped.

'What, mentioning foul play?'

'Yes.'

'Because with all that's happened, this scenario feels a little too farfetched for my liking.'

He looked stunned. 'Lewis's explanation sounded simple enough to me.'

'You've got to be kidding.'

'Why, what is the alternative?'

'That Lewis had something to do with it. That he made the phone call to scare me and then hurt Kitty to try and make us go.'

Sandeep shook his head. 'It does not make sense. If he wanted you to go, why would he put you in a situation where you would have to stay?'

I walked back through the doors into the reception area. 'OK, let's ask him.'

But Lewis was nowhere to be seen. Sandeep checked the men's toilets and asked at the duty desk whether anyone had seen him, but no one had.

I turned to Sandeep triumphant. 'See!'

'I do not understand where he could have gone. He does not even have a car.'

I grasped for my straw. 'He's done a runner because he knew I was onto him.'

'A runner?'

'He's run away, Sandeep. That's enough for me.'

'So what do you want to do?'

'I want to report everything to the police.'

That stunned look again. 'What, now?'

I nodded. 'I'm going to check up on how Kitty's doing and then yes, I'd really appreciate it if you could give me a lift to the nearest Police station. I don't know who's done what or whatever but everything has gone too far.' I pointed at the perpetually swinging emergency ward doors. 'My best friend is lying unconscious in there and it might be my entire fault because I brought her here. Do you understand? I have to do something to stop all of this.'

He finally gave up. 'If that is what you want,' he shrugged. 'It will not come to anything but if you must, you must. You go and do what you have to do and I will wait in the car and then I will take you to the police station.'

'Thank you, Sandeep.'

I watched him shuffle away and then walked through the swinging doors. Kitty had returned; her trolley and machinery now in the far corner of the ward. Everyone was so busy going about their business that they didn't question me as I made my way across to her. She was still unconscious, still flat out with one leg suspended at an angle in a bucket of lukewarm water. Her lips were pale and dry, crisped by an exhausting fight. I came up close to her face, leant over and was surprised to detect the scent of the ocean on her skin.

'I'm sorry,' were the only words that I could clutch out of my throat. I pushed back the tears, tried to concentrate on something else and that is when I saw her chart, clipped on the top of her bed frame next to the sign that read 'nil by mouth.'

? Substantial traces of barbiturates in blood sample. Combination may have induced coma???

My jaw dropped. 'Kitty what the hell have you been up to?'

'Excuse me?'

I wheeled round to find Dr Folds standing at the end of the bed with his arms crossed against his chest. 'I'm sorry,' I said quickly. 'I couldn't stand waiting out there in reception any longer. I needed to see how she was doing.'

His features aged and became rigid, like a strict headmaster. 'Did you know about the drugs?'

'No, I had no idea.'

He stepped closer. 'And what you said about foul play?'

My heart jumped a beat. 'You think something's wrong as well, don't you?'

His expression didn't falter. 'In my experience Stonefish are defensive creatures, they don't use their spikes to hunt, they wait patiently for hours and swallow their prey whole instead. The drugs aside, for it to have inflicted the amount of venom needed to induce this level of unconsciousness it would have had to fear for its life.'

'Do you think there's enough to report to the police?'

He dipped his head judiciously. 'I'd say that was probably the best thing to do in the circumstances. If you want, I can ask them to come here.'

'No, it's OK. I've got a lift sorted out already and besides, I thought I'd better go home and pick up some of Kitty's stuff. There's something I know she'll want to have near her when she wakes up.'

I found Sandeep in his pickup truck in the car park as he'd promised. I climbed up into the cab and agreed with his suggestion that we should head for the station in Quatre Bornes as he knew a few of the officers that worked there.

'How is Kitty doing?'

'She's stable and doing fine.'

He nodded and proceeded to drive out of the grounds. I knew in my heart that if Kitty hadn't been so sick I probably would have changed my mind about reporting the incident now that drugs were involved. We'd been naughty enough in our time for me to know how not to be a hypocrite. But this was different. This was deadly serious and I just couldn't jeopardise her life over a crisis of conscience. I just had to hope that she would forgive me.

The rain had stopped and the road shimmered silver like a wet coat of translucent paint. I relaxed into my seat, resigned to the fact that the roller coaster ride was now well and truly under way and that the only thing left for me to do was make sure my elbows were securely tucked in.

'What exactly are you going to report Lewis for?' Sandeep asked, keeping his vision trained on the slippery road.

'I'm not sure yet. I thought I'd just see what happens when I start explaining the story.'

Tea plantations stretched on forever outside the windows, their low green bushes wafting flavour through the air vents. I hadn't noticed them on the way to the hospital, but then again, I reminded myself, there hadn't been any windows in the back of the ambulance. Storm clouds hung heavy in the air, threatening to engulf us once more. I glanced out the back window and saw the remnants of a warm blue sky disappear above the waves and the sea and the palms trees. Kitty would have loved the view. I could almost hear the *click, click, click* of her camera beside me.

Then I realised that something wasn't quite right.

'The sea should be in front of me, shouldn't it?'

Sandeep shrugged. 'Normally, yes, but I am taking a short cut.'

I thought about it for a moment.

'But if it's on my left that means we are heading south west doesn't it?'

He ignored the question.

'If we carry on this way, surely we'll miss Quatre Bornes completely.'

His attention remained steadfastly glued to the road. 'I think I know the roads in my country better than you.'

The road wound further and further up into the hills and the dense greying clouds. Tealeaf plants evolved into overbearing evergreen bushes that encroached on our narrow path with the heaviness of hard green fruits. The rain struck up again in earnest, crashing down on the roof of the car, producing a claustrophobic din.

'Where are you taking me, Sandeep?'

He refused to look at me. 'I am taking you to the police station just as you asked.'

'I don't believe you.'

'That is up to you,' he muttered distastefully.

My anxiety notched itself up another gear. 'Sandeep, I want to know where we're going.'

He still wouldn't look at me.

I could see the rails of my roller coaster ride disintegrating fast. 'Sandeep, talk to me.'

He wouldn't let me see his face.

I gripped the sides of the seat as my carriage rocketed up into the air. 'Sandeep?'

He left me suspended in a sickening weightlessness with my guts in my ears. I endured an eternity of misgivings before he eventually decided to turn his head and speak.

'Will you shut up, woman!'

I caught a glimpse of my terrified expression in the reflection of his tears.

'Shut up! Shut up! Shut up!'

Chapter Thirty Five

Papa

Can you imagine how hard it was trying to keep a secret that big from a child, especially one as inquisitive as Elizabeth?

There were times when she made my life a living hell. Not only because she grew into the spitting image of Sahana, the permanent ghost from my past, but also because of her incessant questioning. It was a constant battle of wits. I had to be so careful about my words, how I described and explained things to her, since she would find any excuse to try and steer the conversation towards Mauritius. This task in itself made all the more difficult by the fact that English is my third language. I would do something as simple as show her how to cook curry and she would ask a million and one questions about how I knew how to prepare it, what type of people ate that kind of food, where the ingredients were to be found naturally in the world and so on and so forth until she sensed that I was about to crack.

It became worse as she grew older, her questions more insistent and demanding, her demeanour more aggressive and unladylike. I have no idea to this day how she discovered where I came from but she used her newly found knowledge to great effect. For instance, when I took her for a driving lesson on her seventeenth birthday and after I had explained the rules of the road, about the right of way and how to turn right, she nonchalantly asked whether I knew that they drive on the left hand side of the road in Mauritius. I was driving at the time and nearly steered our Vauxhall Cavalier into a muddy ditch. While I calmed down she sniggered beside me in the passenger seat. She knew exactly what buttons she needed to press to get exactly what she wanted.

But please do not get me wrong, she was a lovely child most of the time and I loved her deeply and if circumstances had been different I would have done anything for her. I did relent on occasion, caught in a trap by my own misdoing, usually swearing, and have to teach her a new phrase in Kreol or a proverb to make up for it. When I actually let my guard down, I have to admit I experienced a certain pleasure in sharing my culture and roots with her. Like the day I bought her sugar cane from the market in London. There was something about her face, the way her eyes sparkled when I allowed her in to our secret that warmed me deep inside, that made me remember, made me wish and made me regret.

Ultimately we reached an impasse in our relationship that neither of us had the strength to cross. A tacit agreement was formed the day she left home and we never spoke of my past again. Elizabeth did not ask me another question until the day I died. Throughout all those years, I held her disappointment close to my heart, a constant reminder of my guilt and shame. I had spent so many years avoiding her inquisitiveness that when it ceased I actually experienced an overwhelming grief. When she finally stopped wanting to know I finally became aware that I had lost something special, lost a part of her within me. She became a shadow in my heart. There was nothing that I could do. I had made a promise, to myself, to Shelly and to Elizabeth many years before. Nothing could come in the way of our family. No matter how high the price.

In the end it was death that changed me. When Shelly's eyes betrayed the warning she had received from my doctor I realised that the time had come for Elizabeth to receive the answers to every single one of her questions. She had been made to wait long enough. So, I left her key and I wrote her letter. I made it palatable and I entrusted it to my angel, Shelly.

And now here I am again, back where I started. You know my story. You know more than I ever told Elizabeth. You know more than I ever told my wife. It is ironic because I do not know who you are or why you wanted to know, but I told you anyway. I told you, a nameless face, more than I ever told my own flesh and blood.

I told you because I am already dead and have nothing to lose.

So what kind of man did that make me?

Part Three

Kozé souvan vinn séga

Chapter Thirty Six

Tifi

I freeze. Sandeep drives on through the dusk, a twilight haze falling over the wilderness that surrounds us. Shifting in my seat, I pull my skirt down to cover my knees and button my shirt to the neck. Pressure begins to build on my bladder. He starts humming nervously. I feel for the door handle with my left hand.

Clunk.

He pushes his elbow down on the lock on his door. 'Central locking.'

Out of the window the scenery changes. The road swells to the width of a motorway, undulating in waves as it climbs further north. Bus and coach stations, empty now, stretch off to our left and right; a seeping sea of rolling tarmac.

We drive into a complex of small out buildings and porta cabins. A sign reads, 'Welcome to Grand Bassin – Ganga Talao – Please proceed with respect for this religious site.'

Amongst the shadows I can make out a layered lake of dark mist and looming statues. We are high up here, practically in the heavens, clouds balancing the gods in their boxes, an audience waiting patiently for my finale. An eerie spiritual silence filters through white fog. A place where people naturally speak in hushed tones, where the devil himself fears to tread. The car lurches violently as Sandeep slams on the brakes; a thud and a savage jolt confirming that he's hit whatever it was he was trying to avoid.

'Bloody monkeys!' He shouts across the dashboard.

A light goes on in a building nearby and a figure appears at a window. I try to call out and get as far as inhaling before the back of Sandeep's hand finds my face. I don't see if the person sees me or hears me. Then the truck moves off again towards another group of buildings, pulling up alongside a classic Mercedes saloon.

He turns to face me. 'Beth, before I unlock this door I think that you should know that it would be easier if you came quietly and just did as you were told.'

I stare at him.

'None of us want this to get messy, Beth.'

It's now my turn to refuse to respond.

He frowns and reaches behind him for the lock button. 'I am going to trust that you will not run. I know that you are not stupid.'

I hear the latch click open and I grab my chance, the one chance I know I have before someone else inevitably comes to join him. I use the bottom of my palm to ram up under his nose, slamming his head back against the window. I bring my elbow back and thrust up again into his exposed Adam's apple. I fling the door open and manage to get one leg out before he grabs at my hair and rips a thick tuft away from my scalp. I feel it but it's not enough to stop me from moving. I hear another door open nearby and a cry of frustration as I hot foot it into the darkness.

I run on between trees and bushes that scratch at bare skin, until I am finally satisfied that no one is following me. I pant like a fox after the chase. The branches like crazed limbs in the blackness claw and paw at the spaces around me. Hound dogs on my trail. Strange noises, screeches, hoots and barks prove that the overgrowth is alive and just as frightening as the human world I'm hiding from. I'm aware of a warm trickle down the back of my neck. I can barely make out the shape of my hand in front of my face as I bring my fingertips to my lips and taste iron on my tongue. Crouching down, I sweep about the ground around my feet and discover a damp log and try to recall whether Mauritius has snakes as I sit back onto it. Stretching my legs out on in front of me, I concentrate on steadying myself and getting my bearings. Lifting my face to the heavens and the cloud filled sky, I curse God and my father for not providing me with at least a few stars to navigate by.

I am exhausted; too tired to panic. For a fleeting second I'm even convinced that I've been unwittingly selected for some sick reality TV show; the brief hope that Noel Edmonds or Jeremy Beadle will step out of the undergrowth with a microphone and a stiff drink. I shake my head.

The midges and mosquitoes sink their teeth into my legs. I don't care. Let them enjoy me while I last.

All I have now are even more questions. Questions, questions, questions!

Why did I get in the car with Sandeep? Why had I trusted him? What is waiting for me back in those buildings? Why did I get on the plane in the first place? Why the hell did I come here?

Before I'd been given that bloody letter my life had been fine. Granted, it wasn't perfect, there had been something lacking, but at least it had been safe. Before my father had died I'd managed to survive and carve out a relatively easy going existence without needing to know all the secrets that now felt they had to be heard. Since then I've been told that I am adopted, have lost my job, separated from my husband, abandoned my mother and arrived in a country that doesn't want me. I've located one aunt and found out about another and discovered that I have four cousins named after saints in the bible. I've found out my uncle was murdered at the same time as my father left the island and that my biological mother is in fact still alive. To make matters worse, my best friend is in a coma, her boyfriend is missing and my naivety has led me straight into the clutches of the very people who obviously know the whole sordid truth.

I try to figure out what I am going to do but can't concentrate on the matter in hand. I try to delve into my handbook of survival resources but it's no use.

Instead my brain chooses to think about Patrick. About the way he laughs, about the photograph that sits on my bedside table at home, about his white washed legs dimpled with sunburn, about the bottle of beer in his hand and the merry grin he once had on his face. I am in no doubt that he'd know what to do. He'd been a scout leader and he'd promised his unborn children that they'd be scouts too. My blood has always run cold before at the thought. Not about joining the scouts, but about joining the legions of numb women with thousand yard stares I see every morning taking their offspring to school. There was a time when I couldn't imagine anything more horrific. Patrick as ever could never quite understand. He really believes in his heart that it'd be fun.

I think about my mother, Shelly the Beautiful by Default, and wonder how she'd coped; how she'd managed to bring up a child that wasn't her own, who wasn't even the same colour as her and still avoid getting that dead look behind the eyes. How had she dealt with the knowing looks, the racism, the bigotry and intrusive questions? I suppose I've never really contemplated the extent of her love before. She's always looked after me as though I was her own. I had absolutely no idea before I'd read that letter that it could be any other way. I've always been aware of how she's been labelled; a slag, a whore, a traitor, a woman in love with a big cocked black man. And she's smiled in the face of it all. She's never faltered. She's never once made me question whether her love could be any other way.

'Don't worry your pretty little head about it, Elizabeth,' she says. 'They're the ones who are missing out on getting to know who you are. If there's a problem with your skin, then it's their problem and that's because they're jealous and stupid. You're just far more beautiful than any of them can ever possibly dream to be. You just remember that and they'll never get you down.'

She's fitted into my past like a comfortable glove; well worn, warm and protective, to the point where, to my shame, I've forgotten that she's allowed feelings of her own. I've never appreciated until now how much we've actually encroached on her, dumped all our baggage onto her shoulders and expected her to deal with it, take it all in her stride.

I can't remember my father openly displaying his love for her. I never once caught them in an embarrassing embrace. Now I actually spend some time thinking about it, I realise that he was always more courteous towards her than anything else. He treated her more like a well respected friend than a lover. I never saw them fight, didn't remember them ever falling out. Occasionally he'd hold her hand, or trace the words I love you across the soft fleshy part of her palm but mostly they'd just cuddle up on the sofa when he was at home and watch TV and drink cups of tea. The highlight of their week was the antiques roadshow, the highlight of their viewing month, Crimewatch.

'Look, George, that photofit looks like John from up the road. You know, John at number 28.'

'I do not think that he would be involved in an armed robbery though, Shell, he has only just had his hip replaced.'

I think about my father. There's no way that he'd have murdered or killed anyone. I'd never met a more placid man in my life. The more I think about it, the less likely that avenue of investigation becomes. Maybe he'd have jumped on any bandwagon to escape. Maybe all he really needed was an excuse to run away to a country that would leave him free to think and be what he wanted to be because no matter how hard I tried I couldn't imagine him here. He would never have fitted. He was too big for an island this small. He'd have suffocated with claustrophobia or drowned in the expanse of ocean, too clever for a small island mentality. He'd had trouble enough dealing with the English, let alone one million mixed up Mauritians crammed into a space no larger than Cumbria.

And that's when I realise.

Maybe that's the whole point. Maybe I'm trying so hard to understand everything that I can't see the answer staring me in the face. That in fact, there are some things you just have to accept.

Like sitting in a tropical forest in the middle of the Indian Ocean with a bogeyman on your tail. I can hide here all day but it isn't going to get me anywhere. I can spend hours pulling apart every what, why, how and whatever and still remain in the same position.

Some things just are, no matter which way you look at them. No amount of thinking, considering and therapy is going to change that.

I look up and notice the pink glow of a rising sun. The time of reckoning has arrived.

I stand up, brush myself down, creep forward, back towards the buildings I ran from until I see the warm glow of light from an open door and hear voices talking in a foreign tongue that I wish I could speak. I check myself.

'Elizabeth Stephens,' I whisper silently, 'if you get out of this alive the first thing you'll do is pay for some Kreol lessons.'

Two men, Sandeep and another shadow, lean against the bonnet of the Mercedes. The shadow holds a silver hip flask out to Sandeep but he declines to take it, too intent on throwing glances over his shoulder, towards me in the bushes. The shadow shrugs, places the flask to his mouth and gulps. I wait and I watch for a while and when I realise that they are in no hurry to find me, I decide to move around to the back of the building and see if I have any other chance of escape. I figure that if this is a religious site that there will be priests about, that hopefully it was a priest who'd seen me earlier from the window.

I move slowly and carefully, aware that just one broken branch or brittle stick will completely ruin my plan. I use the murkiness as cover, reaching the window across the tarmac. The light is still on. I can make out movement behind the mottled glass. I can hear music. Indian music. I step up to the door and knock quietly, so quietly that I'm not sure whether I can be heard. A chair scrapes across the ground. Footsteps approach the door. It opens.

Framed in orange light, I am drawn first to the black almond shaped eyes. Then the bridge of my nose, the dark curve of my thick eyebrows, my straight jet black hair, my plump brown crimson lips and glistening honey caramel skin.

'Hello, Elizabeth,' she says. 'I have been expecting you.'

Chapter Thirty Seven

Mama

Her initial reaction is not what I am expecting it to be. Instead of standing open mouthed, she kisses me on the cheek and says, 'Hello Sahana,' and then she walks into the room as though she is owning it. She picks out the chair that I had been sitting on, the one in front of the wall of radios and makes herself comfortable.

My heart is beating fast, even though I am preparing myself for this eventuality ever since I discover that she has come to the island.

'You have your father's eyes,' I say and she replies, 'And my mother's cunning by the looks of it.'

She is quick and I am feeling a burst of pride. But it is fast gone. We have done all that we could to keep her away. We have thrown as many obstacles at her as possible but it has not worked. Now I am being faced with a difficult decision; one that will tear me into two pieces. I close the door and take up a chair beside hers. She is looking at me expectantly.

'So you have found me,' I say.

'I'd say it was the other way around, wouldn't you?'

She is thinner than I thought she would be. And she looks more Western, more European than I expected. It is in her eyes, in the way she is looking at me and at the room. There is none of the shyness that women are being expected to show.

'Would you like a drink, orange juice or tea, perhaps?' I ask.

She asks for water and I walk to the refrigerator in the corner of the room.

'It is a lot hotter here than in England, no?' I say, while I pour her a cup from a bottle of mineral water.

I notice that she is picking at the threads of the leather armrest as she speaks. 'Yeah, it is. Although it appears to rain just as much over here.'

Her accent is not as British as I am imagining it to be. There is a hint of a dialect and something else, almost hidden behind the vowels, something lazy, as though she is not needing to pronounce the whole word.

'The rain will cease soon enough,' I tell her, passing her the cup. 'This is the rainy season after all. In England, it is never stopping raining.'

She smiles, her teeth are white against dark lips and black red gums. 'You remember it then?'

Of course I remember it; the heavy sunless sky that is crushing my anticipation into the tarmac, the bitter wind that is sawing through my bones, the unrelenting stinging of icy rain on my brittle brown skin. 'How could I be forgetting England?' I say.

She is examining me like an eagle as I speak. I can see her eyes focusing, her pupils contracting. I am feeling her trying to strip away the layers, trying to get under my skin. My resilience is making her uncomfortable. She is crossing her legs and folding her arms about her.

'So, what happens now?' She asks.

'I am not sure.'

We sit in silence. She is glowering at me, hot like a fire, inviting me to feed from her anger and frustration. Through the heat I am still seeing that she has grown into a very beautiful woman, although she is needing to eat more and there is a bruise blooming along her chin. She is dressed for an appointment, a very important meeting. There is also a ring on her wedding finger.

'Do you and your husband have children?' I ask.

She is grabbing at her hand to cover the ring. 'Not yet.'

'And what is his name?'

I can see that she is reluctant to tell me. She stares at me, as if she is trying to remember his name. 'Patrick.'

I am pleased that it is a good British name. 'But he has not come with you?'

'No,' she replies.

After all of these years, I am realising that I do not know what to say, what to ask. The woman who sits before me is my child and I suppose I have expected that this day may happen but I am having easier conversations with total strangers in hospital waiting rooms. I look around the room for some kind of inspiration, for something, anything to fill the space. Thankfully a radio behind us bleeps into life.

'Sahana, are you there?'

It is my father's voice, scratchy and old, yet still full of power. I go to the radio, click the receiver and say, 'Yes, papa?'

I glance at Elizabeth. She is twisted in her chair, confusion and questions written across her pretty face.

'There is still no sign of her,' my father says in Kreol. 'I have decided that Sandeep and I will go into the trees and look for her one last time now that it is lighter. Then I do not know what we will do.'

As I look at my daughter the number thirty one is bursting into my mind. The thirty one years that are passing since I last saw her. It is strange because I know that I must not lie, that I am indebted to his generosity for the rest of my life, but I cannot help myself.

'Yes papa. I think that is a good idea. We should try and find her as soon as possible.'

The radio crackles for painful seconds before he replies curtly, 'It would be worth your while to pray that we do, Sahana.'

The radio returns to dead air and I return to my seat beside her. She is picking at her fingernails, chewing at her bottom lip. I cannot imagine what this must be like for her. Sandeep has told me what she has said. I do not know how much I believe but I must trust in the word of my son.

'How much is your father telling you?' I ask, suppressing the desire to reach over and sweep the hair from her dark eyes.

She looks up from her hands. At this angle her face is how I am picturing it to look when she is a child.

'My father never told me anything.'

My eyes flicker to the clock on the wall in front of me. My heart quickens. I suddenly appreciate that we do not have very much time at all.

'How much are you needing to know?' I ask.

'Everything.'

'From the beginning?'

She nods. 'Yes.'

I am unable to recall how many times I have practiced this moment, in the dead of night, alone in my bedroom with all my ghosts to haunt me. I have become increasingly numb to the shame and the guilt that I have lived with every day of my life. I may even go as far to say that this story has killed my heart.

'Very well,' I sigh. 'When I was young and very stupid, I am falling in love with a boy, a catholic boy called George Labelle.'

I settle back into my chair aware that this will probably be the final retelling. Elizabeth leans forward in hers.

'This is a very foolish thing to do, but I am young and my life is not going according to plan. It is never going according to plan. It was supposed to be different to the one that I am finding myself living. I am discovering that being female is the worst thing that can happen to me. I am realising that if I am being born a boy, like my brother, everything can turn out correctly.' This is harder than I am thinking it will be. I stand up and pace to the bookcase. 'So, I am allowing myself to fall in love with someone who I knew would anger those around me. I want to prove to them that I still have some control over my own life.'

I can tell that the brutality of my words are offending her. 'I am speaking with, how do you say...hindsight?' I explain. 'At the time, your father was all that I could think about. I am a child and people grow up and see things for what they really are. Life is not being a bed of roses as they say, no?'

She softens very slightly and nods for me to continue. 'So, your father and I start to see each other. It is all very innocent. There is no sex or anything like that at the beginning. Instead we talk and write each other love letters. Now and then we find an opportunity to kiss. When we are that age, we are too young in our hearts and our minds to do anymore than that.'

I return to the fridge and take a sip from a carton of orange juice. 'Would you like some?' I ask her.

She shakes her head and covers the top of her cup with her hand. 'No thank you.'

I replace the carton slowly, using the time to carefully think about how I will tell her my version of what is happening. There are some things she must hear from me before he is allowed to get to her. 'I am to be married to an Indian man,' I tell her. 'It is early to be married but I am still made to go to India and meet this man called Baba. I know immediately that he is not liking me and I am telling my parents but it is no use. Baba is wealthy and I am discovering very quickly that wealth is more important to my father than his daughter's happiness.'

I watch as she sips tentatively at the water in her cup. 'Baba was a very cruel man and I am finding out after we are married that he would never be able to like me because I am female. He is not even going to bed with me after we are married. He is the type of man who is preferring the other kind of love, the illegal dirty kind. Instead he is beating me, locking me in cupboards and is treating me worse than you would treat a dog.'

She asks me with a hint of cynicism. 'And your father didn't stop it?'

Her intuition and intelligence surprises me. 'My father knew. He is even hearing it and seeing the bruises on my face and arms but he is warning me not to upset Baba. He is warning me that my entire family now is relying on Baba's fortune. I was to be a good girl and live with it.'

As I look down at her I find that a part of me is happy that she is obviously not knowing cruelty in this way, yet another part of me is jealous of her. I could even say that it is angry at her because of it. She is sitting there pretty, looking to me for answers when she has everything that I was never allowed to have. She has her life in front of her, the promise of love and children of her own, the opportunity and freedom to do as she pleases.

'Go on,' she tells me.

I sit back against the desk and try to calm my thoughts. I must do her bidding safe in the knowledge that her moment of reckoning is soon to arrive. 'One day I am in my house, my parent's house and it is a very rare occasion when I am alone. My brother is at school, my father is at work, my mother, grandmother and aunt have gone to the market. Baba has visited us in Mauritius again and I have a black eye, so I cannot be leaving the house and letting people see. Because of my father's job, he is a high ranking policeman, we are one of the few families in the island who have a telephone. When the telephone rings he has taught me how to answer it, so I answer it properly. I pick up the handset and it is one of my husband's business colleagues, a man I have been introduced to before when I was in India. He is telling me that he knows that I am alone and that he is winning me in a game of cards the night before with my husband. He asks me when would be a good time for us to meet.'

I wait for her to comment but she does not. She wants to make this as hard as possible for me to tell. 'I am slamming the telephone down and running away from the house. I am not meaning to run into your father but that is what I do. I thought that I had put away all of my silly notions about love but when I see him and look into his dark strong face and feel his arms around me, I am deciding to give myself to him first before anyone else can take it.'

Her expression is still blank and unreadable. I was hoping that she would give me some help, some understanding but I cannot sense that it will come. 'You have to understand, Elizabeth. I am needing control over what is happening.'

I do not know whether she has envisaged a romantic fairytale love affair. The truth is now seeming so cold and inadequate. That George Labelle was convenient. That he is simply in the right place at the right time. That George

Labelle, her father, is at once my saviour, my rock and my scapegoat. 'I am never doubting that he loves me,' I tell her. 'He is always loving me as they said it should be, that loving is blind and full of trust.'

She looks at me through narrowed eyes. 'So, you never loved him after all.'

I shake my head. 'I do not think that I am ever loving any man, although I am in no doubt that your father is believing that we are in love.'

I feel a deep seated desire to plead with her, to tell her that some people have an amazing ability to trust in what they are seeing with their eyes and understanding only what they are thinking in their own mind. I want to tell her that he is following me even after I am married, watching me as I am watching my favourite type of film but it is obvious that there is no point, that she will not believe me. After thirty one years, Elizabeth's heart is belonging to daddy.

'So how did you end up in England with a baby?' she asks.

As we are nearing the truth I feel my heart starting to race. I am amazed that George is able to keep such a secret away from his child for so long and that he told her in a letter that I am dead. I never once imagined that she is stumbling into this mess without any idea of what has happened. That he is leaving it all up to me to explain.

'I am sleeping with him once and becoming pregnant with a baby. I am carrying you inside me and nobody knows. I am not even telling my family or your father about it.'

She looks at me as though I am a child. 'And how long did you expect to keep it a secret?'

That feeling of anxiety returns to haunt me and knocks me back as if I am being hit with a punch. 'I suppose, if I am being honest, I am pretending that you might go away.'

She laughs but she is not happy. I am pathetic before her. I am nothing that she has wanted or expected. I am so young when she is inside me that she cannot hope to understand what it was like. I know that I do not deserve this punishment but my guilt still makes me offer myself up to her so that she can carve away at me until she reaches my bone, until I bleed for her thirty one years of hate.

'So, what happened exactly?'

I shrug my shoulders, 'Many things,' I say.

She yawns and rubs her eyes. 'I deserve to know the truth.'

'I know you do, Elizabeth. That is why you are here after all.'

Her frustration and anger are rising but as each second passes, she is becoming too heavy to fight me. I remember as I am watching her, about how amusing it all was at first, a catholic Creole and a little Hindu girl that should never be touched. I still cannot believe how much he actually allowed me to consume him, how I was allowed to gnaw away at him, to take all that I am needing with no demand for compensation.

She flays her arms sleepily, just as Sandeep used to do when he was a child and did not want to go to bed. 'What have you done?'

I am sighing with relief as the pills that I am putting into her water are finally taking effect. I move to sit on the armrest and stroke her hair. 'It is for your own good,' I explain softly. 'This is all out of my hands. I must do as I am told just as you should do. We are both being expected to be good girls. A daughter should never wish to be anything else.'

She is protesting and trying desperately to fight back. I wonder who she has inherited that trait from. It cannot be from her father or from me.

'Help!'

She is trying to get out of her seat, but does not have the strength to stand and so falls to the floor and knocks her head on the coffee table. I kneel on the floor beside her and lift her head to cradle it in my lap. As I am lulling her to sleep, I think about the volume of sensations that one human life can contain and bring to another; the memories, the emotions and the pain that this one human being is bringing to bear on me and my life for eternity. As I am holding her, I remember her sleeping in her push chair, two weeks old, with a far better future before her than I can provide in Mauritius. Nothing is bothering her. She is quite happy to lie, stare, work on her smile, smack her tiny puckered lips together, search for the breast, yawn, curl up her fists and sense her fingers. She was beautiful, warm and genuine. I think as I look at her that I am wanting to stay, wanting to see her grow up, wanting to make sure that she is happy and healthy. But I am still a child back then and easily scared by life in the real world; especially the white, damp and unfriendly world that I am ridiculously running to.

I reach under the table and pull out the rope that father has left with me for when he finds her. My heart is cold like ice as I bind her hands and secure her ankles. As I am tying her I try to remember that I must not think about what is happening too much. It is out of my control. This is the price I am promising to pay all those years ago; when my father arrived on that wet Wednesday afternoon in the Spring of 1972. I have to remain aware that even in this madness there is meaning.

She is lying now, on the floor, as peaceful as she had been back then. While my father is outside, climbing the urine soaked stairs up to our council estate flat, I am inside putting my daughter down after another feed, planning to wash a few clothes by hand, wash enough nappies for another few days. I hear the knock at the door and open it expecting to be greeted by one of my Pakistani neighbours wanting to borrow some more curry powder, or one of those desperate little door to door salesmen selling dish mops and bin bags.

He is standing, drenching, dripping and scowling on the doorstep. He says, 'Hello, Sahana.'

An eternity is passing before I offer to let him in, my heart as usual banging against the wall of my chest. I smooth down my hair, pull my Sari back into some proper shape. He followed me through to the living room, clicking his tongue. He stops making the noise when he sees her. She is asleep, always asleep. He turned his back on her without a second thought and begins to speak at the damp and peeling wall behind him.

'I do not want to talk about this. I do not want to know its name. Pack your bags this minute. You are leaving this place and coming home to heal the wounds that you have caused.'

'Papa, I cannot leave her here,' I say.

He does not look around at me. 'I said I did not want to talk about it. You are in enough trouble already as it is, or have you forgotten why you came here in the first place?'

'But papa, I cannot leave her,' I am pleading.

'You will do as you are told. That thing is a bastard, a child of *bann nasyon.* The sight of it disgusts me. You will leave it here and come home.'

'And if I do not?'

He clenches his fists and punches at his thighs. 'If you do not! If you do not I will have no choice but to disown you and leave you to the mercy of others, offer you up to justice to pay for the crimes that you have committed. Then you will lose more than just that thing.'

'But papa, you would not do that to me.'

He is wheeling round, his fury shaking the room, 'I am your father and I can do whatever I want!'

Elizabeth stirs in her push chair, twists her tiny hand into her blanket, smacks her tiny puckered lips together. He is moving towards me, seething and I lift my arm to protect myself from the blow I am sure will come. 'You will leave her and do right by your family, you little whore. You will never speak of her to anyone. You will never speak of her again. You will forget that any of this happened. You will come home and be a good daughter, a proper daughter to your parents and a proper sister to your brother. You will serve us for the rest of your life and work to relieve the shame that you have brought to bear upon your family and our name.' He came right up to my face, so that I am feeling the spittle on my face. 'Or I will tell of what my whore of a daughter did in the fields with *bann nasyon*. I will tell and you will be hung, if not by the courts, but by his bloodthirsty friends and I will sit back and watch it happen with a just heart.'

I remember him standing in the corridor while I gather my things. There is not much, a small suitcase, my purse, my makeup. I am leaning over the mirror and with a shaky hand, I try to apply some lipstick, but I am pressing too hard and it snaps, smearing my chin like bloody toothpaste. I look down at her and try to imprint the picture into my mind for always. She is sleeping, always sleeping, clenching her fists, sensing her fingers. I kiss her on the forehead and brush away the tears. I harden my heart and I am joining him in the corridor where he is pacing up and down and up and down. I do not leave a note or a message for George. I do not want him to be able to find me. In this way, I actually believed that the story would end.

But it does not. Not until I am finishing it.

I kiss my daughter on the forehead and brush the hair from her eyes; make her presentable for when he sees her again. For when he is coming to drag her body into the room next door. Where her fate is waiting.

Chapter Thirty Eight

Tifi

The moment I wake up I'm in pain. I am also shocked to see that Juliet is sitting on the floor beside me. She's tied up just like me; her hands and legs are bound by rope, a scarf is covering her mouth. She's the youngest of four children, the younger of the two that were left when Frank died and George ran away. At eleven years of age, she knew more about death and loss that I would ever want to appreciate. She looks at me now, for help, for understanding, an answer to why this is happening and I'm physically unable to respond even if I did have something to tell her. I have absolutely no idea why she is here or what the hell is happening.

I try to remain calm and get my bearings. It's still early morning I think. The light in the room is still dim; the sun isn't high enough yet to penetrate the windows. I can hear birds and cicadas chattering away as though this is just another day. I look down my body and make sure everything is where and how it should be. I can't see any blood or ripped clothing which is good, however, my bladder is full to the point where my abdomen is aching. It makes it all the harder to concentrate. Back in the normal world, I'm usually unable to find something as simple as a parking space if I'm trapped in my car and needing a pee. I try to relax my stomach muscles and count my blessings.

At length, I call out through the material, managing a muffled cry for assistance. I'm not sure whether anyone is outside. I can't hear anything but the constant chirruping of wildlife. I don't recognise anything in this room either. The walls are bare, painted a sick khaki colour that reminds me of hospital teacups. The floor is concrete and cold. A lone chair sits in the middle of the room, facing us as though it's waiting for something to happen.

I have been known to imagine escape routes for various disasters whenever I enter a new building; decide where best to hide in the event of an earthquake or a flood, stupid things like that. It is what Patrick always referred to as my morbid fascination with catastrophe. It's funny but I've always known exactly what I'd do when the five minute warning sounded. Even back in the apartment in Flic en Flac I'd noted the gas bottles, the proximity of our neighbour's balcony, unsecured security bars and the length of the drop to the floor outside. But now that I'm in most need of a survival strategy, my damn brain eludes me.

Juliet is beside me now, sobbing through her gag. There is a wet patch on the floor where she's been sitting. I feel the heat of our combined embarrassment as she rests her cheek on my shoulder. We cannot hold each other so this level of contact will have to suffice. I'm too scared to move now anyway, frightened in case I pee myself as well. I cry out again and this time we hear footsteps on the other side of the door. Juliet sits herself up straight as it opens. The man I saw passing Sandeep the hip flask has come into the room. He is holding a gun; a small revolver. He closes the door behind him and moves to sit on the chair in the middle of the room. He reminds me instantly of the child catcher in Chitty Chitty Bang Bang, except this time his skin is black and wrinkled like old leather forcing a memory and a childhood chill to play its icy fingers up the length of my spine.

'What is all this noise about ladies?' he asks with perfect British flare.

Juliet and I remain in silent synchronised hypnosis, our attention drawn by the gun.

'Well?' he sneers.

He sways the revolver this way and that as if to prove a point and I know my eyes are compelled to follow, betraying my fear. He wants me to show him how vulnerable I am. He wants me to try to talk to him through the gag so that he can be sure that I am intimidated by him. I refuse to play along. I flicker a glance at Juliet; her thoughts are still trapped in the barrel of the gun.

He gets up from his chair with the agility of a Billy goat and strides towards me, chuckling to himself all the way. It is obvious that he is practiced at coercion; there's even something about his swagger that tells me that this whole scenario is run of the mill stuff for him. He squats down in front of my face, making it quite clear that the gripe he has is definitely with me.

'If you scream,' he says flatly, pressing the gun to my temple, 'I will shoot you.'

His breath stinks like a wheelie bin in the summer; of stale cigarettes, fermenting alcohol, peanuts and cabbage. His green turquoise pupils pierce into my head enabling me to make at least one link as he drags the scarf over my chin with his other hand.

'I need to use the bathroom,' I tell him, nodding my head quickly at Juliet. 'We both do.'

He looks at me with such distaste that I blush and look away from him. He lowers the gun and yanks the material back over my face with musty fingers. Then he stands, straightening his back carefully as he does so and walks out of the room. There is no backwards glance or any indication that he has heard our plea. I try not to panic. Somehow I have to concentrate. I have to piece together the parts of the puzzle.

The only thing I know for certain is that this man and Sandeep are related. One step further and a logical assumption would be that Sahana is also a part of this big happy family. Take another step and it even includes me.

The door swings open again and this time we are greeted by an overly morose Sandeep who thankfully does not feel there is a need to threaten us with weapons.

'I am to take you one at a time to the bathroom.'

He will not look at me but I can look at him; a small scab of encrusted blood under his nose fills me with confidence and pride. He walks up to Juliet, pulls her to her feet and lifts her over his shoulder into a fireman's lift; the same fireman's lift which I once thought he had offered me out of friendship.

He puts his hand out and grabs the door handle; he does not turn around as he speaks. 'If you move while we are out of the room, he says he will kill you.' His voice is robotic, lifeless. As he disappears out of the door with my aunt, I can't help feeling amazed at how well trained some people can allow themselves to become and also how gullible I can allow myself to be.

When he returns he slings Juliet unceremoniously to the floor and then moves towards me. I realise that she is still bound and gagged and panic briefly at the practicalities of what lies before me. His expression gives nothing away as he levers me up over his shoulder. Bone greets bladder and I nearly lose it, only just managing to hold on, the pain excruciating, throbbing out from within.

Fuck.

He bounces me, I swear, for three full hours, an eternity across the room, through the doorway and into the radio room I remember from the night before. Every jolt sears like a hot knife through butter. He chucks me into a chair and sets about untying the rope around my legs.

'One move from you this time and your aunt will be the one being punished, you remember,' he says in his deadpan voice before pulling me once again to my feet.

He grabs my shoulders, turns me around and then shoves me through another doorway where a solitary toilet without a loo seat greets me like a long lost friend. Sandeep affords me a little dignity by shutting the door and leaving me to undergo the krypton factor challenge of getting my knickers down alone.

I look about me, at the peeling damp white paint and the enormous golden cockroach that is twiddling its antennae at me from on top of the empty toilet roll holder. I know that the drugs must still be in my system because I do not scream. I take my time, counting out the seconds, revelling in my brief moment of consolatory relief. And that is when I see everything clearly. Well, almost. The old man is Sandeep's grandfather, the man who owns the company. And from what Sahana told me, the man she must obey, her father. And that means that Sandeep might even be her son or her nephew. A half brother or a cousin for me.

He opens the door when I am finished and ushers me back to the chair. I close my eyes as he reties the rope around my ankles, unwilling to let him see that I know his secret. My stomach starts to gurgle in protest of the whole situation, urging me to retch, but I won't let it. I've lost far too much self respect for one day already. Without a word he carries me back to the makeshift prison cell, hurls me to the floor to lie alongside Juliet, wipes his hands down his trousers and marches out of the room, slamming the door behind him.

Juliet is praying, clicking her fingers over a row of imaginary rosary beads. I can't help but feel calmed by her faith in the fact that something or someone will protect us; the hope of divine intervention. However, the moment she opens her eyes, I perceive quite correctly, it turns out, that she is also willing to hedge her bets. We manoeuvre ourselves to sit with our backs to each other, searching out the other pair of hands. They meet and touch, pressing reassurance and encouragement into palms, before groping at ropes that secure them. We hear noises outside, stop, wriggle away a few centimetres, wait, then return once we're sure that no one will enter. The cord is fast and unforgiving, the skin of our wrists screaming at us to stop.

And then release. I'm the first to rise and tug the scarf from my face. We hug fiercely, as wrestlers, crushing our bodies together to form our own bonds from this ordeal. Selfishly, I realise that I'm glad that she's here; that I'm fed up of dealing with all of this crap on my own.

'*Korek?*' she whispers.

'Yes, I'm fine. A little sore but nothing too bad physically, although my mind's in a bit of a mess.'

'Mine too.'

'How long have you been here?'

'I arrived yesterday, I think,' she tells me. 'That man came to my house yesterday afternoon. He said that he was a taxi driver, told me that you were at the hospital with your friend and that you'd sent him to pick me up. I didn't think twice about getting in the car and once inside he offered me a bottle of water and that's the last thing I remember until I woke up here on the floor with you asleep beside me.'

'Did he mention anything more about my friend?'

'No, not really, from what I can recall. He just said that she'd been involved in an unfortunate accident.' There are heavy bags under her eyes; supermarket carrier bags loaded with fading sleeping pills and anxiety. 'Do you know what all of this is about, Elizabeth?'

The answer trips off my tongue as though I'd known it all along. 'This is all about why my father had to leave the island. It's all about why he never told me about Mauritius.'

'Ki-été?'

'It's all about who killed Frank.'

'Bondyé Ségner, Mari Zozef!'

We stare at each other, both shocked by the statement that just fell out of my mouth. My internal panic button begins to sound that we have now reached the threshold of a black security alert. It warns my organs and I that we are now facing a real war on terror.

'We need to get out of here, right away,' she says, spinning around in a circle, chasing her tail.

'Do you know where we are?' I ask.

She stops moving. Her expression is blank. 'I've no idea, I wasn't conscious when I arrived.'

I pick up the chair and place it under the window on the other side of the room. The glass is mottled; I can't see any movement outside. 'I think I remember that the sign said Grand Basin or something like that,' I tell her.

Juliet shakes her head. 'You must be wrong. Grand Bassin is the name of the Hindu temple in the middle of Black River Gorges. It's one of the most religious Hindu sites outside of India.'

'Well, I'm sure that's what it said on the board when we drove in. There was a lake and statues and ridiculous amounts of tarmac on the run up to the main entrance.'

She remains incredulous. 'Why would they take us there? It wouldn't make sense. My friends come here every year on pilgrimage. I can't think of anything more sacrilegious.'

'I think I can, ladies.'

The child catcher is standing in the doorway with the gun levelled at my knees. He appears so small from way up here. I can see his bald patch tinted red by years of henna abuse. I'm sure that if I could extend my leg far enough I could squash him into the ground with my heel.

'Please get down off the chair.'

I look down at him until I know that he appreciates what I'm thinking, then oblige, holding my arms out and stepping as demurely as possible onto the concrete floor.

'Now move over there,' he says, shepherding us like sheep, with the barrel as his staff. 'Into the corner, that's it. Now sit down.'

Juliet reaches out to grasp my hands in hers.

'It is a good thing I came to check on you,' he says with a note of genuine relief. 'It wouldn't do to have you getting out and upsetting the priests now would it?'

'I don't know, it might give them something to talk about,' I say, eager to show that I am still resilient to him.

He laughs. 'I like your spirit but it does you no favours. No one will ever find you here.'

'That's where you're wrong actually. People will be looking for me, policemen from England, my husband, my family in La Reunion, they'll be on their way too. Someone will report us missing soon enough and then they'll come looking.'

He takes a tentative step towards me, brandishes the gun in my face. 'But will you survive long enough for them to get here? That is the question little girl.'

His stench is overpowering. His vile expression wavers in mid air before me, his bottom lip slightly curled out, catching dust from the wrinkles in his forehead. Juliet clasps my hands even tighter. I realise that she won't have a clue what is being said.

'Did you really need to bring my aunt into this?'

'I didn't bring her, you did,' he replies. 'I didn't even ask you to come here. You did this all on your own. I do not remember inviting you here to destroy my life and that of my family.'

He waves the gun in a flourish and moves away into the centre of the room. Touché.

'I've no bloody idea what you're talking about. I didn't come here to destroy anyone. I just came to Mauritius because my father's final wish was that I find a fucking field to scatter his ashes in. I don't give a shit about your frigging family. I already have my own mother, a husband and a country I can call home for God's sake. Why the hell would I want yours?'

'Because I have money, little girl. You don't think I'm that naïve surely.'

'This is all about money?'

He sits back down on the chair, his face aglow with a smug grin. 'Of course, isn't everything?'

I can sense my heart become heavy as he says it. I know I need money to feed and clothe myself and keep a suitable roof over my head, but it's never been something I covet, as the be all and end all of my plans and dreams. Money has never really been that important to me. It makes everything that is happening around me seem so much more absurd.

'What the hell is going on?' Juliet asks.

'All will become very clear for you very soon,' he tells her in French.

The atmosphere in the room crackles and sparks. The child catcher sits back in his chair and taps his foot. He is waiting for her to arrive.

'You murdered Frank because of money didn't you?' I ask, pre-empting his finale.

He is caught off guard and wavers slightly before answering. 'Money was definitely part of it, yes.'

'And his death is tied up with why I am here, isn't it?'

'Yes. Now stop with your silly questions.'

He talks as though I know the secret, as though I am some nasty predator that he has managed to catch in his net.

'And Sandeep is your grandson?'

He looks to the door and then down at his watch. The gun is lying along his thigh, still pointing towards us.

'Yes, but he has nothing to do with you.'

'He's not my brother?'

The floor beneath us begins to tremble with his rage. 'You are nothing to him, do you hear me? You are nothing to him or to this family. You are dirt, the vilest creature on the face of this earth to me. You are the bastard child of an illegal and immoral coupling that has already brought far too much of a burden of shame and evil on us all.'

And then, with perfect timing, the door behind him opens and in walks Sahana.

Chapter Thirty Nine

Mama

Father is looking at me with that face he always uses when he wants me to do something for him that I do not want to do. I walk towards him and he is holding out his hand, so that I stand by him in the middle of the room. He is needing me here so that he has my blessing when all of this comes to an end. It is funny to think that he is still pretending that I have some control over what is happening when I am not having any since Bhupen my brother is born, forty two years ago.

She, Elizabeth is sitting on the floor in front of me with her aunt, the two of them holding hands and cuddling close in a way that I am wishing once that I am close enough to her to do. There is strength in her features, her eyes, that is unnerving and at the same time reassuring. My grandmother is telling me that when I was a baby I am strong and hungry for life. She is telling me that the minute she saw me she knew that I would survive, she said that she could tell immediately that I will live longer than the others that came before me. It is this same assurance that I am seeing in my daughter's eyes. She is reminding me so much of her father as well; haunting my thoughts with what may have been.

'Mauritius was a turbulent place to be in the late sixties and early seventies,' my father is explaining to her and her aunt in French. 'A new political party was making my life, as a policeman and the government's life very difficult, trying to break up the order of things on the island and your uncle Frank was a member and very vocal leader of this radical group. He and his friends are holding rallies, encouraging rioting and looting and telling people that the Hindu led government are corrupt. In the end we decide that we have to ban their party and send the ringleaders to prison.'

'You panicked when they started to win seats, you mean,' snaps the aunt.

My father waves her comment away as if it is being a bad smell.

'One day, I receive a telephone call from an anonymous person who tells me they know a very interesting secret that it would be in my interest to hear. The man tells me that he knows that my daughter is having an affair with a Creole man. He says that if I give him money he will keep his mouth shut and will not ruin me, my career and my family.'

He is looking up at me from where he is sitting and smiles, squeezing my hand silently so that my knuckles are rubbing against my rings. 'He says that he can even prove it to me, if I come to a field just before 7 p.m. that evening. He assures me that he can make my daughter appear in a way that will prove her guilt. So I went along to see, absolutely sure in my heart that he would be wrong and that I could arrest him. But something else happens instead, doesn't it Sahana?' His smile is broadening as he revels in my discomfort. 'Why don't you tell them what happens next, my dear?'

I am being fifty years old, yet in his presence I feel as though I am ten years old again. A stupid ignorant little child who must do as daddy is telling me, who is nothing now that my baby brother is being born.

'I am receiving a note that I am thinking is from George, telling me that I must meet him urgently in our sugar cane field at 6 p.m.,' I say.

'So what do you do?' he asks theatrically.

'I go to the field to see him,' I reply, as rehearsed.

'And what happens?'

The memory of that fateful evening is flooding back into my head. I have held it so close for so long, wondered what would have happened if I had not gone, wondered what my life would be like now if I had just been a good girl and done as I am being told to do.

'The *boutik* is closed, which I am thinking is very strange, but it is not stopping me from walking down the path to our meeting place. But instead of seeing George, there is a different man sitting on the rock, chewing on a stick of sugar cane. In the other hand he is holding a knife, a long hunting blade which he is turning this way and that to catch the sunlight.'

My father mirrors the movement gleefully with his gun. 'And what happens then?'

'The man is laughing and saying to me, 'Do you know what it means to cut down nine segments of sugar cane?''

'And what do you say?'

'I say, yes, that it means nine months in jail.'

My mouth has gone dry again but there is not a fridge in this room, or a bottle of water.

'And what else does he say?'

'He says, 'I hear that you keep my brother George entertained.'' I am trying to mimic his voice the way I remember. 'You the daughter of Chief Inspector R. Sundaram. A married woman, no less, the wife of Mr B. Chandels, of Chandels Textiles who is trying to buy a

Catholic owned textile business so that he can put fifty Mauritian men on the street and replace them with cheap labour from his homeland.'

I remember that he stood so close to me that he is spitting small bits of cane into my hair as he speaks. 'He tells me that his brother maybe an idiot but he has good taste in women.'

'And then what does he do?'

The horror returns, sweeping through me like an evil demon, freezing my heart, taking the strength from my legs. My child rises before me, holds out a hand to help me and I am drawn towards her but his hand still holds fast. He will not allow me to fall for her. He insists that I am telling the story the way he wants it told.

'I am laying down with him like a whore.'

The aunt screams. She is shaking but I cannot tell if it is terror or anger. Her eyes are closed to me now, and she is panting loudly, as though she is having an attack. Elizabeth, my daughter, is trying to calm her and in between words she is throwing me a look that I have never seen before. It brings tears to my eyes.

'He laughed as he is pulling up his trousers and doing up as his belt,' I went on. 'He is laughing because he is thinking that this is all I am good for.'

'And then what did you do?' my father is prompting with a smile.

I am not wanting to say it, but he forces me. The aunt still has her eyes closed, is chanting some Catholic prayer under her breath and I am tasting metal in my mouth. I can see it in front of me, the stone in my hand and the slimy red flecks on my dress. I can even smell it in the air, as if I am there and it is happening all over again. 'I do not know why I did it. I am just angry. I am being angry with him, with my husband, with my father, with my brother, with everyone who tells me what to do. I am the one who is killing Frank Labelle. I am his murderer.'

'No!'

The aunt gets up off of the floor, her body possessed by some other creature, her hands outstretched. She is wanting to hurt me. I cannot help it but I am hiding behind my father, seeking the protection that he has always denied me. He puts his hand down for the gun and it is sliding away in slow motion. Elizabeth is rising too, making for the door behind us. I catch a glimpse but do not alert my father. For a fleeting moment I am hopeful that she is escaping but as she is opening the door, Sandeep is waiting there to wrestle with her. He puts his leg between hers and is curling his foot around her calf, pushing her down onto the concrete floor.

Somewhere in the room an old wooden ruler is broken. The sound is high pitched yet underwater. In the same moment Elizabeth starts to retch, bile tearing up her throat. I want to run to her but my father holds me back. He has the gun again now and has tamed the aunt to sit at his feet. Sandeep steps back, his face powdered white with snow. He is staring down at the girl as she is writhing on the floor. Everyone is transfixed, nobody moves. I sense the fire within me. The heat is swelling and unsheathing the sword. I have to watch until it stops. I have to watch as the black angel is piercing her sword straight through my heart.

Chapter Forty

Tifi

'Elizabeth?'

'Elizabeth? Wake up, can you hear me?'

'Hhmm?'
'Elizabeth?'
'Dad?'
'Thank god.'
'Dad? Is that you?'
'Yes, Elizabeth, it is me.'
'But you're...'
'Yes, yes, I know. Look, calm down, relax. I cannot explain in too much detail. We have not got enough time.'
'Am I...?'
'No, dear, no, heavens no, you are not.'
'So, where are we?'
'I am not sure. I have not been able to figure it out yet.'
'Dad? I can't see anything.'
'I do not think you are supposed to.'
'And the pain is gone in my arm.'

'That is normal too I think.'

'Oh, Dad, I can't tell you how much I've missed you.'

'And I have missed you too, Elizabeth.'

'I can't believe how good it is to hear your voice.'

'Same here.'

'Have you been here ever since you left?'

'Yes, I think so.'

'And are you happy?'

'Well let me say that I am not sad.'

'Well, that's good I suppose.'

'Quite.'

'Did you know about Frank, Dad? Did you know that she was the one who killed him?'

'No. I swear that I had no idea.'

'Do you think it's true, you know, what she said?'

'I do not know. It may be. It may be not.'

'So you never sent me to Mauritius to find out?'

'That was not my intention. As far as I was aware, when I left everything was normal.'

'So what was your intention?'

'To tell you the truth, I am not sure anymore. When they told me that I was going to die, it just felt like the right thing to do.'

'But after all those years of keeping it a secret? I really don't understand. And now look what's happened.'

'I know, Elizabeth. I have been an idiot.'

'You can say that again. And come on, Dad, could you have fallen in love with a weirder bloody woman?'

'It was a long time ago and people change. Anyway, just be grateful I did not follow her back to Mauritius.'

'Why couldn't you have explained any of this while you were still alive?'

'It was easier to write it in a letter.'

'Easier for whom may I ask?'

'For me I suppose.'

'Well, thanks.'

'I have told you that I am sorry.'

'That's all well and good when you're dead.'

'I know.'

'So what happens now?'

'What would you like to happen?'

'Me? I'd like to get out of this mess alive and go home, if that's at all possible now.'

'I will see what I can do for you. I am sorry, Beth. Truly I am, for all of this trouble that you are going through. I really thought I was doing the right thing by telling you the truth. I never at any time thought it might end up like this. I am really sorry that I have been such a failure...'

'Fucking Hell my arm hurts. Make it stop again, Dad, would you. Dad? Dad?'

'Elizabeth, try to lie still, your arm is being badly broken.'

It is a woman's voice this time. Hers. Sahana's. It takes me a few moments to realise that my legs are bound again. I open my eyes and look about me, eager to concentrate on anything but the pain that is tearing at the left hand side of my body. She's talking. Sat on a chair in front of me. Close. Really close. So that I can smell cardamom as she speaks.

'..as he lands, he spills some of the Ganges from his head into a big crater. The Ganges becomes very angry and to appease him, Shiva promises that people from the banks of the river will return one day to live on the island and honour this sacred lake called Grand Bassin.'

My arm juts out in front of me, wrapped tightly in bandages and secured in a half roll of cardboard with elastic bands.

'I need a doctor!'

My right hand is handcuffed to a metal pipe.

'I need to see a doctor right now!'

I only manage to bring my knee up a fraction before I knock the cast, cry out and have to lower my leg.

'For goodness sake, Sandeep, shut her up.'

His form lumbers into view, casting a shadow over me and the wall. He brings his palm across my cheek, pounding against the bruise that he left there the day before. In the silence that follows, he presses the tape to my mouth.

'Now, go and check outside, make sure nobody is hearing her,' Sahana says.

I hear a door open and close on the far side of the room. Beads of sweat congregate along my eyebrows, behind my temples and trickle mercilessly down my back.

'Frank never raped me.' Sahana whispers urgently, like an infant confiding a naughty secret. 'I am making that bit up afterwards. I had to come up with a story as to how you were made. It is seeming like the easiest explanation.'

The sweat is in my eyes now. It feels as though someone has coated the inside of my lids with sand.

'Frank was waiting for me in the field and told me that he was going to tell my father about George and me. That a friend of his is telling him about us and that the two of them are thinking that they can get money for our secret. He is telling me that he knows that I am rich and that I will pay.'

She looks over her shoulder nervously, presses closer to my ear. 'I am arguing with Frank in the field and he is shaking my shoulders and I am trying to make him stop and he is shouting and I am shouting and then his eyes,' she hesitates for a second, swallows a bad taste. 'He falls to the ground and I am covered in bits of him. He falls at my feet, his knees buckling and his eyes, his eyes, his big brown eyes are staring back at me.'

I can sense her body shaking. I want to say something but I cannot. I try to blink and cut my eyelids with glass.

Her lips are practically brushing my cheek as she continues. 'He is standing there, in front of me, side stepping out of the way of the falling body. He has the stone in his hand and his face is red; flaming red.'

My stomach heaves. She couldn't mean...?

'He drops the stone and I am doing a stupid thing, I do not know why. I am picking it up so that blood is now on my hands. I cannot think, just two pairs of eyes staring, staring...'

I try to quell the rising panic in my chest.

'He killed Frank. He is hearing the argument and he is killing him. He is believing that it is Frank who is my lover. So it is he who is giving me money to run away and hide. Telling me that I am the chief suspect, that no one will believe it any other way now that the blood is on my hands. His own daughter. He is not doing it to protect me, but to protect his investment, the future of our family, his own reputation. He is telling me that I must go like a good girl.'

I breathe a sigh of relief. Now it all made sense. In a sick way it all became plausible.

'But he is not knowing that I am also running away with George. He is even thinking that you are Frank's baby. To this day he is thinking that you are Frank's baby. Not George's. That is why he is not believing you when you say why you are here.'

Her warm breath is in my eyelashes. I'm so relieved to know the truth that I want to kiss her.

'Your father is never knowing of this. I am thinking that it is best that he does not know, otherwise he may not come with me and protect you. If we had not gone, I do not know what would be happening to you or me. Maybe you would be taken away and given to strangers and I am being banished from home for always. As it is, my father finds me and brings me home and I am leaving you with George to grow up happy. Then my father is making my husband give me a child to make me happy. And everything is good until you come here and ask questions about sugar cane fields and love affairs. Then, you see, you are being the link to the killing, you are talking to everyone and finding out things and it is only a matter of time before people piece it all together and me and all that my family have worked for is being lost. That is why this is happening, Elizabeth.'

She starts to cry, the anguish and frustration filtering through her. 'It is all out of my hands, I must do as I am told, Elizabeth. I do not know how else to behave. If I could change it I would, but I have a duty to my son now. I was given a second chance and I cannot risk losing Sandeep. He is what is most important to me, especially now that his father has passed away and left only me to look after him. I cannot allow my past to ruin all that he has achieved.'

I notice for the first time that Juliet is not in the room with me. There is no sign of her. I am alone with Sahana.

'Your aunt is being taken away first,' she says, reading my thoughts. 'I am saying that I am wanting to spend a few more moments with you, since you are after all being my daughter. That way you are going second. Father is allowing me to have this time with you.'

I don't know how she wants me to react. It's not as though I can talk to her or ask her questions. This is all for her own amusement I suppose, a way of cleansing herself before they do whatever it is they have planned to do with me. I look up at her as she sits above me and I know I just look goggle eyed. This is beyond me. All I can think of is how my shitty boring life back in England doesn't look half as bad as I thought it was after all. I'm actually starting to think at this juncture that death would be a welcome relief. At least I'd be able to finish my conversation with dad.

I try to shift my position again to avoid cramp setting in, knock my arm once more and a white hot blade of pain pierces through the nerve endings of my funny bone. Funny, hah, hah. As I bite down on my tongue she says, 'I am sorry for everything that has happened, Elizabeth. It is never my intention for any of this to happen. This chaos is not my making. It is being the way life is. Everything will be better soon enough. I promise you of that.'

Then she gets up from the chair and walks towards the door. Before she reaches it, however, she looks over her shoulder one last time, frowns and returns sheepishly to my side.

'I will peel off the tape if you promise to be quiet,' she says.

As I nod, her fingers reach out towards me, gnarled knuckles and wrinkly skin. She rips and the glue takes away any hairs, leaving my lower face to smart like the rest of my body.

'I am needing you to leave me with something.'

'You need me to leave something for you?' I reply incredulously. 'How about my fucking life, you loon.'

'Now, now, Elizabeth. Do not be ruining this. Be a good girl,' she answers, brushing the hair from my forehead.

'A good girl? A good girl?' I shake her hand away, endeavour to maintain control over my voice. 'What the hell are you talking about? I didn't ask for any of this. You've got me handcuffed to a pipe with a broken arm and a black eye and I've got to be a good girl? God, if only I'd thought to use my Judo on you the minute I walked through the bloody door.'

She kneels down to face me, astonishment filling the crevasses of her weary lined face. 'You know Judo?'

I shrug. 'Yeah, what about it? I did it years ago. Dad insisted I learnt how to fight when I was a kid.'

She smiles sadly.

'What?'

She holds her hand up in front of my face and rubs her wrist. 'You are seeing the lumps on my wrist?'

I strain to see through bleary eyes. 'Yes?'

'I broke my wrist on a tree in the school playground when I am a little girl. I am trying to karate chop it like I see in the movies. Your father is the only one who is seeing me do it. It is our secret. He is knowing that I always wanted to learn how to do it properly.'

I watch her rub her fingers along bumps and grooves. The scars from a life she wished she'd had. I realise that there is still so much I need to know. It is ridiculous that this should be the end.

'He's not seriously going to kill me, is he?'

Tears begin to well again. 'I am afraid that is so, Elizabeth.'

'But you can't let them.'

'I am having no choice.'

'Of course you are having, I mean, you have a choice. You chose to keep me. You chose to take my father with you. You chose to protect him and me from the truth. Don't tell me that at your age, that now you don't have a choice?'

She wipes the back of her hand under her nose and snivels, gets back to her feet. 'I have no choice. It is you, or it is being me and my son. I stand by you, I lose everything that I know, everything that is mine and that I have worked for.' She cuts off another piece of tape and smoothes it over my mouth. 'Father will never forgive me and I do not want to know what he will do. We will never be safe and I will lose my son.' She shakes her head and backs away towards the door. 'I am sorry, Elizabeth.'

Then she leaves the room, leaving me to suffer the nightmare of my last moments alone.

In a vain attempt to calm my mind, I decide to start ranking the possible methods of my demise in order of preference. This morbid curiosity actually enables me to concentrate on something other than the physical agony I have to endure. An array of deadly methods crawl across my mind like the conveyor belt in the generation game; a pick axe, a thin metal wire, an overdose of barbiturates, a rope, a pillow, a knife; no cuddly toy in sight.

In the end I manage to whittle the list down to three. Firstly and most obviously, I could be shot. I already know that they have a gun, so maybe it will be a quick and painless death with a bullet in the back of the head. Or, maybe, less appealingly they will make me look at them as they pull the trigger so that it looks more like suicide when somebody finds me. Either way this would be the quickest and easiest way for me to go so it is my number one choice. In second place there's strangulation. It would take longer and I can't guarantee that I wouldn't struggle and prolong the agony but it would be a lot less messy than the gun method and enable me to have an open coffin at the funeral; if I have one. Then in last place, I remember the lake outside and hope to god that they are not planning to drown me. I reckon that would be the worst way to go. I don't like water at the best of times, but to float down into the depths and have time to be scared of the darkness. I wouldn't like that at all. No sir'ee, I wouldn't like that. Not one little bit.

The door opens again and this time in steps my favourite half brother I never knew, Sandeep. He marches towards me, a man on a mission and releases my handcuffed hand before pulling me to my feet. In an instant the blood rushes to my head, Niagara Falls in my ears and as I am lifted, I fall into the wall, my arm exploding like a rocket firework, shooting bile up from my stomach to burn the back of my throat. He lets me sway in mid air, doesn't even reach out an arm to still me. Even through the tears, he recedes before my eyes and I see him as a small boy, about five or six years old, stamping his feet and wobbling his bottom lip for attention. I can even see me in him and wonder how it would have been if it had been the other way around. Would I have been doing this to him to protect my family and my fortune? Did he have a better childhood than me? Could I ever conceive swapping places with him?

'It is time to go.'

He grabs my right arm and pushes me forward towards the door, through the radio room and out into the fresh air. It is pitch black outside, a space filled with shadows and semi-darkness.

'If you had not argued with your friend, none of this would be happening. You would be on a plane home now and I would not have to be doing this.'

He nudges the gun against the ribs of my left side as he speaks, knocking my broken arm and encouraging the tears to flow. I realise that there's no other sound but that of our footsteps this evening. There's no bird song, no crickets, no frogs; just an eerie silence and the crunch, crunch, crunch of our shuffling feet on the gravel.

I strain my head as far back as it will go, look up at the sky and see that the stars are out in force tonight. The Milky Way twists and turns across the sky, desperately trying to break through the dark matter that encases her. I contemplate running, making a last ditch attempt to get away; centre my mind by calculating how far I can manage with my feet tied and one arm on fire. But then I look forward and notice that Juliet is still alive; she is in front of me with the old man. He is jabbing his fist into the small of her back and making her hop with her tethered ankles. She doesn't deserve to be here. She hasn't done anything wrong. This should not be happening to her. It's all my fault that she's been dragged into this. I wish that I could turn the clock back, that I could undo the harm that my inquisitiveness has caused.

Faces pop into my mind. Kitty, Mum, Dad, Patrick. Unwritten endings. Stolen farewells. I curse my father for sending me here. I curse my mother's stupid fear of ghosts and the afterlife. I curse that bloody meddling Catholic priest. I curse Kitty for opening her legs and her big mouth. And I curse Patrick for not being here, for not saving me in my hour of need. What good is a husband anyway if he can't save you from the psychopathic clutches of your evil biological mother, her murdering henchman and demonic offspring?

I laugh. It's muffled behind the gag but the sound is exquisite. It rises from within me, a deep chocolate noise that resonates in my rib cage, tickling my heart from within. I notice that Juliet hears it too and is trying to twist around to see me. She recognises the sound, as I do. A most incredible laugh. I feel his bear claws around me and a warmth that spreads out from my heart, out along my veins, through my capillaries, fanning out onto my skin, dulling the ache in my limbs. The child catcher thumps Juliet in the back again and she topples forward, falls to the ground and the heat now wells inside me. I can feel my stomach acid burning, adding fuel to the flames.

The old man is pushing her with his foot, making her scrabble along the ground to the water's edge. The lake. It looms out in front of me, a vast expanse of molten silver in the moonlight. It ripples and laps at the side of the path, burping in preparation of its next meal. In the quiet I can even hear the splash of fish; fish big enough to eat a child. Sahana appears from the shadows of the trees, a ghostly figure in a billowing dress. She holds out a stone wrapped in rope to her father.

'Here you are, just as big as you are asking.'

My throat closes. I'm being strangled from within; by my own tongue, my own voice. Every tendon in my body is pulled taught, ready to snap. My blood is boiling, bubbling hot like larva.

Juliet is twitching, struggling, pining to be saved. Unwillingly I watch as the old man's fingers encircle her legs; as knots are tied and secured. He pushes her hips and her upper back steadily over, rolls her to the edge of the lake, over a bed of rotting rose petals. The night sky turns electric blue.

My right arm comes up, fist clenched, knuckles sharpened and ready. I bring it back, swing it 180° and execute a perfect blow, crunching Sandeep's nose into his skull. My elbow follows suit, 45° downward; slams into his abdomen so that I hear and feel his guts explode with a dull thud. I tear the tape away from my mouth.

'Stop! Don't do it! For God's sake, don't do it.'

The child catcher looks up at me, his green eyes reflecting the ripples of the water. And I'm laughing again, not my laugh, but his laugh, my father's laugh; deep, resounding, powerful. I circle around to check that Sandeep is still down, watchful as he desperately attempts to press away the ache in his solar plexus. I reach down and pick up the gun. Sahana and her father do not move. Juliet starts to wriggle away from the water's edge. I hop forward to help her; all the while keeping the gun trained on our would-be assassins. I rip the tape from her mouth. She coughs and splutters but she's safe, alive. I scream at the top of my lungs, cry out like Tarzan, call to the gods above to see us and save us. Lights start to go on in buildings around us, reflecting on the water like fireflies. We hear the pitter-patter of religious flip flopped feet running on tarmac.

'No!'

Sahana screams too and launches herself at me. She hits me full on the left side and in the wave of pain that overwhelms me, I let the gun fall into her possession. Three pairs of eyes turn towards her. Then others across the water join them. Now she's standing beside a colossal statue of Shiva, his palms open, his features stern, garlands of fragrant marigolds hanging from his fingertips. She's pointing the pistol at each one of us in turn, even at her father, at her son, at the shadows, at the echoes in the moonlight.

'How could you? How could you?' she chants over and over again, in English, in French, in Kreol.

No one replies. The old man lowers his hands over his ears and closes his eyes to shield himself from further spectacle, denying his daughter with one simple gesture. Sahana edges back into the darkness as the noise increases around us. I can hear a siren, the high pitched shriek of a banshee.

'Elizabeth, you're bleeding,' Juliet is speaking softly. 'Your side, you've been shot.'

I touch my waist, reach around and discover the warm sticky patch of flesh under my ribcage. The ground slides forward. In the distance I can make out teeth, they're familiar, like crystals, flashing in the twilight. The night falls faster, a pea soup of numbness flowing gently over me. I see Sahana step forward, clear in the centre of my blurred vision and level the gun at my head. Her skirts are dancing in the breeze, flaming orange in the murk, and a yellow smudge beneath her eye. The sea is in my ears, rolling me in waves. I hear a voice.

Mai tuma ha pyar karta hu.

And I swear I see Shiva unfold his legs and stand tall behind her. With ease and agility he lifts his foot in the air above her and brings his full force down upon her head.

Epilogue

Elizabeth

'Ayo, Marie. Haven't you finished with the mayonnaise yet?'

'In a moment, Juliet, keep your hair on. There's hardly any left anyway since the boys have been at it.'

Marie and Juliet cast a stony glare over the four boys - Matthew, Mark, Luke and John - as they shove rolls of curry filled *farata* into their perpetually hungry mouths. Pierre, Marie's husband, a brick wall of a man chuckles silently and pours himself another glass of cold Phoenix beer.

'This is truly delicious,' my mother, Shelly, mutters beside me, wiping a chilli induced tear from her eye and reaching for a glass of water.

'No, no, Mrs Labelle, you must eat bread,' Lewis says, passing her a piece of his roll. 'Place this on your tongue and suck it. The pain will go away faster this way.'

My mother duly obliges, smiling uncomfortably with a wedge of bread stuck in her teeth.

'Hey, why don't we put on some music,' Kitty asks. 'This is supposed to be a party after all.'

Obediently, Lewis clatters his cutlery onto his plate, disappears into the house and brings out a ghetto blaster and a sega CD.

‘Put that track on, Darling, you know, the one that I really like,’ Kitty calls, before popping another *gato-pima* into her waiting jaws. She’s sat at one end of the table in her wheelchair; her leg stuck out from under the table cloth in a permanent goose step.

‘Here, try one of these, you’ll like it,’ she tells Patrick, holding out the dish of deep fried chilli balls. He takes it from her and all eyes around the table turn to watch him innocently crunch down into its blistering centre and then erupt in laughter as Patrick’s face glazes over. Pierre slaps him on the back, offers a glass of beer and declares jovially, ‘Now you can say that you are real Mauritian man.’

My husband drains the glass in one and manages a courageous smile through watery eyes.

Click, click, click.

A few of Juliet’s friends have joined us. A Muslim man and his daughter have brought along a rice cooker cascading with yellow spiced Biriani. A Hindu couple, old school friends of Juliet have made cakes and pastries for pudding. A reasonably corpulent Chinese looking man who sits at the other end of the table has donated a large Tupperware dish of *mein frite,* fried noodles with beef and spring onions. As I look at him he pushes himself up from his seat and wiping his sweating brow with a hanky announces that, ‘It is time for a toast.’

The gathered assembly agrees through forkfuls of food and by the clinking of glasses.

‘As I am sure you are all well aware by now, my name is Jerome and firstly I’d like to say what a great honour it is for me to be invited here today to join in with your celebrations.’ He looks like a sage and aged sumo wrestler, a weeble, rocking backwards and forwards in an attempt to stay upright. ‘George Labelle was a very good friend to me all those years ago. I remember him as a very kind and thoughtful young man who looked beyond what was expected of him and who had a good heart.' He raises a wobbly finger into the air, 'I would like it known that I for one never doubted his innocence and never believed the lies that they tried to spread about him. I always knew that there had to be more to what happened. I knew that he'd never run away like that for no reason at all.' He lowers his arm and wavers a moment, reaching out and clasping the table to steady himself once again. One of the boys, Luke, I think, rushes up to help him, but is waved away as the old sumo focuses his attention on me.

'I am only sorry that I never tried more to find him. We are such a long way away from everywhere else here that it is difficult for us to see the world as big as it is. It is normal for us to think of the world as Mauritius and when people are not here, it is easier for us to behave as though they do not exist. I am sorry, Elizabeth, that I didn't do more to resolve the rumours. I know now that I should have persisted and put our own prejudices away to find you and keep you out of harm's way. Please accept our apologies for letting you down and not bringing you home sooner.'

Everyone was looking at me and I blushed, glanced down at my dark hands and saw my mother's white and bejewelled fingers linked within them; a welcome reminder of my other home.

'You should have been able to grow up here, in your homeland, instead of in exile with your father. I can't imagine what it must have been like for you, not knowing where you came from, not knowing who your real family was. I can only offer you an apology and be the first to raise a toast to your return, to your and George's return to your home.'

Chairs scrapped back as glasses of wine, beer and coca cola tinkled. I nodded politely; squeezing my mother's hand.

Click, click, click.

It's been a month since I woke up in hospital to witness her crying beside me. The poor thing had found out about the kidnap live on the ten o'clock news back in England, the evening we'd been found. She'd rung Patrick immediately and demanded that he escort her to Mauritius and my bedside that very night. I'd been rushed to the same hospital where Kitty was coming round from her deep sleep and after a few hours surgery on the bullet wound that my half brother kindly donated, was wheeled into the same private twin room as my best friend.

We received flowers and cards from well wishers from all over the world, from Mauritians, from religious leaders, even a letter from the Prime Minister of Mauritius anxious to offer his apologies and keen to explain that what I had endured was in no way a true depiction of modern behaviour on the island.

In this day and age, I suppose it's not unsurprising that there's been a lot of media interest in our story too. Juliet and I have turned down numerous invitations to appear on chat shows and in interviews about what happened, while Kitty has actually agreed to take part in a Discovery Channel documentary entitled, 'When Stonefish Attack!' once she and Lewis have had a chance to enjoy their honeymoon.

Yes, they got married in a registry office last week in secret. It's strange to think that he really was telling the truth and that the whole stonefish event truly was an accident. Even the drugs, it turns out, was just Kitty doing what Kitty does best. I must admit, I'm not entirely convinced, but that's the way life is sometimes. Sandeep's defence states that the decision to kidnap Juliet and I would never have been taken if Kitty hadn't stepped on that bloody stonefish and guaranteed that I couldn't leave the island and leave her behind. It was Lewis's quick thinking at the hospital that actually avoided him being kidnapped too and resulted in the police foiling the plan at the eleventh hour. Fortunately for Juliet and me, he'd overheard a conversation between Sandeep and his father about Grand Bassin and had put two and two together and come up with four. I suspect I'll be expected to eat my fair share of humble pie over that for some time to come.

The police say that it may take a long time for the whole affair to come to trial since it will be difficult digging up the evidence needed to prove the conspiracy surrounding Frank's death. They say that until then, all they can promise is that Sandeep and his father at least will be kept safely behind bars; that they won't be trying to drown Juliet and I anytime soon. They've already pleaded guilty to kidnap and conspiracy to commit murder although both are attempting a diminished responsibility defence. They're hoping to prove that Sahana forced them into doing it; that she was mentally unstable and that she threatened to destroy their property empire and their status if they didn't comply. The newspapers have been filled with stories against her too. Aunts, uncles and cousins have oozed out of the woodwork to tell tales about her wayward ways. She's not available for comment because no one knows where she is. She disappeared into the undergrowth when I passed out from the bullet wound; shrank away into the dark forest never to be seen again. The police assure me that they have looked everywhere for her and now believe that she must have fled the island. Interpol has been informed of course, but I don't hold any hope that they'll catch her. In fact, I'm praying that they don't.

I know it sounds callous but there's a certain poetic justice in her enforced exile that reassures my heart; the irony that she'd given up so much over the years in the name of loyalty, protection and obedience only to discover that in practice it had a very different meaning where the rest of her family was concerned. That by sacrificing me and my father, by not standing up for herself and not doing right by Frank, she created a situation that would come back to haunt her in the end. It angers me on the one hand that she believed I could be so easily dispensed with, yet on the other, I'm warmed by the fact that I was blessed with a second chance at maternal love. This is what will keep me sane. For my mother's sake I can't allow Sahana to succeed in destroying me. All I can do is pity her and hope that she survives; even wish her the same luck that my father received. There's not really much else to say on the subject, except of course that I'm now left in no doubt as to who the real coward was after all.

Once the party's over this evening, Juliet, Marie, mum and I are going to scatter my father's ashes on top of a hill called Candos. Juliet says it's where he used to play when he was a young boy. Patrick and I walked up there very slowly yesterday to check it out and it's perfect for him. There's a fantastic view over the sugar cane fields and town where he grew up and it faces the massive expanse of Corps de Guard Mountain, below which he fell in love for the first time and helped to make me. I'm looking forward to it if I'm being honest. I'm glad I've been strong enough to take a little control over the situation and it'll be good to lay this chapter of mine and his life to rest before we go home to England tomorrow.

Everyone assures me that everything will be a whole lot easier after the trial has finished. Until then, they tell me, I have to learn how to be patient, how to take it one day at a time. I know they're right but it's obviously easier said than done; the cast and the bullet hole acting as constant reminders of what has happened. There is one thing, however, that I can take some solace in while I wait for the wounds to heal. I'm not angry at my father anymore. Of that I'm absolutely sure. I've done a lot of soul searching and I've discovered that it's useless being angry at him. When it comes down to it, how can I be angry at someone who genuinely thought he was doing the best he could for me? My father, no matter what other faults he may have had, kept me safe and enabled me to grow into the kind of person who can handle whatever life throws at them. The last few months have definitely proved that to be true. Ultimately, what more could I have asked of him? What more can any child ask of their father?

THE END

Glossary

Mauritian Creole (Kreol) evolved through an interpretation of the French language by the myriad of races brought together on the Island. As a language it depends very much on a phonetic understanding; therefore certain spelling can vary between dictionaries and in everyday use. This glossary has been created as an aid to reading Sugar Cane and is not a definitive dictionary of Mauritian Creole (Kreol).

Alala!	An exclamation of annoyance.
Alé do!	Roughly translates as 'Oh, come on!'
Ayo!	An exclamation of anger.
Bann blan	Derogatory term for Franco-Mauritians.
Bann dimounn Morisyen	Mauritian people.
Bann lascar	Derogatory term for Mauritian Muslims.
Banzanfan	Children.
Bez sa !	Swear word to denote frustration or anger.
Bondyé Ségner, Mari Zozef!	Lord God, Mary and Joseph!
Bonswar	Good evening.
Bonzour	Good day.
Bouillon bred	Boiled edible plant leaves.
Chien mechant	Guard dog – literal translation – nasty dog.
Dakor	OK.
Dal-pouri	Flat bread made from dhal lentils.
Dilo	Water.
Dimatin	In the morning.
Diri blan	White rice.
Disel pima	Salt chilli paste usually spread of guavas.
Diswar	In the evening.
Faratha	Flat bread made from flour and oil.
Frer	Brother.
Galan kolonn	Term for men who show off to women.
Gato-brinzel	Aubergine fritters.
Gato-piman	Chilli cakes.
Gato-pomdéter	Potato fritters.
Goyav de Chine	Type of guava.
Gros pois	Peas.

Kann	Sugar Cane.
Karipoulé	Chicken curry.
Ki fer?	Why?
Ki kouyonad ?	What nonsense/ What the hell's going on?
Ki manyer ?	How are you? How do you do?
Ki-été?	What?
Korek ?	(Are you) alright? How are you?

Kot Anglé pasé, larzan pousé: Where the English pass, money grows.

Kot to alé?	Where are you going?
Kouyon	Idiot.
Kozé bayo!	Speak!
La boutik	House/home.
Lapolis	Police.
Lentilles	Lentils.
Madras	Derogatory term for Mauritian Tamils.
Mai tuma ha pyar karta hu	I love you (in Hindi).
Malbar	Derogatory term for Mauritian Hindus.
Mama	Mother.
Mang lakord	Mango.
Manman!	Mother !
Mari sa!	Exclamation of shock or admiration.
Mein frite	Fried noodles.
Mersi	Thank you.
Mo disik dou	My sweet sugar.
Mo kontan twa	I love you.
Nasyon	Derogatory term for Mauritian Creole.
Non	No.
Pa dir mwa!	Don't tell me!
Padkwa	My pleasure/ it's nothing.
Papa	Father.
Péna problem	No problem.
Pima	Chilli.
Poisson salé	Salt fish.
Pom damours	Mauritian tomatoes.
Roti	Flat bread made from flour and oil.
Rougay	Spicy tomato sauce.
Salam	Goodbye.
Satini	Chutney.
Sori, mo koko	I'm sorry, my coconut.
Sousou	Chou chou – type of vegetable.
Tanto	In the afternoon.
Tifi	Girl or daughter.

Tir lizyé	Ritual to get rid of the evil eye.
Trwa-z-er	Three o'clock.
Vini vit!	Come quickly!
Wi	Yes.
Zak	Jacques fruit.
Zallot	Shallot.
Zanvyé	January.
Zasar	Achard – a type of spicy pickle.
Ziromon	Pumpkin.
Zoli	Pretty.

Acknowledgements

My thanks must go to my husband, Robert, without whom I would never have had the confidence to put this story onto paper, let alone print. To Julie, my sister, for reading and re-reading, fishing out spelling mistakes and grammatical errors from beneath my unseeing eye. To my mother, Marie-Louise, for staying forever in my heart and helping to make me the fighter I am today. To Paul, my father, 'the other half of me, the half that no one could see on the outside,' for his love, understanding, additional proof reading skills and cheque book. A Grand-mère, for giving her daughter the Mauritian fire, teaching us how to ward off the evil eye, kill chickens and roll faratha. A Luis Belmar López, por haber dejado a una extranjera escribir su primera novela mientras que trabajaba en una tienda de muebles sin clientes. To all those people who offered their help and advice, who read my story and believed in me especially when I didn't – Fizz, Sarah, Laval, Jase, Penny, Joan, Bel, Beth...too many to mention you all, but you know who you are. To Elizabeth Haylett Clark at the Society of Authors and Jenni O'Connor at Kaiku Communications, for helping me see the light. To the agents, editors and publishers who saw something in me and Sugar Cane. And last but by no means least, to Mauritius and her children, a wonderfully magical island and people, where the beauty of the human spirit survives no matter what is thrown at it.

Thank you all.

Further Reading

If Sugar Cane has inspired you to find out more about Mauritius, I can heartily recommend the following books for further reading:

Mauritius, Reunion and Seychelles (Lonely Planet Country Guide) by Deanna Swaney, Robert Strauss, Sarina Singh and Josephine Bindloss (28 Feb 2001)

Journey to Mauritius by Bernardin de Saint-Pierre first published in French 1773, translation, introduction and notes Jason Wilson 2002 (Lost and Founds Classic Travel Writing, Signal Books, Oxford 2002)

Mauritius: Its Creole Language - The Ultimate Creole Phrase Book and Dictionary by Jacques K Lee, Green Print, 3rd Revised edition (28 Oct 2008)

A guide to the plants in Mauritius by Rachel Atkinson and Jean Claude Sevathain, Mauritian Wildlife Foundation (December 2007)

Rights and Development in Mauritius – A reader edited by Sheila Bunwaree and Roukaya Kasenally, Ossrea Mauritius Chapter (May 2007)

Creating the Creole Island, Slavery in Eighteenth-Century Mauritius by Megan Vaughan, Duke University Press (Durham& London 2005)

Un Chef a la Maison, Les Secrets de la Cuisine Mauricienne by Sandy Daswani, Serengeti Publishing Ltd (2007)

Slaves, Freedmen, and Indentured Labourers in Colonial Mauritius by Richard B. Allen, Cambridge University Press (2007)

Paul et Virginie by Bernadin de Saint-Pierre, J'ai lu (5 April 2004)

Contact E E Fry

If you enjoyed Sugar Cane, you can find out more about the author, leave a review on Amazon or goodreads, tweet her, follow her fan page on facebook and even find out what she's up to next!

Email: sugarcane.book@gmail.com

Tweet: @sugarcanebook

Like: www.facebook.com/sugarcanebook.e.e.fry

Blog: www.sandybredpublishing.blogspot.co.uk

Goodreads: www.goodreads.com/EEFry